NICHOLAS ROYLE has published five collections of short fiction, including *The Dummy & Other Uncanny Stories* (Swan River Press), *London Gothic* and *Manchester Uncanny* (both Confingo). He is also the author of seven novels, most recently *First Novel* (Vintage). He has edited more than two dozen anthologies, including twelve earlier volumes of *Best British Short Stories*. He also runs Nightjar Press, which publishes original short stories as signed, limited-edition chapbooks. His first work of non-fiction, *White Spines: Confessions of a Book Collector* (Salt), was published in 2021. Forthcoming are *Paris Fantastique* (Confingo) and *Shadow Lines: Searching For the Book Beyond the Shelf* (Salt).

BY THE SAME AUTHOR

NOVELS
Counterparts
Saxophone Dreams
The Matter of the Heart
The Director's Cut
Antwerp
Regicide
First Novel

NOVELLAS
The Appetite
The Enigma of Departure

SHORT STORIES
Mortality
In Camera (with David Gledhill)
Ornithology
The Dummy & Other Uncanny Stories
London Gothic
Manchester Uncanny

ANTHOLOGIES (as editor)
Darklands
Darklands 2
A Book of Two Halves
The Tiger Garden: A Book of Writers' Dreams
The Time Out Book of New York Short Stories
The Ex Files: New Stories About Old Flames
The Agony & the Ecstasy: New Writing for the World Cup
Neonlit: Time Out Book of New Writing
The Time Out Book of Paris Short Stories
Neonlit: Time Out Book of New Writing Volume 2
The Time Out Book of London Short Stories Volume 2
Dreams Never End
'68: New Stories From Children of the Revolution
The Best British Short Stories 2011
Murmurations: An Anthology of Uncanny Stories About Birds
The Best British Short Stories 2012
The Best British Short Stories 2013
The Best British Short Stories 2014
Best British Short Stories 2015
Best British Short Stories 2016
Best British Short Stories 2017
Best British Short Stories 2018
Best British Short Stories 2019
Best British Short Stories 2020
Best British Short Stories 2021
Best British Short Stories 2022

NON-FICTION
White Spines: Confessions of a Book Collector

Best {BRITISH} Short Stories 2023

SERIES EDITOR **NICHOLAS ROYLE**

SALT

SHEFFIELD

PUBLISHED BY SALT PUBLISHING 2023

2 4 6 8 10 9 7 5 3 1

Selection and introduction © Nicholas Royle, 2023
Individual contributions © the contributors, 2023

Nicholas Royle has asserted his right under the Copyright, Designs and Patents Act
1988 to be identified as the editor of this work.

*This book is sold subject to the condition that it shall not, by way of trade or otherwise,
be lent, resold, hired out, or otherwise circulated without the publisher's prior consent
in any form of binding or cover other than that in which it is published and without a
similar condition including this condition being imposed on the subsequent publisher.*

This book is a work of fiction. Any references to historical events, real people or real
places are used fictitiously. Other names, characters, places and events are products
of the author's imagination, and any resemblance to actual events or places or
persons, living or dead, is entirely coincidental.

First published in Great Britain in 2023 by
Salt Publishing Ltd
18 Churchill Road, Sheffield, S10 1FG United Kingdom

www.saltpublishing.com

Salt Publishing Limited Reg. No. 5293401

A CIP catalogue record for this book is available from the British Library

ISBN 978 1 78463 299 1 (Paperback edition)
ISBN 978 1 78463 300 4 (Electronic edition)

Typeset in Neacademia by Salt Publishing

Printed and bound in Great Britain by Clays Ltd, Elcograf S.p.A

CONTENTS

To the memory of David Wheldon (1950–2021)

NICHOLAS ROYLE

INTRODUCTION

TAKING THE FORM OF A HIGHLY SUBJECTIVE ALPHABET OF THE SHORT STORY

A is for anthologies, as distinct from collections. Most people seem happy to go along with the convention that a multi-author volume is known as an anthology, leaving 'collection' to describe a book of stories by a single author. Anthologies are how many readers come across short stories and, indeed, new short story writers. Anthologies may be themed or un-themed, consist of all new stories, or a mixture of original pieces and reprints, or be all reprints. Some editors, or series, combine different forms - stories with poetry and essays, for example - but if you love stories you might feel that amounts to taking up space that could have been given to more stories. Some great anthologies: Alberto Manguel's *Black Water: The Anthology of Fantastic Literature*, Ramsey Campbell's *New Terrors 1* (and *2*, for that matter), Daniel Halpern's *The Art of the Tale: An International Anthology of Short Stories 1945-1985*, *The Slow Mirror and Other Stories: New Fiction by Jewish Writers* edited by Sonja Lyndon and Sylvia Paskin, John Burke's *Tales of Unease*, *Chick-Lit: Postfeminist Fiction* edited by Cris Mazza and Jeffrey DeShell, Kirby McCauley's *Dark Forces*, *P.E.N. New Fiction I* edited by Peter Ackroyd (and follow-up volume *II* edited by Allan Massie - what a shame there were no more), Giles Gordon's *Beyond the Words: Eleven Writers in Search of a New Fiction* and a million others.

B is for JG Ballard, but it could have been for Iain Banks, AL Barker, Clive Barker, Djuna Barnes, Stan Barstow, Alan Beard, John Berger, Jorge Luis Borges, Pierre Bourgeade, Elizabeth Bowen, Ray Bradbury, Richard Brautigan, Christopher Burns, Ron Butlin or Dino Buzatti.

C is for chapbooks. Given that the short story is the best literary form (see F is for form), we need a way to publish individual stories with their own covers, cover art and International Standard Book Numbers (ISBNs). Fortunately we have one. It's called the chapbook. Not all chapbooks have ISBNs, but if publishers go to the trouble and expense of acquiring them, they are then required to supply copies to the copyright libraries, and the libraries are obliged to add them to their collections. That's nice for authors and readers, as chapbooks are often limited editions and, so, when they're gone, they're gone. But, when they're gone, they're still available to read at the British Library and other copyright libraries. Chapbooks publishers are often shoestring operations, looking on wistfully as publishers of poetry pamphlets rake in Michael Marks Awards For Poetry Pamphlets worth £5000. There's no equivalent award for publishers of fiction chapbooks, which could be seen, looking at it in a glass-half-full sort of way, as a gap in the market for philanthropists.

D is for Elspeth Davie, but it could have been for Roald Dahl, Marie Darrieussecq, EL Doctorow, Andre Dubus or Patricia Duncker.

E is for experimental fiction. (See O is for Oulipo.) The short story is the perfect form (see F is for form) for experimental writing. Short stories are by no means easier to write than novels – indeed they may be harder to write and get right – but there's less at stake, for both writer and reader. If you're the writer, it might take you a morning, or a week or a month, to get a story right, rather than the six or twelve months or more that the novel might require. So, if you want to gamble, if you want to take a risk, there's a less at stake. If you're the reader, what are we talking about? Ten minutes, twenty, half an hour? You, the reader, can also afford to take a risk. If it doesn't work for you, what have you lost? Half an hour at the most. Have you got ten minutes or twenty minutes or half an hour for BS Johnson or Imogen Reid or Simon Okotie or Joanna Walsh or Will Eaves or Paul Griffiths or Robert Coover or Rikki Ducornet or Tony White or Giles Gordon or David Rose or Susan Daitch (see X is for 'X ≠ Y')?

F is for form. Form is how we distinguish between fiction, drama, poetry and non-fiction, and other forms, and how we further distinguish between novel, novella, short story and so on. I'm deliberately not including 'flash fiction', because it's such an awful term, which has somehow taken hold and spread, like dry rot. To be clear, I'm talking about the term, not the work published under that umbrella, but the very nature of the term, with its implications of speed and ephemerality, is, I think, unhelpful. Might it not encourage writers to dash off pieces of so-called flash fiction rather than work at them patiently? David Gaffney, who has published several excellent collections of very short stories, doesn't dash them off. He writes longer stories and then chips and chisels away at them until they are 150 words long, or whatever. I don't really know why we need a special term to describe stories that are shorter than average, but if we do, what's wrong with short short stories, or very short stories, or micro fiction? Anything, frankly, rather than flash fiction. I do recognise that I have a bee in my bonnet about this.

G is for Giles Gordon. Gordon (1940-2003) was mentioned twice in the *New Statesman* – in a diary piece and subsequently on the letters page – while I was writing this piece. On each occasion he was described as 'agent Giles Gordon'. It's true that he was a literary agent and a very good one, with happy clients, but it would be a great shame if we lost sight of the fact that he was also an accomplished and entertaining novelist and short story writer (he also wrote poetry and a memoir) and anthologist. In his short stories – and in his novels, for that matter – he often experimented (see E is for experimental fiction) with style and form, and as an editor he supported writers of experimental fiction (see A is for anthologies). With David Hughes he edited ten volumes of *Best Short Stories* between 1986 and 1995. One of his own stories, 'Couple', was published as a chapbook (see C is for chapbooks) by Sceptre Press of Knotting, Bedford.

H is for horror. Ghost stories are perennially popular. Is it their brevity that appeals? Maybe, partly, but what about big horror novels, Peter Straub's 500-page *Ghost Story*, for example? They have their legions of fans, too. Is it that Jamesian (MR, not Henry) idea of sitting around an open fire and being told a story? Is it a mixture of that and the same reason why experimental fiction and the short story are such a good fit (see E is for Experimental fiction)? Horror is an emotion, an uncomfortable, sometimes extreme one. To evoke it in the reader is to take a risk. Alison Moore's 'Small Animals' is only ten pages long, but it's so intense and your nerves are jangling so much, you wouldn't want it to be even a page longer. Robert Aickman's 'strange stories' do tend to be longer: twenty pages, thirty, or more. A sinister atmosphere develops, a sense of doom pervades. Will it work, you might ask, in the back of your mind, will he pull it off? The answer is always yes.

I is for idea. Which is how most of those stories we are told around the fire (see H is for horror) actually begin – with an idea, a 'what if'.

J is for the Jacksons. You'll know Shirley Jackson, author of 'The Lottery' and many other dark stories, but you might not be familiar with her near namesake Shelley Jackson, author of the 2002 short story collection *The Melancholy of Anatomy* and of the story 'Skin', published on the bodies of 2095 volunteers, or 'Words', each of whom has had one word from the story tattooed in a specific location of their own choosing. I'm lucky enough to be one of them. My word is 'After'.

K is for Jamaica Kincaid, but it could have been for Franz Kafka, Anna Kavan, James Kelman, Heinrich von Kleist or Hanif Kureishi.

L is for Clarice Lispector. Her short story, 'The Imitation of the Rose', reprinted in *Other Fires: Stories From the Women of Latin America* edited by Alberto Manguel (see M is for

Alberto Manguel), is an account of mental illness as powerful, in its own subtle way, as Charlotte Perkins Gilman's 'The Yellow Wallpaper' (see U is for Errol Undercliffe).

M is for Alberto Manguel. They say you shouldn't meet your heroes – actually, don't they also say you shouldn't even have heroes? – but I met Manguel, the editor of *Black Water: The Anthology of Fantastic Literature* and *White Fire: Further Fantastic Literature*, and he was charming, generous and entertaining. We bonded over sky-blue shoelaces.

N is for Gary Numan. I remember reading, as a 16-year-old, probably in *Smash Hits* or the *NME*, about Numan's dabbling in literature. The Tubeway Army frontman, who captured the imagination of fans with his lyrics about electric 'friends' and 'Machmen', had written science fiction stories before he started recording music. I wanted to read those stories. I still do.

O is for Oulipo. (See E is for experimental fiction.) Oulipo – short for *Ouvroir de littérature potentielle*, which translates as Workshop For Potential Literature – was formed in France in 1960 by writer Raymond Queneau and mathematician François Le Lionnais. They encouraged the practice of writing under specific constraints. Many writers have enthusiastically taken up the baton, some of whom are featured in *The Penguin Book of Oulipo* edited by Philip Terry.

P is for *Penguin Modern Stories*. This quarterly anthology series edited by Judith Burnley ran from 1969 to 1972, featuring three to five writers in each volume, with between one and three stories from each writer. It finished after twelve volumes. Stories were appearing for the first time in the UK and were by a mixture of established writers and new names. Design was by David Pelham, using bold, solid colours, a different one for each book, with the number appearing in large, white type on both front and back covers. You see them now and again in charity shops and second-hand bookshops. If you're lucky you might spot a multicoloured box set including volumes one to six. The series kicked off with William Sansom (see S is for William Sansom) joined by Jean Rhys, David Plante and Bernard Malamud. Other notable writers who appeared as the series proceeded included Sylvia Plath, Margaret Drabble, Giles Gordon (see G is for Giles Gordon), Elizabeth Taylor, BS Johnson, William Trevor, Jennifer Dawson and Gabriel Josipovici. If you do see one – a box set or a single volume – they're well worth picking up.

Q is for questions. I like to be left with more of them than answers. The short story is perfect for that.

R is for Alain Robbe-Grillet, whose status as a short story writer is out of proportion to the number of stories he actually published. The slim volume *Instantanés* published by Editions de Minuit in 1962, and issued in translation as *Snapshots*, contained six stories, two of which, 'La plage' ('The Beach') and 'Dans les couloirs du métropolitain' ('In the Corridors of the Métro'), have been reprinted in various places. Both stories exemplify a tendency towards repetition of image and narrative within a story that is characteristic of the *nouveau roman* (new novel), of which Robbe-Grillet was a key exponent. The unfurling of waves on a beach and the constant motion of an escalator create infinite loops within which we see actions appear to repeat themselves, with uncanny effects.

S is for William Sansom, but it could have been for Saki, James Salter, Greg Sanders, Bruno Schulz, Ellis Sharp, Alan Sillitoe, Clive Sinclair, Muriel Spark or Robert Stone.

T is for tense, which is what I become when I think about a certain highly regarded writer, who wrote – more than a decade ago now, but I can't get it out of my head – of his displeasure at how often the present tense was being used in the contemporary English novel. I took his first short story collection down from the shelf, curious to see if it included any stories in the present tense. It does: two. The use of the present tense in those two stories does not especially distinguish them from the other stories in the collection. The present tense is there for writers to use, whether in the novel or in the short story. Use it well and readers will be happy.

U is for Errol Undercliffe. Horror (see H is for horror) maestro Ramsey Campbell's 1973 collection *Demons By Daylight* was, interestingly, divided into three parts: 'Nightmares' opened the collection and 'Relationships' closed it. Caught between the two was the curious and fascinating 'Errol Undercliffe: a tribute', which comprised a short biographical note about Undercliffe, 'a Brichester writer whose work has only recently begun to reach a wider public', a first-person piece narrated by 'Campbell' entitled 'The Franklyn Paragraphs' that reads, at least to begin with, like a memoir, and a short story, 'The Interloper', by Undercliffe. I put 'Campbell' in inverted commas, because 'The Franklyn Paragraphs' is Campbell's fiction, as is 'The Interloper', of course, since both Undercliffe and Brichester are his invention. In 'The Franklyn Paragraphs', the narrator visits Undercliffe's flat after the disappearance of the Brichester writer: 'The wallpaper had a Charlotte Perkins Gilman look; once Undercliffe complained that "such an absurd story should have used up an inspiration which I could work into one of my best tales."' (See L is for Clarice Lispector.) Campbell's opinion of Charlotte Perkins Gilman's 'The Yellow Wallpaper' is higher than Undercliffe's: he included it in *The Folio Book of Horror Stories*, which he edited for the Folio Society in 2018.

V is for Boris Vian. Another author with a pseudonym (Ramsey Campbell also published a novel as Jay Ramsay), Boris Vian was a novelist, short story writer, poet, musician, singer and critic, who published some of his work, a string of controversial crime novels, under the name Vernon Sullivan. Of Vian's four short story collections, two were published posthumously (he died young, at 39). *Le loup-garou* (*The Werewolf*), the second of these, kicks off with 'Le loup-garou', in which a wolf turns into a man, but only on the full moon, a clever inversion of the myth. 'Martin m'a téléphoné' is a jazz story, about picking up gigs in clubs. 'Les chiens, le désir et la mort' was originally published under the Sullivan pseudonym and is one of the strongest stories in the collection, a fatalistic noir piece about a taxi driver who picks up a fare he probably should have left waiting on the sidewalk.

W is for Paul Willems. Belgian novelist, playwright and short story writer Paul Willems (1912–97) published two collections towards the end of his life. *La cathédrale de brume* was the first of these and is available in English translation, as *The Cathedral of Mist*, from US-based Wakefield Press. Willems came from near Antwerp, but wrote in French. 'Requiem pour le pain' begins with the narrator's cousin explaining to him that the reason his grandmother told him to break bread with his hands rather than cut it with a knife was because the moment a knife touches bread, the bread cries out. Moments later, the cousin falls out of a window to her death and the narrator's grandmother reassures him that his cousin will be in paradise, more precisely in a pension in Ostend for dead little girls. Ballard (see B is for JG Ballard) was a fan of the Belgian artist Paul Delvaux. Maybe he also knew of Willems' work. Ostend, the narrator of Willems' story tells us, is submerged by the sea during the night. Only in the morning do the waves recede. This reminds us of the opening of Ballard's story 'Now Wakes the Sea': 'Again at night Mason heard the sounds of the approaching sea, the muffled thunder of breakers rolling up the near-by streets.' Another of Willems' stories, 'Tchiripisch', is set in Bulgaria, but the narrator of that story remembers a dream he had in Ostend. He could hear waves breaking on the beach (see Z is for Curtis Zahn) and it seemed to him that they uttered two words, one as they broke and another as they withdrew, taking back the first word. What the words were was not, in the end, revealed to him.

X is for 'X ≠ Y'. This story, by the American novelist and short story writer Susan Daitch, was published in *Bomb* magazine in 1987, according to bombmagazine.org, where you can read it online, but I read it in *After Yesterday's Crash: The Avant-Pop Anthology* (Penguin) edited by Larry McCaffery, which gives the story a copyright date of 1988. It's a tense, effective and,

I think it's accurate to say, experimental account of a plane hi-jacking from the point of view of a passenger. McCaffery's anthology also includes an extract from Steve Erickson's novel *Arc d'X*, which I mention in spite of its being a novel extract rather than a short story simply because Erickson is so good, and a story by Marc Laidlaw, 'Great Breakthroughs in Darkness (Being Early Entries From *The Secret Encyclopaedia of Photography*)', that uses a similar alphabetical device to this essay but doesn't get any further than 'Acetylide emulsion'.

Y is for Elizabeth Young. Best known as a critic (her critical essays were collected in *Pandora's Handbag*), Elizabeth Young was also a brilliant short story writer, who died too young (in 2001, at the age of 50) and before she could publish enough stories to think about putting together a collection. In the 1990s I had a number of opportunities to invite her to write new stories, which she duly supplied and which appeared in anthologies like *Darklands 2*, *The Ex Files*, *The Time Out Book of London Short Stories Volume 2* and elsewhere. Her story 'Shrinking' in *The Time Out Book of New York Short Stories* is one of the best stories about multiple personality disorder, crack addition and therapy that you are ever likely to read.

Z is for Curtis Zahn. The US author's collection *American Contemporary* was published in the UK by Jonathan Cape in 1965. His sharp observational gifts, with his eye focused mostly on Californian society of the 1950s and 1960s, and some of his ideas - in one story, doctors surgically remove a character's conscience - might remind readers of Philip K Dick. A couple of lines about the call of the surf - '. . . the surf called to us monotonously above the murmuring of marsh birds in the great swamp'; 'But now the surf came to us, reminding us of our task, confessing in its tortured tumbling that aggressions had been stored up for some time' – remind me also of Raymond Chandler and my favourite line from *The Big Sleep*: 'Under the thinning fog the surf curled and creamed, almost without sound, like a thought trying to form itself on the edge of consciousness.' When reading the 1968 Penguin edition of *American Contemporary* earlier this year, I felt that my thoughts about Curtis Zahn's stories were trying to form themselves on the edge of consciousness, so hard were they, in some cases, to pin down, but maybe this was deliberate. One story, 'A View From the Sky', was reprinted in 1971 in *Anti-Story: An Anthology of Experimental Fiction* (Free Press) edited by Philip Stevick, included in a section headed 'Against Subject: fiction in search of something to be about' (see E is for experimental fiction). In his introduction, Stevick writes, 'Nearly any classic story can be said, with a kind of simple accuracy, 'to be "about" some abstraction . . . There is, however, no intrinsic reason why a short fiction, or any other literary work, should be so constructed as to provide us with an answer to our preliminary question of what its subject is . . . Is it possible to have a fiction that is coherent on its own terms but so tentative and exploratory that its writer seems never entirely clear what its centre is, not even at its end? Can we ever assume that a writer knows what he is doing but does not know what his subject is?' (See Q is for questions.)

NICHOLAS ROYLE
Manchester
July 2023

MILES GREENWOOD

ISLANDS

ONE TIME, A daughter was born to a mother and a father on an island. their way of life was an old one. they lived with the land to grow just enough food for themselves and their neighbours, and their neighbours did the same. yam coconut soursop callaloo breadfruit. almost-ripe mango swelled the trees and could be smelt on the fresh air. goats cows and chickens too. nature provided more than food as well. birds would offer their song in the day to a backdrop of the cool breeze rustling the leaves as it swept through the green hills. crickets would chirp at night, frogs would croak and rain would beat on the zinc roof of the house that the daughter the mother and the father lived in, nestled in the hills of the island.

the daughter thought this life was hard. all she did was work.

fetching water from the spring high up in the hills in the morning

chop sugar cane and cut grass to feed the cows in the afternoon

she would cut some of the sugar cane to taste the sweet sweet juices on her thirsty tongue don't tell the mother in case she get a beating with a stick of choice

sweep the house

wash the clothes.

the daughter thought she could manage this life if it wasn't for the mother and father having more daughters and a son. now the daughter had to look after the sisters and the brother. now there was no time and no money for school to get the book learning that the daughter loved.

yes, all she did was work

she had to learn to cook and feed many with what they grew from the land

soup made with green banana and yellow yam from the garden

hot pepper and thyme from the garden

pumpkin from a neighbour

carrots from a cousin

fish brought from the market at the old harbour by the father.

the daughter seasoned the fish and fried enough for the family and the neighbours so that none went hungry. she served it with roast breadfruit and steamed callaloo. they all ate.

the mother

the father

the sisters

the brother

the neighbour

and the cousin

the daughter was becoming a woman. a pretty one with bright eyes with a hint of sadness to them. she had dimples that sat each side of her cheek whether she smiled or not. some thought she was the prettiest woman on the island. the daughter had no time to worry about this pretty business. her mother had spat on the ground and told her to return from the shop with spices before it dried. the shop was run by a father but a son stood behind the counter that day. a handsome man, she thought. older than she. nice smile. she could feel the beating she would get from the mother with a stick of choice for ignoring her warning.

don't talk to strange men

don't look pon them

don't think of them.

but the son was nice. many thought it, but he was the first

3

to say that she was the prettiest girl on the island when she walked into the shop that day. he was going foreign, he said, and he would like to write to her. this was the most exciting thing she ever heard. this son was taking a boat across the big blue sea to another land and of all the daughters on the island, he wanted to write to her.

the son did write to the daughter. he wrote of a cold island with brick houses two, three storeys high with fire inside. more white people lived there than the daughter could imagine, he said. more letters followed. a longing crept into her chest.

then that letter came.

the letter that said the son wanted the daughter to come foreign and marry him. this was the most exciting thing she ever heard. this was the scariest thing she ever heard.

what business did she have in foreign

why could she not go foreign and marry the son

she was too young to marry the son

she was a woman now

she would have to ask the mother and the father

she could feel the beating she would get from the mother with a stick of choice for ignoring her warning.

don't talk to strange men

don't look pon them

don't think of them

don't marry them.

ask the mother and the father she did. no beating came. the father's face turned serious and sad. the mother kissed her teeth before the silence. then the daughter had to wait to catch fragments of hushed conversations from the bedroom of the mother and the father.

too young

a stranger

a beating

better life

silence.

the mother and the father held the daughter like they did when she was born to this world. the father pressed a five pound note into her hand and said no more. she got on the bus with the neighbours who were heading to the market for fish. she would not return with them. she was to go further.

don't look back

fix yuh eyes forward.

the bus creeped down the bumpy, winding road from the hills. the daughter noticed the soil change from the deep red of home to a yellow like the yam in her soup. the bus reached the old harbour and the neighbours left one by one, each squeezing her hands and wishing her well. then strangers replaced them on the road by the big blue sea that followed the coast to the city.

don't look back

fix yuh eyes forward.

the son crossed the big blue sea by boat. she was to cross in an airplane with the birds in the sky. a mixture of fear and excitement tumbled around in her belly as she was pressed back in her seat as the plane ramped up to top speed. a woman next to her prayed to her god to take everyone's lives in their hands. may they guide and protect us.

amen.

the plane floated into the air and the daughter shared in everyone's relief. she could see the island and the hills. if she squeezed her eyes she might see home, the father the mother the sisters the brother.

don't look back

fix yuh eyes forward

but with her eyes fixed forward, the daughter didn't notice those unseen threads unravelling around her.

the foreign island was so cold that the daughter felt frozen to her soul. even when she saw the son, and he wrapped her in his coat and under his arm, she could not stop her bones from shivering. he told her again that she was still the prettiest girl on the island. she wasn't sure whether she believed him with all these pretty people on this cold island.

the daughter and the son took the two-storey bus to the son's three-storey house. she soon realised that the son occupied one box room in the three-storey house with nine other people from the island and other islands. this wasn't what the daughter expected of the foreign island with its brick houses white people and fires.

the daughter began to unpack while the son looked on with expectation in his eyes.

yuh bring breadfruit and callaloo, he asked.

she forgot. in the last letter the son sent to the island from foreign, he asked her to bring breadfruit and callaloo. she thought it strange that he would want breadfruit and callaloo when he has all those bricks and white people, and she put it so far to the back of her mind that it got stuck there.

why she forget, the daughter asked herself.

she expected the son to get angry and could feel a beating

with a stick of choice, but now the son would be the punisher instead of the mother. she didn't know this son she was to marry after all. but he just looked sad.

it's ok don't worry yuhself, he said in his gentle way she would grow to love over time.

the son wanted to get busy and so they got married quick at a local church in borrowed clothes from neighbours, surrounded by the son's friends. the daughter was nervous and curious about this busy business. she didn't enjoy it the first time but it wasn't so bad the second. before she knew it,

one child

two child

three child.

and then she was vexed. all the daughter did was work.

she washed and ironed clothes

she sent the children to get their book learning while the son went off to work in a factory

she cleaned the two-bedroom house they now lived in

she went off to the hospital to look after white people who said evil things to her she would come home tired. but she still had to make soup.

green banana, yam, dumplings, thyme, hot pepper and chicken all from the market. she can't afford any fish to fry. she can't get breadfruit and callaloo on this cold island.

why she forget the breadfruit and callaloo.

all she did was work. and they still struggled to pay the bills. one day the son had an accident at work.

hit by a truck, they said

he won't walk again, the doctor said.

the daughter had to take another job sewing clothes while the son and the children slept. sometimes she felt a temptation creeping in her heart to look back and ask, before a sadness distracted her. sometimes eye water rolled down her face.

don't look back

fix yuh eyes forward.

the children grew. they got their book learning. they got jobs too. had their own families. grandchildren to love and the son and daughter loved them with all their hearts. loved them enough to warm the cold of this island. the daughter was able to retire. she was able to make soup for grandchildren.

why she forget the breadfruit and callaloo.

no matter. the grandchildren ate and they were happy and she loved them. there's one grandson that held a special place in the daughter's heart. strange boy. nice boy. quiet. head full of thoughts and questions.

where does the green banana come from

where does the yam come from

where does the hot pepper come from

strange boy.

when the grandson grew older. he told the daughter that he wanted to go to the island and the hills and to the home. this made the daughter nervous.

why him want to look back.

but there was an excitement like what she felt when she left the island to go foreign. she had to unfix her eyes and look back.

back to the ocean

the road

the hills

the family

the home.

she told him, when yuh the plane drops from the sky it will
feel as though it will drop into the sea but the runway will
catch yuh. then take the road from the city along by the big
blue sea until yuh reach the old harbour. from there take the
bumpy and windy road into the hills where we grow fruits of
all kinds. make sure yuh try the breadfruit and callaloo. when
the earth turns a deep red colour like rust, you will be near.
ask for directions to the father's house at the shop.

the grandson followed the daughter's instructions. when he
arrived he thought it was the most beautiful place he ever saw.
hills cloaked in green trees bearing fruits he didn't know. a
cool breeze wrapped around him carrying the smell of ripe
mango. a smell he did recognise from the markets of the cold
island but this smell was fresher. sweeter.

he did not find the father or the mother. he did find grave-
stones at the front of a house he was told was the father's. he
did not find the daughters. they had moved away, he was told.
some to other parts of the island. some to foreign islands. the
grandson did find the son of the father, the brother of the
daughter though. the son greeted the grandson as if he was
his own.

held him tight

looked him up and down

took him in

gave him a cold coconut to drink from

introduced him to a family

children

grandchildren

cousins

they prepared a meal of

saltfish

callaloo

breadfruit and dumplings.

the meal tasted familiar and unfamiliar. like a distant memory half forgotten. the food was shared with the whole family and with neighbours. nobody went hungry. everyone was looked after. he listened to the bird's song in the day, the frogs croaking and the crickets chirping at night only for them to be silenced by the rain that beat on the zinc roof of the home.

the grandson went with the son to chop cane and cut grass to feed the cows in the morning.

is this your land, the grandson asked.

nuh, this is our land, the son said. extending his arms over the hills to foreign islands.

when they returned through the village, the son introduced the grandson to everyone.

this is my nephew from foreign, he would say

this is yuh cousin, he would also say, about everyone it seemed.

the grandson fell in love with this life, this family and this island. but he knew that he must return to the cold island. part of him would always be on this island, in these hills though. and one day he would take his children too. but for now, he had to go back.

and he would bring breadfruit and callaloo.

LYDIA GILL

THE LOWING

It was only a short walk from the farmhouse to the barn.

The moon was a bright hole in the sky, letting a thin veil of light creep into the dark. The farmer had no torch.

The dog stood up in the kennel.

'Heel.' The farmer's voice sliced the air with white and the dog folded to the floor.

A persistent wind had blown the snow over and over itself, until it swooned in tired drifts against the drystone walls. Now the snow lay thick and lifeless, pricked by splinters of frost, face upturned to the sky.

It was the silence that had coaxed the farmer outside.

For three days and nights the cows had been calling for their calves. Each year, the weaning began with the relentless lowing of the mothers, their restless stamping, their udders swollen, their saliva hanging in threads and falling to the ground.

And each year the farmer forgot how the sound would take hold of his limbs, pull him out of sleep, and rake its claws across his skin, until he allowed himself to be held and rocked. And where the noise had pierced him, pain leaked out. Milk streaked with blood.

But now there was no noise.

❧

It was only a short walk from the farmhouse to the barn.

The calves were not far away, gathered and soft. The smell of their fear seeped across wheels of hay, the sweet earth of it, reaching into the shadows of the byre, searching for their mothers.

The calves were not far away at all.

But the snow was deceptive in its quietude. Secretly deep and unyielding. The farmer's boots staggered into drifts, and stuck. Each step wrenching, one foot to the next.

The dog stood up in the kennel. 'Heel,' said the farmer.

Somewhere a cow bell rang. It was nothing at first, the clear roundness of the sound, the familiarity. How it smelled like the sun on grass. How the warmth of it spread through him like a child's laugh. How it lingered in the air, waiting.

But they didn't bell the cows anymore.

And the sudden knowing of this resounded through the farmer, discordant and cold. He shook himself down, billowing white lungfuls of air into the night, his eyes searching the darkness.

But the darkness would not move.

The moon had fallen behind the looming trees, and stars began to crowd the sky, watching with pinprick eyes. Waiting.

It was only a short walk from the farmhouse to the barn. Past silage bales that sagged and split into piles, grass growing from their openings. But the farmer hadn't reached the barn yet. His boots were heavy with snow, his legs were heavy with cold, and he felt the weight of the dark upon his back.

The dog stood up in the kennel. Cocked its head. Licked

its teeth. 'Come here, boy,' the farmer reached out. 'Boy,' he growled. The dog stood still in the kennel.

The wind softly brushed the snow. Brushed it into a sheet at the farmer's feet. And on the sheet were three drops of blood, each one closer to the barn. An invitation written on white. A calling.

One. Two. Three.

Beyond, something lay in the snow. A twist of gore. A gleam of blood. A clot of flesh. The warmth of it steamed into the air.

A cow bell rang.

The farmer creased into himself, stumbling back, the bone of a cry caught in his throat, his hands feeling along the loose stones of the wall. The stones fell away. They would not hold him. The wind had dropped, and the trees held onto their outlines, arms outstretched and willing.

It was only a short walk from the farmhouse to the barn. And the cows knew this too, as they watched from their dark places. Shifting bulks of shadow in the heart of the barn.

The farmer fell to his knees. Gave himself, face down, to the snow. Something made of blood was in his way.

The dog stood up in the kennel. 'Heel,' growled the dog.

A cow bell rang. Rang just as the farmer reached to touch the thing of blood in the snow. And when he looked at the heft of his hand, he saw the dirt that lived in the grain of his skin. What was frozen melted under his breath. And the round of his cry left a hole.

It was only a short walk from the farmhouse to the barn.

A short walk, even for a woman with a child hidden in

the depths of her. Hidden from the dark and unknown edges of the farm. From those who separated mothers from their young.

It was only a short run, for a woman pursued. But she had never reached the barn.

It was only a short walk from the farmhouse to the barn, so it didn't take them long to find the farmer in the morning.

And they remarked how the dog was watching from the kennel. And how it looked as if the snow had left a blank space. How it had erased something.

And they wondered why the farmer had made his way to the old barn in the night. The cows had all been sold a few years back.

'After,' they said, and coughed against the thought of it. Coughed out the remembering. The remembering of the cold that had carved her into stone. Of the frost that had swirled all her blood into fronds. And the things in the snow that they would never name.

Beyond the drystone walls of the farm, the moors swelled into skin-white hills and trees grew in patches, untamed.

As they lifted the farmer's frozen body, they were surprised at its lightness. And how his hand stayed reaching for the barn.

And how he barely left an imprint in the snow.

DAVID WHELDON

THE STATISTICS REBELLION

THE BUILDING, OF local Pennant sandstone, is tall and narrow. Once a hotel associated with the nearby railway station, it is now part of the university; it houses the epidemiology and medical statistics departments.

It was four-thirty on a Friday afternoon in late spring. In a large class-room, once the lounge of the hotel, some twenty preclinical medical students sat behind their desks, restive and anxious for the seminar's end.

The course's subject was statistics. I was present. I can't recall much about that particular seminar except that dense little clouds were gently passing across the sky. At one moment the room was in full sunlight: the next it was in shadow. This alternation of sun and shade was frankly soporific. Tall Martha, sitting next to me, yawned and looked out of the window. The window was in the tripartite Venetian style as that was understood by nineteenth-century British architects. The air inside the room was close even though the window's sashes were all open. The seminar droned on.

Tall Martha shook back her long, dark hair and began to fiddle with the Facit machine on the desk in front of her.

We all had Facit machines on our desks. Do you remember Facit machines? They were obsolescent even then. Our Facit machines were electro-mechanical calculators, dark-green pre-transistor monsters which we used for our studies in statistics. They were very heavy. The size of small typewriters, they had a cast-iron chassis. Each stage in any calculation involved cogs and shafts, gears and pawls, in different arrangements, and each stage produced a specific cascade of noises. This was actually interesting. With experience it became possible to guess, by hearing alone, the general nature of the equation someone had keyed into their Facit. Tall Martha and I sometimes used to amuse ourselves over sandwiches at lunchtime by staying in the classroom and experimenting with these sequences of sounds.

So much for the Facit machines.

The lecturer was poor; his voice was monotonous and his delivery was dull. Worse, he would usually overstay the hour of the seminar and would plod on into overtime. So, as the hands of the wall-clock turned to five, there was no certain relief that the teaching would come to an end. At ten past the hour the students would start to fidget and put away their papers. And that would usually be the signal for the end. His misplaced enthusiasm for the gloomy science would draw to a slow conclusion.

Just before the start of the seminar Tall Martha turned to me. 'I need to leave on time today,' she said. Her brow was thoughtful. 'For no reason in particular. It's just that when that minute hand reaches ten past five I feel like a delinquent schoolgirl kept in detention,' she said.

'Were you often kept in detention, Marth?' I asked.

'Quite often,' she replied, in a matter-of-fact voice. 'Chiefly when I was at Stoke Damerel High. As you'd expect, they kept firm naval discipline.' We were both standing at the open window, leaning on the sill, looking down at the activity on the railway station's platforms. A little tank engine was doing some light shunting in the goods yard. It was mildly interesting. 'I never seemed to learn my lesson: I can't think why. In fact I couldn't give an aylesbury even now.'

There was a brief silence.

'Why did you get detentions?' I asked.

'None of your business, David,' said Tall Martha, with a rueful half-smile. 'A girl has to keep some secrets of her early life.' Her brow furrowed again. 'Though on one occasion – when I was about twelve – a catapult was involved.' Then she groaned. 'Yes. We have to find a way to stop Lord Charles dead on the stroke of the hour. Then I shall head out for the hinterlands.' *Lord Charles* was the name she had bestowed on the statistics lecturer. It was apposite. Tall Martha was adept at finding suitably apt names for people she didn't much like. The lecturer really did have the odd mannerisms of a ventriloquist's dummy, and his idiosyncrasies of speech were not unlike a ventriloquist's. (Martha, incidentally, was also mistress of the retort discourteous. 'You'd be the one who'd use a log table to multiply by ten, and get the answer wrong,' she once said to someone she found painfully slow on the mathematical uptake. Now she crossed her arms and examined the decorative mouldings on the ceiling with a critical eye. She tapped her foot.)

I thought of Lord Charles. 'Be kind to him, Marth,' I said. 'Be as merciful as a lady medical student can be. Beneath that bone-dry carapace and under that monotonous voice he's probably very shy and sensitive. Many statisticians are.'

Tall Martha continued to examine the plaster mouldings (her arms still crossed) as she considered my request. 'He's about as shy and sensitive as a Brillo pad. No. I'll show him no mercy. Come five o'clock we have to find some way to stay his pitch,' she muttered.

At that moment Lord Charles entered the room, busily erased the obsolete chalk ciphers on the blackboard and said: 'Today we study scatter plots. One of the more obviously useful aspects of a scatter plot is its ability to demonstrate nonlinear relationships between variables. If there is time I shall touch on scatter-plot matrices.'

Shortly after this I turned off mentally and began to drowse. Finally, I fell asleep. The wind had dropped and the day was growing hot.

Suddenly I was wakened by a short whistle from the steam locomotive; someone simultaneously touched me on the elbow. It was Tall Martha. I sat straight and looked at her. She had a secretive smile on her face. Her intelligent eyes were alert and mischievous. I knew she had something carefully planned.

Lord Charles was busy at the blackboard, now filled with chalk drawings of scatter plots. Tall Martha passed me a folded piece of paper. I unfolded it and looked at a couple of lines of blue-black ink. In her rather untidy backhand I read: *Program your Facit to work out the square root of 10. Dead on five o'clock set the machine going. Pass this note on. M.H.*

Tall Martha and I smiled at each other. I refolded the note and passed it to Diana Rushfield who was sitting beside me. Diana read it, smiled, refolded it and passed it on.

Three minutes to five saw the class fully alert: in fact it was more alert than it had been all afternoon. Lord Charles seemed a little taken aback by this unusual alertness but continued his teaching.

And that was it. On the stroke of five (by the sonorous sound of the Memorial Tower bell) every Facit machine in the room began that interminable calculation. The busy chugging noise was insistent if inane, enhanced as it was by the laughter of the students. The air was blue with the smell of electrical sparks and hot lubricating oil.

√10

3.16227766016837933199888935444327185337195551393252168268
5750485279259443863923822134424810837930029518734728415284
0055148548856030453880014690519596700153903344921657179 2
5994065915015347411333948412408531692957709047157646104 43
69257879062037808609941828371711548406328552999118596824 5
6420332696160469131433612894979189026652954361267617878135
0061388186278580463683134952478031143769334671973819513185
6784032312417954022183080458728446146002535775797 0282864
4029024407977896034543989163349222652612067792651676 0310
4843669779375692615572050036989490946942185000735834884
464388273110928910904234805423565340390727401978654372593
9641726001306990000955784463109626790694418336130181302
894541703315807731626386395193793704654765220632063686587
197822049312426053454111609356979828132452297000798883523
75958532857925136296468651149767521712345955923803937562512
5369855194955325099947038843990336466165470647234999796 1
3234340302185705218783667634578951073298287515794521577165
2139626324438399018484560935762602031676804240795894693
4247814145806514304533258897144676931113759240470507701 8
5460439272128358941921437984326343229410069841773833560 7

26911107125549274561841707758654442076025678341820374148
29455461534720993410591702356226115911404732754291627011127
03017816958732447241098614929595088080751785265560628316
835297689579890021578592912442089113168034811561162320 . . .

Lord Charles took in the situation.

Then, his face expressionless, he put down his stick of chalk and left the room.

SHARON KIVLAND

THE INCORRUPTIBLE

YESTERDAY, MAXIMILIEN ROBESPIERRE tried
to kill himself with a pistol. My beloved succeeded only in
shattering his lower jaw. I was told that in the room of the
Committee of Public Safety, he lay on a deal table until a
doctor was summoned to attempt to staunch the bleeding
from his jaw, from his ruined face. His wound was fearful.
Even his yellow stockings were spattered with his blood. His
last recorded words may have been 'Merci, monsieur,' to the
man who gave him a handkerchief to wipe away the blood
on his face and clothing. I was not present to wipe his lovely
face as I would have desired. I grieved then and I grieve still.
He asked, you know, for clean linen, they said, indicated by a
gesture. He was wearing his sky-blue satin coat, his beautiful
redingote.

Today, oh grief, 10 Thermidor, he was taken to his death in
the Place de la Révolution. His face was swollen and dread-
fully pale, and he kept his eyes closed. Twenty-two men were
executed, including his brother Augustin, dear handsome
'Bonbon', the calm, proud, and always elegant Saint-Just, and
brave Couthon, who suffered in agony for fifteen minutes as
his paralysed body was arranged on the board by Sanson, the
executioner, who in clearing the neck of my beloved to meet

the blade, realised his head would not fit the into the guillotine with the bandages that were holding his shattered jaw in place, and Sanson tore them off, causing him to produce an agonised scream, a final howl, until he was silenced by the fall of the blade. The blood flowed. The son of the executioner said he roared like a tiger. Oh, it was swift, his death, but not swift enough, no. His coat had come off or the executioner had taken it from him. My heart broke when I heard this.

The mob howled, oh, how that cowardly rabble howled, releasing such terrible cries of rejoicing. Had they forgotten that he spoke for them, the *sans-culottes*? Had they forgotten those whom he defended, the enslaved, Jews, actors? That he called for the abolition of slavery? His enduring compassionate zeal for the oppressed, his sacred love of homeland, his deep horror of tyranny? That he expelled the enemies of the Revolution from the assemblies? That he broke the chains that bound the people? That he wept for those who perished and for those who were the instruments of their death? His generous ambition to establish here on Earth the world's first Republic? Or his tender, imperious, and irresistible passion, his sublime and holy love? He was without prudery or affectation. He was taken to burial in a common grave in the cemetery of Errancis in the Parc de Monceau. Danger mattered nothing to him; he declared his heart to be free from fear but in the moment of his death, I feared, how I feared, that finally he felt afraid. The mob should have accompanied his death, protested or mourned it, but instead they called him a monster. Sanson did not hesitate to hold up his head to the crowd.

He was modest, despite what some said of him. I must insist on this. When he came to Paris, he had but few belongings – a puff and powder for his hair, which was always immaculate, that his hair should be well kept was more important to him than food and drink, his wooden shaving-bowl, clean linen, always clean linen - he was so fastidious, a pink satin waistcoat. He knew how to make lace and to sew, to knit; he had learnt these skills from his grandmother. On the day of his death a bucket of animal blood was thrown against the door of the house where I had given him the most delicate concern, an abundance of little attentions. He told me once that I had the soul of a man, that I would know how to die as well as I knew how to love.

Some said that my adoration ruined him by exalting his pride, that our household made him invisible, that we sequestered him. Yet our house was always open, with a constant passage of visitors. I made curtains of blue damask for his bed from an old dress of my mother's to allow him privacy. He trod underfoot vanity, envy, ambition, and all the weaknesses of petty souls. He was never censorious. He was indulgent towards error. He was tender, he was respectful. I hated Condorcet for saying he led a sect among women, that there were always women around him, that he was a priest at the head of his worshippers. I hated the stupid woman who proposed he and she drown themselves in the Seine to cleanse him of the sins that sullied his reputation. Hah! she did not even know her alphabet, that one.

There was gossip, such calumny, about us. They said I passed myself off as his wife, that I ruled over him, that I was his mistress, that we had married in secret in the presence of Saint-Just. Yet how could one who was so absorbed by his work for the Committee of Public Safety have had the time for love or marriage, even though I desired both? There was a deep reserve in his character. His only happiness lay in the happiness of the people. However, he was assailed by enemies and his life was a perpetual battle. No, he could not afford to play Céladon with me, yet, while he lived, we walked often in the Champs-Elysées or in the woods at Versailles, walking Brount, his faithful dog who would sleep under the table while his master worked on into the night, tirelessly.

Often, I was content to sit watching him in the pleasant *salon*, where he and his visitors talked quietly at the end of the day. I would take out my sewing. I would serve refreshments. Sometimes he would read from Montesquieu. His hair was brushed back, he wore a high stock, a large jabot and collar, with striped revers, a coat with a dark collar, a patterned waistcoat open at the throat, or a green tailcoat, with a sash, yellow silk breeches, boots. I remember the care he took with his clothes, he wore lace cuffs, changed daily, yet he was not a dandy nor a libertine. He was never shabby, in dress or in behaviour. His manners were always without ostentation. Danton, that great oaf, described his face as resembling that of a cat who has tasted vinegar. His expressions were accentuated by his green-glass spectacles, which hid the movements of his face, for at times he suffered from a tic. Yet, I thought of his dear head rather as that of a tiger, magnificent, noble and strong.

Always abstemious, he thought the love of champagne to be a failing and resisted attending parties in consequence, though he did have a weakness for sweetmeats. And he especially loved oranges, which he could peel with one hand. As a young man in Arras, he wrote a poem in alexandrines about the cakes in the bakery above which he lived.

Money meant nothing to him; he was the most austere of men. For him, the equality of possessions was a chimera, even less necessary to private happiness than to public felicity. To the festival of the Supreme Being, he wore a hat decorated with ostrich feathers dyed red, white, and blue, carrying in his arms a bouquet of poppies, sunflowers, sheaves of corn, and he said then that evil comes from the depraved man who oppresses his neighbour or allows him to be oppressed. They dared to call him a tyrant, the one who declared he would wage war to the death on tyrants and conspirators, against the vile agitators, the mercenary scribblers. He saw the ruins of the Republic and spoke of taking hemlock. He would not sacrifice his virtue. He asked what could be done against a man who was right and who knew how to die for his country. He bequeathed the terrible truth of death, and he was lost, condemned without trial. The flowers I planted in the court-yard had dried up in the heat of the days of *Thermidor*, the burning days. We knew it was the end. My mother hung herself. My sister and I lay on the floor of our house weeping.

I survive him. I withdraw from the world. I will wear black for what remains of my life. I am his widow in all but name. Grieve with me, mourn. Without him, our Revolution is lost.

10 THERMIDOR II
10 THERMIDOR CCXXXI

DJ TAYLOR

SOMEWHERE OUT THERE WEST OF THETFORD

MRS GROTE LIVED on the last pitch of the final row of the park, squeezed up on four brick casters next to the barbed-wire fence and beneath the overhang of the elm trees. Some of the caravans had neat gravel surrounds and wind chimes that rattled constantly in the Breckland gales, but hers was just a big oblong box with the paint ribboning off the window frames and patches of withered grass where she threw out the tea leaves of a morning. The front half had no curtains and late at night you could see her long, angular torso bobbing around the living space or sitting bolt upright in a deckchair watching TV. The Grotes were Fen people who had headed east fifty years ago, and traces of this heritage lay around the caravan where there were, in addition to an eel hive, three or four rush baskets that could be folded up into themselves like a Panama hat. You could see it, too, in Mrs Grote's long-sightedness, the way in which she always seemed to be regarding something that was a hundred yards away, out on the edge of a bare horizon bounded by endless grey sky. She was a tall, gnarled woman in her late seventies with a brown-stained skin who looked as if she had been carved out of a tree, and conspicuous, even for the backwater in which she had come to rest.

Billy used to see her late in the afternoons, walking back along the verge from Brandon with her grocery bag, tottering a bit yet determined, not caring about the HGVs that went hurtling by on their way to Lynn. Sometimes there were two bags, which gave her equilibrium, and she swung them vigorously in either hand, like a porter carrying cases up a hotel stair-flight. On the third or fourth of these occasions, when the rain was coming down hard and the twilight was stealing up out of the road-side thickets, he stopped the van, leaned out of the nearside window and said: would she like a lift?

'I'll not say no,' she said, so he swept a hand down to displace the drift of newspapers and sweet wrappers from the passenger seat and reached over for the grocery bags, which mostly harboured packets of rice and tins of steak and kidney; the kind of things people who lived on caravan parks ate, he thought, and pretty much the contents of his own larder. The look on her face as she climbed in beside him told him that the lift was hers by right, that he had no other purpose in life except to drive her home.

'Seen you around the site, haven't I?' he said, in case she should think him to be some anonymous way-layer of old ladies.

'You might have,' she told him, and he was reminded of the women who had taught him at school, calm and indifferent, treating insult and olive branch alike with the same grave unconcern. For the rest of the journey – it was only a couple of miles down back lanes that were already melting into darkness – she sat rigid in her seat, saying nothing. Back at the park he took care to drive her right up to the door, which was on the row down from his own pitch, but the solicitousness went unmarked. 'I'll thank you again,' she said, bags balancing her big frame, not looking at him as she stepped out into the mud, and he watched her head away up the half-dozen wooden steps, prod at an envelope that the postman had left hanging in the slot that made do as a letter box and stand looking at it as if he and the van and everything else in the world had ceased to exist. Then, just as he was starting to back the van away down the path, she turned back on her heel to stare, the letter still in her hand, and he saw that he had done the right thing.

After that he started looking out for her, in a small way. He was elsewhere most of the time driving the oil truck out to Oxburgh, Wisbech, Soham, places even further afield, but sometimes, coming back of an evening, he'd leave a milk carton or a packet of Jaffa Cakes on the topmost step of the caravan, out of the wind, and be rewarded, next time he saw her, with another frosty nod. Mariette, who came over a couple of nights a week from Brandon, and to whom exchange was a two-way thing, was amused. 'What d'you want to give that old girl pints of milk for?' she wondered. 'Anyone can go get a pint of milk.' But Billy judged that he was responding to solitude, not need.

'She's got no one,' he rationalised. 'Or' – correcting himself – 'no one I know of.' That much was true. It was a wet autumn that year, darker too, and Mrs Grote, plodding home along the verges, bags in hand, looked more wraith-like than ever, gaunt and sepia-toned, as if she had just risen up from one of the beet fields that ran alongside the road. One afternoon, when he'd left a packet of digestives on the step, she asked him in for a cup of tea.

'Your name's Billy ent it?'

'Billy Martin.' The tea was a queer tan colour, but not the worst he'd had.

'You like eels?'

'Never have tasted them,' he conceded.

'You come round here one night,' she instructed, as if this was the greatest favour ever done by woman to man, 'and I'll cook you some eels. Can bring that girl, too, if you've a mind.'

But Mariette refused to go with him. She had better things to do than dine out in Mrs Grote's caravan. 'You're soft,' she said. 'You'll be painting up her windows next and not taking a penny.' Billy didn't like to admit that this idea had already occurred to him. The eels, like much else in this part of Norfolk, tasted of river water and woodsmoke, but he did his best. Mrs Grote fidgeted around the caravan, opening doors and closing them, putting kettles on to boil and then thinking twice. There were framed photographs on the damp wall of old men pulling sedge out of the Fen dykes, ancient families – the girls in pinafore dresses, the boys in flat caps and hob-nails – brought together before cottage doors. On the couch by the window the *Radio Times* lay open at the day's date with inked crosses running down the margin.

'You see after me,' she said, pronouncing it *arter* and accepting one of his hand-rolled cigarettes, 'and you won't lose.'

'Don't mind if I lose or not,' he said, a bit affronted by this directness.

Come November there were fewer people on the site and the days started earlier. Most mornings he was up and gone by 7, van parked up at the depot, taking the truck out on the A11, the A47 and the roads beyond it, up into Lincolnshire, westward into the square fields of blackened Fenland earth. The people he delivered to lived in odd places, on run-down farmsteads where no farming seemed to be done, down out-of-the-way lanes hedged with cow parsley where fallen branches crackled under the tyres. Mariette, thinking the oil-delivering foolish and underpaid, wanted him to get a job in town. Meanwhile, he was discovering things about Mrs Grote. One of them was that the floor of her caravan was slowly disintegrating into the mould of old leaves and litter beneath it. This could be fixed with some hammered-down squares of plywood, but there was nothing he could do about the second thing, which was Mrs Grote's habit of taking a turn.

The first time this occurred they were coming down the caravan steps together, so he could stop her fall and put her back on her feet. 'This happen before?' he asked, worried by the way her legs seemed to unravel beneath her.

'Now and again,' Mrs Grote allowed. But the second time was so bad that Billy was unable properly to rouse her from her chair and, in collaboration with Mr Morgan, the site's owner, brought the paramedics out from Thetford.

'You got anyone we ought to call?' Billy wondered, after the paramedics had been and gone, leaving instructions for Mrs Grote to attend her GP's surgery the following day.

'Could ring my *darter*,' Mrs Grote suggested, pulling a slip of paper out of the mass of old envelopes that lay next to her sink and indicating by the way in which she flopped down again in her chair that the job was Billy's.

Mrs Grote's daughter came over the next afternoon. She was a tall, surly woman with oiled-up hair raked back over her scalp who drove a battered estate car with a Stars and Bars transfer on the back window and a bumper sticker that said

BEWARE: RATTLESNAKE INSIDE. Billy left them to it. When the woman came out a few minutes later, she gave him one of those disbelieving, are-you-still-here looks.

'I suppose you're one of the ones she said wouldn't lose.'

He jerked his shoulders, wanting to give as good as he got. 'No concern of mine what you think.'

'Well, she's not got anything to give, that's for sure,' the woman said, bitterly. He realised now that he had seen her before, and that she worked in one of the pubs in Brandon. But no glint of recognition dawned on the other side of the hedge.

'Don't you and her get on?' You got this a lot out here: women who never set eyes on sisters who lived in the next street; teenage boys camped out in hostels while their parents looked on. Everyone in west Norfolk seemed to be estranged from somebody.

'Do me a favour,' she said as she got back into the estate car, whose rear end, he now saw, was half-fallen away and held together with streaks of solder. 'Don't phone me unless it's real bad, OK?'

He decided that he would get back at Mrs Stars and Bars somehow, that he owed it to Mrs Grote and the eel hives and the pictures of the old men out ditching and dredging, this dead world in which she now played no part. December came and things slowed down. The beet fields were picked clean, and the rooks sat in the leafless trees not bothering to explode into flight if they heard a noise. Out across the meadows the weakening sun caught the mist and pulsed through it, turning the landscape ghost-like and ominous. Mariette was supposed to be coming for Christmas, but her texts had dried up. The people he delivered to had started to give him presents now:

jars of jam; bottles of home-made wine; plastic boxes of chicken wings from Tesco. He left the non-perishable gifts in a heap on his fold-up table like pirates' plunder

'What's the matter with your daughter?' he asked once – they were out at Castle Acre, to which she had consented to be driven one Sunday afternoon. The fog was coming in from the west. Up there on the escarpment, dozens of feet above the crumbling stone, they looked like a pair of medieval sentries staring out across the debatable lands where warring armies lurked.

'Never had anything to say to each other,' she said. He knew he was lucky to get this far. His own mother would not have said as much. He thought for a moment she was going to have one of her turns, sink down onto the wet grass and start gasping for breath, but unexpectedly she righted herself and they went back to the van.

The park had not forgotten Christmas. There were fairy lights up in two or three of the caravans that remained occupied, and Mr Morgan had erected a Christmas tree inside the front gate with a plastic star stapled to its topmost branch. He got the text from Mariette on Christmas Eve as he stood inspecting the oven-ready turkey in its plastic sack, worrying what you did with it. No details were offered beyond the apology, but Billy knew what had happened. Like the storms, which cruised up from the Wash in angry clouds that were visible thirty miles away, he had seen it coming. Hastening over to Mrs Grote's caravan – she might not care to join him over the turkey, but she would like to be asked – he found her tossed to one side of the deckchair with her eyes off at a slant, so that was that. He called the ambulance and told Mr Morgan in his shack and then went away, thinking that whatever happened next was none of his business.

Later, when the dusk was welling up in the field-bottoms and the breeze had begun to agitate the wind chimes, he went back to the caravan and, finding that no one had bothered to fasten the door, stole guiltily inside. One or two things that he had missed that morning – a solitary paper chain hung over the far wall, a row of Christmas cards on the shelf next to the cooker – now caught his eye. Wanting to feed his curiosity about Mrs Grote, the person she was and the things she owned, he bent down and opened the big cupboard on the cooker's further side. Here there were a dozen empty whisky bottles and about the same number of steak and kidney pie tins. He was wondering about taking one of the pies on the grounds that it would be preferable to the turkey when he saw the scuffed-up padded bag. On the front, in big, flagrant capitals, Mrs Grote, or someone else, had written JEANNIE GROTE, and he realised that in all the time this had been going on he had never known her name.

'OK, Jeannie Grote,' he said quietly to the silent caravan, feeling the notes crinkle in his hands. There were not so many of them, but they were high-denomination – twenties and fifties; about £1200 in all, he reckoned. He rolled them into a wedge that filled the space in the palm of his hand, took a sip from the half-inch of liquor that remained in one of the whisky bottles and then put them back in the bag. Later still, when the evening was far advanced and even the light in Mr Morgan's cubbyhole had been extinguished, he crept out of the front gate, where the Christmas tree had lurched slightly to one side and was shedding its needles, went fifty yards down the road and cast the padded bag into a storm drain, gripped by an emotion that was not quite grief and not quite exhilaration, but something else, something sharp and combustible, flaring up into the dense Norfolk sky.

BRIONY THOMPSON

THE NIGHTS

Jean

At the battered table, Jean sits, grey head bent over paperwork. A half-drunk tea rests by her hand, the rim of the mug slightly chipped. The slowness of her movements speaks of exhaustion. I'm getting too old for this, she thinks.

'And so are you,' she says, peering over her glasses at the grizzled collie dozing by the fireplace. The heat from the log burner just takes the edge off the chill in the careworn kitchen. In a box beside the hearth, a tiny lamb is curled up asleep. Its snuffling breaths are muffled by the cardboard.

Jean casts a glance at the wall clock. Another couple of hours before the next feed. The bottle is already made up, waiting by the sink.

The shrill of the telephone cuts into her thoughts. She rises stiffly, leaning both hands on the tabletop to push herself up. The phone is balanced on the edge of an old dresser, amongst more piles of papers, some coated in dust.

'Jean, it's Billy, frae Dykeshaws.'

'Hello, Billy. Everything all right?' Billy would not disturb her for nothing. Like her own farm, Dykeshaws would be flat out at this time of year, working the lambing.

There is a pause, while Billy's breath rattles into the

receiver. 'Mebbes. There wis a light. Awa up the fell. Rab seen it frae the pens.'

Inwardly, Jean sighs. 'Thanks, Billy, I'll have a look.'

'Aye.' The old man rings off, satisfied.

Jean stands for a moment. She stretches out a calloused finger to brush a stray cobweb from her sister's portrait, half-hidden amongst the clutter. 'You would make short work of it, putting this place back in order, wouldn't you?' Mary was never much help with the outdoor tasks, but she kept a good house.

Shrugging on her overcoat and sliding her feet into wellies, Jean peers through the narrow window beside the door. Leaning close to the glass, to banish reflections from the lit room, she can see up the hill. It rises away from the farmhouse in a gradual slope. The blackness outside is not uniform, but full of contrasts. Jean thinks perhaps she does see a movement, up beyond the gorse. She lifts a hand to adjust the position of the glasses-frame on her nose, blinks and looks again. Maybe it's her tired eyes playing tricks, but there have been rustlers in the area. It pays to keep an eye out.

She turns to where the old sheepdog is watching her, alert now. 'It's alright, Jessie. You can stay here.' She stoops to caress the soft place under the dog's raised muzzle. 'Keep an eye on the wee one.' The lamb shifts sleepily, releasing a waft of lanolin from the box.

The door handle is stiff. It takes a second try before Jean manages to turn it. Stepping out into the damp evening and pervading smell of sheep dung, she pulls the heavy plank door closed behind her. She does not bother locking it.

Anna

In the cluttered porch, Anna is preparing to go out. Her jacket is zipped to her chin, the hood of her sweatshirt pulled up, hiding her dark hair. Her fingers check the torch in her left-hand pocket, though she doesn't need it. Yet.

'Don't stay too late,' she can hear her mother calling. 'Wrap up. . . It's still cold. Don't forget to wear your gloves.'

Blah and blah and blah, she thinks. 'Yes, Mum.' She lets just a hint of exasperation enter her tone. It won't help to pick an argument now.

'Bye!' She tries to sound carefree, as she quickly steps out to the shrubby garden. For no reason, she avoids the gravel path, stepping sideways onto the patchy lawn to pick her way silently to the open gateway.

A shape detaches itself from the shadows. Silhouetted for a moment against the light from the living room windows, Calum's form is familiar.

'Hi,' he says briefly.

'Hi. You got away okay then?' Anna looks up at him. He's grown taller lately.

'Yup. Told Mum I was going to Dave's.'

'I said I was going to Rosie's.'

In the deepening gloom, Anna can't make out Calum's expression. She can tell he's grinning though.

As they step out onto the track, a sudden shriek from up ahead makes them both start.

'Just an owl,' Anna says.

Calum is close beside her. Their arms brush slightly as they walk, their skin warm under identikit black puffer jackets. For a few steps they are silent.

'Were you revising today?' Anna asks, eventually.

'Nah. Had to help my dad.' Calum has no interest in taking over the family farm, but he is not exempt from the work. 'Once I get my licence, he'll have me driving the tractors. Then I'll never get away.'

She lets her fingers brush the back of Calum's hand, creep round to thread through his. Calum's pace slows slightly; she can feel his eyes on her.

'Did you bring a torch?'

'Yeah. I'll wait 'til we're up at Black Peter's – save the battery.' Don't want to be up there in the pitch-dark, she thinks.

They fall silent again. The heavy farm vehicles, with their oversized tyres, have worn deep treads into the surface of the track. A hump of tufty grass runs down the middle. They keep to one side of it, where the ground is comparatively level.

An uneven hedgerow runs alongside. Beech and hawthorn mostly, it has been here for generations. The bright new growth on show hides old, twisted trunks beneath. They are revealed in the occasional open hollows where, as a young child, Anna built dens.

Her eyes follow the track ahead, as it crosses the familiar folds of hillside. She finds herself tensing, becoming aware of the shadows around them. Calum must feel it. She senses him glancing her way.

Anna is used to the unlit isolation of this place, at home with it. Tonight though, something feels different. There is a discord in the air. She can taste it on her tongue, like when you bite into a sour berry. Instinctively, she moves closer to Calum. They are moving beyond the hedge now, her house out of view, so he slides an arm round her shoulders. She leans into his solid warmth.

Claire

Pulling the curtains closed, Claire pauses to peer through the creeper that drapes trailing limbs across the window. She's always meant to cut it back. Doesn't know where to start though. Through the leaves, her attention is caught by a light up on the fell – a sudden bright flare. It appears, then is gone.

Claire shivers slightly, then relaxes her shoulders. Probably one of the farmers. They never seem to sleep. People think the countryside is peaceful – at least that's what she thought, but that's a fallacy. Five-thirty this morning the first tractor rumbled past. Still, the silence bothers her more.

Dragging the curtains firmly shut, so there's not even a crack left between them, she checks the lock is turned on the front door. There is only one log left in the basket, she notices, heart sinking. It will have to be an early night then. It's too late to eat now anyway. She'll just have a cup of tea, a piece of toast.

Claire rubs her eyes. They feel dry and gritty. It has taken almost two hours to settle Rory tonight. She clenches her teeth, remembering the attention he drew, howling away down at the village shop today:

'Puir bairn, he's teething!'

'Look at thaes wee rosy cheeks!'

'Ah coud tak him hame wi' me.'

'Go ahead and take him home then!' she imagines herself replying. 'See what it's like!' But, of course, she didn't say that, doesn't mean it. The memory of her mother's lecturing replays uncomfortably: 'There's no point running away. You'd be better off here, where you've family and friends.'

There are voices outside on the track. Quiet, but Claire has good hearing. It's those kids, off to their hideout up at Black

Peter's place. Probably think no-one knows. Well, Claire won't tell. It's not so long since she was young herself. And they're nice enough. She's had Anna babysit Rory a couple of times, not that she ever leaves him for long. Calum she doesn't know so well, but he's polite when she sees him waiting at the top of the track for the school bus.

Black Peter, there's a conundrum. 'Conundrum': Claire rolls the word round on her tongue. She was a literature student, once upon a time. She chuckles thinking of that, although she doesn't really find it funny.

'Who was Black Peter?' she asked Jean Scott one day. The elderly farmer often drops by with logs for her stove or a snippet of news. Checking up on me, Claire thinks. But she's glad, all the same.

'He lived here when I was a lass.' Jean explained. 'Used to labour on the farm come harvest or lambing times.'

'Why was he called Black Peter?' It seemed to Claire like a name you might find in a story.

A shrug. 'Just a nickname. They like their nicknames round here. Jim-the-Cheese, that was another.'

This is all she can glean about Black Peter, except someone tells her he moved to a care home. His old cottage stands empty, a popular hangout for local kids. Nowhere else to go, is there? They just want some privacy.

Everyone knows each other's business round here. Just yesterday Margaret from the new bungalow had turned up at the door with a flyer for a book group at the village hall.

'Ye'll want tae git oot tae meet folk.' She didn't even say it like it was a question. 'Must be awfie lanely, jist yersel an the wean.'

There is a tapping at the window. Deliberately, Claire

ignores it. It's that creeper. Maybe she should try the book group. It would save on the logs.

Jean

Emerging from the farmyard, Jean pauses. Ahead of her, off to one side, she can see the glow from the lambing sheds. She'll look in on the way back.

Down in the valley, she can hear a car engine. The vehicle is hidden amongst the trees. For a few seconds its whine echoes off the hillsides before fading into the distance. There is a light on at Claire's cottage, up from the village. Jean often wonders how the young woman is managing. It's not easy out here, especially when you're new to it.

The valley is rich with night sounds: the rustle of livestock, a stream gurgling close by, the faint scrape as a pebble is dislodged, perhaps by some rodent. A bat flits past her ear. Jean does not flinch. There is a colony in the barn - pipistrelles. Through the clamour of small noises and movements, she hears nothing unexpected. Too far away then. With a nod, she starts up the track.

To her right is the but-and-ben where Black Peter lived. That was a while ago. The roof is made of corrugated iron, though it's too dark to make that out. Rustic, they would call it now. It's sound though - Jean keeps an eye on the place. Can't risk anything happening to the children that play there.

Someone is there now, by the low wooden door. Jean can see a movement. She slows to a stop, a chance to catch her breath. And to observe. She can hear conversation but can't make out the words. Then a sudden exclamation:

'Ow! You try. It's stiff.' A muffled giggle.

Jean smiles to herself. Anna Tait. She knows the voice.

Grown up fast. Or maybe it's that the years pass quickly for Jean these days. She can still picture the wee long-haired girl that used to come to the farm with her Mum to buy eggs. Anna must be almost finished high school now. And that will be Calum Laidlaw with her. Jean is out often enough, checking the livestock in her old Land Rover, to know what happens around here. They must have wrestled the door open. She can see a torch beam inside. Reminded, she checks the torch in her own pocket. She resumes walking. Quietly. No need to frighten the youngsters.

The sky is turning now from dark blue to black. There has been no more sign of movement on the hillside, but Jean can sense something. The night feels charged.

Anna

'It's not too bad . . .' Calum's tone sounds dubious. It's a while since they were last here and someone has been in, left the room piled up with litter.

'You shift that mess. I'll put out the blanket.' Anna busies herself with her rucksack, but she's not really concentrating. She's sure she heard something outside, a scrape, barely there. Probably a rat, she tells herself. Not exactly reassuring.

'You want a Coke?' Calum is already sitting on the blanket. His face is all shades and hollows in the light from her torch.

'I'm fine, thanks. Cal, can you smell cigarettes?'

'Maybe. Those village kids, probably, smoking up here.'

Anna hesitates, dips her head to hide her awkwardness. 'Rosie told me a story. You know – when we used to come up here after school to hang out?'

'Don't tell me, it's a ghost story.'

'No, just something she heard. Forget it.'

45

'I'm only joking.' Calum's voice is soft now. He pulls her down beside him, so their legs are touching. His clothes smell of detergent.

'Just. . . people say they've seen him here, Black Peter, I mean. Recently. These kids saw him through the window. They were scared – in case he knew they'd been in his house – so they hid. When they came out, there was no sign of him, just a smell of cigarettes.' Anna stops. She's gabbling. Calum is staring at her, or maybe it's the torchlight that makes his face look so intense.

He reaches across, touches a strand of her hair. It's hanging loose where she's pushed her hood down. Anna holds still, aware of her own breathing. 'Black Peter came to the farm once.' Calum's eyes narrow, retrieving the memory. 'I must have been really wee, four or five maybe. He was ancient – he'd have to be about a hundred by now. Dad brought him in for the moles, you know?' Anna nods. A row of dead moles often used to hang along the fence by the cottage. Shrivelled by the elements. Revolting, but you didn't really notice them, after a while.

From somewhere up the fell, a sudden bang erupts, loud and instantly recognisable. Time seems to pause, then they are scrambling to their feet; Anna is stifling a cry. Again, the sound echoes across the hillside beyond the cottage.

'Shh! Listen,' Calum is whispering, his hand on her arm.

They freeze, waiting.

Claire

Propped up on a pillow, Claire has the bedcover pulled almost to her chin. One hand pokes out, clutching the novel she's trying to read, her thumb holding the pages open at the fold.

She should sleep, but her mind is buzzing. Her own fault for drinking tea before bed.

At night, it's harder to escape the doubts. Who am I kidding, hiding out here? How will we live? The refrain can be relentless. But on the early spring mornings, when the rain holds off, sunlight picks out the secret dips and textures of the land; sheep call in the fields; birds of prey hover above the fell, wings braced on the air currents. Then, she feels the draw of the place.

Abandoning her book, Claire slips from the bed. She shoves her feet quickly into her slippers. They already feel chilly. Her cardigan is draped over a chair. Slipping it on, she treads softly over to the bedroom window.

She can see straight across the valley. There must be a moon, though it's hidden from view. There is still enough contrast in the night to make out the looming silhouette of the fell against the sky. And there is the light again. A sweeping arc across the upper slope. Then a crack of sound. And another.

For a moment, Claire is rooted to the spot, her eyes staring into the night. Then, wrapping her cardigan tighter around herself, she tiptoes hurriedly through to check on Rory.

Jean

Moving quietly, Jean follows the mud track that curves up the fellside beyond the lambing sheds. Her eyes have adjusted to the murk. She can make out the shrouded humps of gorse and the snaking line of the dyke. From the field below, the rasp of a cough. A sheep.

She becomes aware of a deeper blackness standing proud of the scrub. Then, turning briefly in her direction, a face, somewhat pale, in contrast to dark clothing and a low-pulled hat. She can smell it now, from a full field away: gun oil.

Jean can tell it's a man, even from this distance. It's almost always men, though it's probably not acceptable nowadays to say so. She stands to watch. To make sure.

The night blanches. A beam of light slices the arterial darkness, just for an instant. Lamping. Jean waits, a frown creasing her face. She is expecting the shots when they come.

⁂

Glassy pairs of eyes spread across the exposed landscape. Rabbits, petrified by the artificial glare. And then the gunshot, severing the silence. A second shot, then stillness. Even the wind seems temporarily absent.

The hunter is darting forward, searching the grass for corpses. They lie, legs positioned for flight, circles of matted fur darkening where the shots have gone in. He crouches quickly, uncomfortable perhaps, knowing that he is watched; heard. Then he is striding over the fell. Another few moments and the roar of an engine cuts across the valley. He is gone.

ELEPHANT

BECAUSE THEY'D ALWAYS called Edward 'Jumbo', the same way they've always called me 'Coco', nobody in the family would for some time state dogmatically that Edward was in fact turning into an elephant. But it was obvious even on the first day he came back from those distant and unspecified parts. A detective and a lawyer led him out of a steaming jungle and home to claim an inheritance he knew nothing about. How could he know anything about it? He'd been sent to school in Switzerland at the age of four and had disappeared without a trace at the age of eleven. It was rumoured by those who make rumours that he had run off with a travelling circus but this has never been proved and Edward says little about his past. Even if I ask him these days he just twists his trunk round and deposits me gently but firmly on the ground and trundles off to a mud pool to hose himself down and play in the water. He never gets tired of doing that and I suppose that's one nice thing about being an elephant – there are certain things you just don't get tired of doing, unlike humans, who can get tired of doing anything, including such necessities as cleaning the teeth at least once daily. In witness to this truth I call to the witness box Lady Dallows' breath, which on many a chat-filled evening has whispered into my ear and unavoidably my nostrils: 'A gin and tonic, Coco, a large one.' By the time she'd reached the end of that little request I had almost been suffocated by the ghastly ruins of her old, old breath. A breath, it was said, that went back a thousand years to the days when the Dallows, or Dalloites as they were then known, had been conquistadores in the magnificent empires of the far west, where magic and ritualised philosophy had sprouted cities full of wizards who suddenly and sadly faded away at the puff of a blunderbuss and the bolt of a crossbow. The Dalloites had done horrible things for money in those days and without their own religion they would probably have felt very guilty. As it was, they blamed everything that was happening on a weird and ancient prophet, who they said was a good sport and used to carrying all sorts of burdens for other people. The Dalloites helped themselves to new treasures and just so as they could always help themselves without further interference from these spellbinding men and women, they killed them off and became very rich. But not all very rich enough. When some of the Dalloites wanted to get richer they started killing each other off. Fortunes were shuffled and reshuffled like decks of cards until only a few families remained and they were firm and pointed and rich and rare as pyramids. After all, they said, if everybody's rich, where's the elite?

Lady Dallows has confided all this history in me now for a number of years. She always tells me old family stories after about a third of a bottle of gin, almost as though there were a pencil mark on the side of the bottle marked 'story time' and she had no choice but to begin. Afterwards she gives me a little smile which I suppose I should describe as 'secret' and she says: 'There now, Coco, what do you think of that?'

I always feel like saying, like admitting, that I cannot give an honest answer to that question because I have built up a prejudice against her breath, which is a compromise between old butter and dead flowers, whose stalks have been left standing in a vase filled with water. I usually say: 'Amazing story, Madam, truly amazing.'

It was the late Lord Dallows who taught me to say things like that. He was a moody man who went madder than usual last year, summoned his doctors to his armchair, where he had been languishing and ailing for several years, and asked them outright how long he had left to live. One doctor told him three years, one told him twenty years, the third discovered a rare and new disease in him and stated without reservation that he would be dead within the week. This actually came to pass, in fact, for one week later I found Lord Dallows seated in an armchair on top of a hill with his brains blown out by a pistol still smoking like a cigar between his fingers. There was a Hell's Angels jacket thrown around his scarecrow shoulders while his twiggy limbs were encased in hard black driving leather. The circumstances, the details of the way that Lord Dallows was dressed, of course never came to the dubious light of the newspapers. Lady Dallows saw to that. The rocket-bike the Lord had kept, unridden and unseen, was also made to disappear. Lady Dallows was powerful enough to contradict the nature and truth of history, so she did.

What could not be hidden, of course, was the dying and eccentric request by Lord Dallows that his long lost son, Jumbo, be run to earth, if he was still on Earth that is, and that he be brought back to the Estate and set up in the household as the rightful and titular head of this old and therefore noble family.

Lady Dallows threw a private tantrum of confusion. She shuddered at the memory of the monster she had given birth to. It was the worst thing that ever happened in her life.

In a calmer frame of mind some time later she read out the contents of her Lord's request at the dinner table. It was a momentous occasion. Only the close family were present. Lady Dallows' daughter, Cynthia, a serene nymphomaniac, was there. She had her hair piled two feet above her head, so that, beside her, her little husband looked even smaller and squarer, just like a little gleaming computer, who, programmed with three vodkas and never any more, could be made to smile and shine at Cynthia, who sometimes called him 'Compo the Genius', which he adored. She didn't call him that very often so he was always listening and hoping to hear her say it to him. This held their marriage together, despite Cynthia's bodily needs to be open to the world. Mercifully, Compo had been programmed to understand only certain things, the rest he was blind to.

Lady Dallows was in many ways happy with the way her daughter's marriage had worked out. Only on those rare occasions when the newspapers caught Cynthia on the arm of a rock of crack dealer, were there cries of outraged indignation at the table and Cynthia would go into tearing tirades against the salaciousness of the press. On these occasions she would stroke Compo, twiddle the dial of his nose, make him chuckly and call him her one and only genius. Compo looked forward to these odd scandals, I'm sure, because on such a night he could hear his wife call him Compo the Genius not once but many, many times. Scandals strengthened their bonds. Also on these occasions Cynthia would make the frustrated point that she was unable to sue these rags since they were so far beneath her. Lady Dallows would nod her head as though agreeing with the sentiments of that statement, the angle at which she held her ivory cigarette holder, a poised forty-five degrees above the lip, said that she knew something different from the conversation that was taking place, however.

After such discussions and after Compo and Cynthia had left for their respective wings of the mansion, she'd say to me with a grim laugh and a wiggle-waggle of her empty glass: 'Play it again, Sam!'

By now I knew what that meant. She meant: 'Pour it again, Coco!' Sometimes she'd even say: 'Pour it again, Coco!' and I'd rush over and fill her glass. I have consequently always been amused and amazed at the power of trivia on the besotted mind. However.

There were just the three of them to dinner on the night they discussed the Lord's will and request that his only son and heir, Edward Dallows, known as a child as Jumbo because of his enormous size and bizarre appearance, be tracked down, no matter the cost, found, brought back to sit in power in the old Dallows chair, where he would be master of all he surveyed and even beyond.

'I don't know if they'll find him and I don't know what sort of man he'll turn out to be.' Lady Dallows spoke weakly and bit her lower lip, thin and mangled like a serrated saw. She was staring at a photograph of the four-year-old Edward. I was pouring sherry and got a good look at the picture. It showed a huge little boy with small round eyes and a nose that swept down the front of his face so far that his mouth was all but invisible.

'An impossible birth,' Lady Dallows murmured to herself. 'A huge boy! Monstrous creature! The Lord knows where he came from!'

She bit her lower lip again and drooled a little blood-red sherry into its wounds.

Cynthia gave a guarded and dubious: 'Mmm.'

She was somewhat bitter that at any moment an elephantine brother might be produced and rise a notch in the status stakes above her, for she knew that with the passing of years she would be just that much more desirable if she were not just rich but stinking rich and head of the house of Dallows.

Lady Dallows realised all this and she was in a dither. The Estate must remain in the hands of the family. She knew as a peasant knows that he is not even a peasant without his dirt patch. That was old knowledge with her, perhaps a thousand years old for a thousand years ago the Dallows themselves had been peasants before they crossed the line in their minds and became conquistadores.

After the family had left, she confided in her glass, sometimes preferring to talk to it rather than myself, whose hand it was guided hers to the glass, that being one of its major tasks.

If Cynthia were head of the family, everyone would be head of the family. It would change from week to week. And who knows, one of them might even get Compo out of the way. Then chaos would be let fly. No system, no regularity, only an army of glistening gigolos, whose ambitions burned more brightly than their lust for Cynthia, whom I suppose must have her little interests outside of the Estate. She's no elephant but she's no great beauty either.

In the past, some newspapers had tried to make Cynthia into a beauty but without too much success because at the same time as they were launching her on that well-beaten path a certain movie queen of Nordic extraction was in the process of becoming a liberated Mormon woman.

She was doing this, she said, so that instead of having to keep divorcing her husbands she could keep them all. 'But do you want them all?' a frowning reporter had asked and she had given her famous reply: 'Of course, darling, I want them all. They're all so cute.'

Well, Cynthia had nothing to match anything like that, so the campaign to make her a beauty had soon fizzled out.

'Play it again, Sam!' Lady Dallows said and I filled her glass and she began talking to me as she so often did when we reached the mark on the bottle. 'Do you know, Coco, that the Dallows Estate has never fallen? It has remained! Why, Coco?' I knew the answer to the question but it was not for me to answer it. Lady Dallows went on: 'Because it has gone on but changed in shape.'

This was, it seemed, true. In one century it was a warrior, in another it was mercantile, in yet another it had mastered systems to control the world and divert the ebb and flow of energy, and all the time it looked as steady as a fairly steady old woman in a high-backed ornate armchair, whispering to me: 'Play it again, Sam!' It was no wonder I considered the Dallows an amazing family. Of my own I know next to nothing. I was born and raised in the kitchen. I'll never grow up and I'll never grow old. Nobody knows my age, I'm five feet two inches tall and I have one of those faces that people describe as ageless. I have somehow learnt or have always known that I come from a distant place whose name I can only once in a blue moon pronounce. I somehow connect the name of the place with a dream I had once in which I saw thousand thousand fires blazing. I don't usually dream, so I've always remembered that particular one.

When it was known throughout the Dallows-speaking

world, which was everywhere, that the search for the missing Edward 'Jumbo' Dallows was on, a thousand or more unemployed men stepped forward and claimed to be the missing man. Lady Dallows saw them all and a sorry bunch of charlatans they were, although each of them received a glass of gin and a pat on the back.

During this waiting period a lot of drink was consumed in the mansion. Lady Dallows was more drunk than usual. Cynthia was drinking more than customary while Compo wondered what he should do after he had drunk his three vodkas and his wife had not once pronounced him El Compo the Genius. It was a frustrating time for them all. For me it was as usual a time of hard work, ruinous breath, old stories and jokes repeated in a musical range of several octaves.

'O Co-co!' a neighbouring minor Lord sang out at the table one night when he wanted a drink. After I had filled his glass he kept singing out my name like that for the whole duration of the dinner party, whether he wanted a drink or not. It was most peculiar and caused Compo to later remark, perhaps a little louder than usual, that Lord Minor and his military friend, Major Burke, were a pair of schizophrenic sopranos, whose performances for the benefit of society should take place on a mountain top in the distant Himalayas before an audience of drooling yetis. This shocked Cynthia and then filled her with delight. 'Oh, Compo,' she said, 'you are a Genius!' Compo was in computers and because he was, he knew few pleasures that did not come from hard work and pointless analysis. Now, suddenly, to receive, gratis, this savoury morsel of affection, he was in ecstasy! He was so happy that the little watch on his wrist began pulsing with a small red light, which I understood was one of his own inventions for programming the system to remain moderate, and consequently on top and in charge and making pots of loot. Heaven help the world if ever he lost his watch!

Thus it was, that with such scenes and with terrible bated breath, the triumvirate of Lady Dallows, Compo the Genius and Cynthia the 'Thrust' - as she was known in some of the better guerrilla circles - waited for word on the long-lost son none of them really wanted to return.

They didn't wait that long and it was just as well for all concerned. An American private eye phoned from the far, far west one night just after Cynthia and Compo had retired to their respective wings of the mansion. He informed Lady Dallows that he had found a 'Jumbo', whom he could prove was Edward Dallows and who indeed admitted he was.

'Bring him home!' was all Lady Dallows had to say on the subject. She sensed this man would be her son and she knew one glance would tell her all.

Lord Edward Dallows the 57th came home in a very big car, a car as big as a small lorry. He was sitting in the back of it, I thought at first smoking a pipe, but I was wrong because, on closer inspection, I saw that he was in fact bringing his long nose down to his mouth as though to feed himself.

We all stood in a row on the lawn waiting to receive him. A small band played 'Men of Harlech', although this had nothing to do with anything except the absurd and erroneous whim of a minor cousin, who because he had once served dinner with brown napkins was said to have 'good taste'.

Edward fell out of the back of the lorry. He landed on all fours and stood up slowly on his hind legs as though he wasn't really used to walking that way. We all stood silently, apart from the band that is, waiting as he came lumbering forward to greet his long-lost family. They trumpeted out their greetings to him and Edward answered in kind with a jolly movement of a small round eye in an enormous head. His voice was slow and strange like a record played at a speed too slow. At first his voice gave the impression that it was about to run out or fade away into complete incoherence, but this didn't happen. In fact Edward could keep on talking and moving his merry eyes for as long as anyone else and most probably longer. At this time he was between seven and eight feet tall, I estimate. The wild, distant and foreign climes from which he had travelled had obviously left their mark on him for his colouring was grey and his skin wrinkled like a pair of trousers the wearer has been forced to sleep in. The look of shrivelling prunes in the eyes of Lady Dallows said that this was indeed her little monster come home to retain his title and take up his place as head of the house of Dallows. And so once more it seemed the nature of the Dallows Estate was to change.

How well I remember the night of the first dinner party held in honour of Lord Edward Dallows the 57th. He leaned over to me and said, very quietly for such a big 'man', 'Please place a bucket of cold water next to me, Coco.'

I nodded and brought the bucket of water. When the ladies and Compo and all the minor and semi-majors saw me hoist the bucket on to the table next to Edward they all smiled and assumed that champagne was naturally the order of the day, but how wrong they were and how short-sighted. A few moments later, when they were all drinking crystal glasses of cold water, their faces took on a pained look and they waited for something to be said and for their livers to receive a worthier stimulant. At last, Lady Dallows, no longer able to contain herself, said: 'Coco, why are we all drinking water?

Don't you think a Dallows 49 would be more appropriate?'

I spoke up quite boldly as I knew I had to on such occasions and my words filled the banquet hall and were heard by all present.

'Your Ladyship, the motto of this house is: I Drink As My Lord. The first drink is thus the choice of the first Lord and those who are loyal are bound to drink with him. Lord Edward Dallows the 57th chose to drink from a bucket of water.'

Lord Edward withdrew his nose from the cool of the bucket and said in that slow speech of his: 'This is true! I Drink As My Lord – that was written on my school blazer all the time that I wore one as a boy.'

There was no denying the truth of all this. Finally Lady Dallows voiced the question pertinent to herself and the largest proportion of those assembled at the table.

'Do you intend to drink water all night, Edward?'

Lord Edward shook his great flapping ears. He hadn't got much hair left.

'Not all night. I will stop drinking after I finish this bucket off, but you, all of you, must drink as you see fit.'

This was Edward's first political statement and it caused a liberal murmur to ripple around. They could drink whatever they liked but he, the Lord, would drink water only. This did seem strange at first but after Lady Dallows had downed a third of a bottle of gin, a glass of water and several other fizzes, she declared Edward's statement 'a very healthy eccentricity' and eccentricity was of course to be respected and tolerated especially if the eccentric were head of the Dallows Estate. Edward became known as a water drinker and that was the end of it. He was Lord as his father had been.

After this dinner party a furtive conference took place at the bottom of Staircase Five, known as the Pearly Way because of its long white shimmering twisting banister, which seemed to mount up and up and up until it seemed to disappear completely out of sight and many was the weary gigolo who with Cynthia cradled in his arms mounted those stairs like an eternal Rhett Butler with an eternal woman to carry up to infinity. This was a strange place for Lady Dallows, Cynthia and Compo to meet. I served them drinks from a pearly tray which was fitting for the setting and did not go unnoticed by Lady Dallows despite her preoccupation with the newly arrived head of the household.

Cynthia asked: 'Has he always looked like that?' Lady Dallows sighed and sipped her drink: 'Not even Switzerland could turn a Jumbo into a Lord.' Then she smiled quite sweetly, although her breath was totally rank: 'A big body with a little brain can hardly be so alarming, can it? After all, elephants perform in circuses. But we will see, we will see.'

They drank to that as though they were not yet conspirators but could one day be should the need arise.

I left them there and returned to Edward who was still seated at the head of the empty table with his nose swishing around inside an empty bucket while his little eyes looked quite merry and bright.

'What are they saying about me, Coco?' he asked.

I answered: 'That they mustn't be disturbed by the way you look and that small brains in big bodies are not to be feared.'

Edward laughed.

'Are you disturbed by the way I look, Coco?'

I shook my head. 'My Lord,' I said, 'you are turning into

an elephant, which is quite a rare phenomenon for people who are not accustomed to such things happening. As for myself I have heard of several Eastern dynasties whose forefathers were fire-breathing dragons and only the other night there was a film on television in which Lawrence of Arabia was accused of having a mother who mated with a scorpion, so I am not at all disturbed.'

Edward nodded and I saw he was contented and wished me to be his friend.

'You are a wise man,' he said.

'I Drink As My Lord Drinks.'

Edward nodded and said cheerfully: 'I think you do, Coco, and I'm glad. Have the staff prepare a bed for me at the bottom of Staircase One. Make sure there is a good thickness of straw on the floor and a bucket of water close by for thirst and fun.'

I saw these things were taken care of.

The family of course could not help but notice these changes. They stared at each other in grim and resigned silences as they realised the extent of their toleration of a 'very healthy eccentricity'. They went speechless before the buckets of water that seemed to be found everywhere, even in the library where Edward could sometimes be found trumpeting with laughter over a major masterpiece which was said to have changed the lives of millions of people. However, most of the time he preferred to stay out of the house, away from the bric-a-brac and gossip.

Once when he was not in the mansion I remember the triumvirate assembled like ghosts for breakfast. Morning wasn't their best time, except for Compo who ran quite smoothly between the hours of nine and five, after which time he was just waiting to hear himself named a genius. Lady Dallows plunged her fork into the scrambled egg and said: 'Where's Jumbo?' She often called him that behind his back. I said: 'He's playing in the pond at the bottom of the rose garden.'

She frowned. 'Oh, he is a dull child.'

Cynthia raised her eyebrows, 'Mother, he's not a child any more and you can't send him off to Switzerland again. He's Lord and head of the Dallows whether we like it or not.'

Cynthia did not really like it because although their lives hadn't changed that much since Edward's return she now felt there was no party atmosphere in the house and Edward didn't seem like 'getting on' and 'having fun'.

'He's not much fun, is he?' she said at last.

Nobody said anything to that, so she fixed her eye on me. 'Well, is he, Coco? He's not much fun, is he?'

'Madam,' I said, 'if you went down to the mud pool and saw Edward Dallows the 57th playing in the mud, you would say he was happy as a lark and having lots of fun.'

She scowled and shrugged as though to say: What else do you expect from an elephant?

Personally I had begun to like Edward very much and he was really happy when once I threw a bucket of water over him. He thanked me profusely and said nobody had ever done anything so nice for him before. After that I was always throwing water over him and watching it run down the sides of his enormous grey body.

At that moment Edward came rumbling into the room and the family gasped. The final changes had taken place. He had changed from a big balding man into a baby elephant or a small elephant at any rate. He nuzzled his trunk into my hand and I slipped him a small green apple which I kept in my pockets these days.

'Thank you, Coco,' he said in that strange voice of his, which I think was becoming increasingly difficult for the family to understand. 'It's nice of you to remember that I like these fruits.'

'There's a whole orchard of them outside,' snapped Cynthia who had evidently understood this exchange.

Edward nodded. 'But it's not the same as being remembered, is it? And besides,' he added with a chuckle, 'you know an elephant never forgets, especially when he himself has been forgotten.'

'You weren't forgotten,' Lady Dallows hissed like a snake, 'you were brought back from the wild to claim an inheritance you've done nothing to earn. We haven't had a party in the house since you've been back and just look at the way you're dressed . . .'

Her words trailed off and Edward, still munching his apple, said: 'I came back of my own free will to claim my rightful inheritance as stated in the last will and request of my father and your husband, the late Lord. As for the way I'm dressed, I'm not dressed, I am just like I look like. I am an elephant and you must accept that because I am the new and rightful Lord. You do not have to drink as your Lord, you may drink as you will.'

They said nothing. There was nothing they could say, but all, it seemed, suddenly noticed that Edward was growing small tusks.

After this small but significant exchange the family held several parties one after another. They were well attended by all the majors and minors. However, now a different atmosphere prevailed. It was one of gossip and intrigue, for even when someone asked politely after Lord Dallows, the family found it difficult to give an answer. They did not state that he had become an elephant and so the company assumed that he wasn't or wouldn't be until Lady Dallows actually confirmed a new page of history by proclaiming the 57th Lord to be an elephant. The Dallows household dragged their feet in champagne slippers, which didn't make any difference to anything really because they'd always been like that.

Edward himself, however, began to make some changes around the mansion. Plantations of marula were sown and watched over carefully by a team of gardeners. Edward told me he loved the plum especially when it was fermenting on the branch. Along with these agricultural changes he introduced into the grounds a herd of elephants not unlike himself. When Cynthia conveyed this ultimate piece of news to Lady Dallows, the ageing woman had little reply.

'I suppose,' she said, 'he's got to play with animals of his own sort, after all. It's out of my hands anyway.'

Cynthia then realised that her mother was retiring more and more from public life and possibly going mad. A mountain of romantic novels beside her mother's bed seemed to confirm her suspicions. In desperation she turned to Compo, who stared at her with expectant eyes. It had been a long time since she had thrown a meaty compliment in his direction and he was starving.

For me these were great days and my own life had changed. I was no longer pouring drinks for the family but throwing buckets of water over Edward and his friends. This was more tiring than serving drinks but much more fun because I didn't have to play unless I wanted to. In fact, I was virtually free to do what I liked for the first time in my life, and of course confronted with the opening of my own destiny I didn't know what on earth I should do.

One hot afternoon I fell asleep beside the mud pool and there was nothing unusual about that except that when I woke up it was dusk and I was rolling and swaying some way off the ground. I took my bearings slowly. I was on Edward's back at the head of a herd of elephants and we were rolling through the undergrowth. Edward slipped his trunk up to me.

'OK up there?' he asked. 'You fell asleep. I thought you might like a ride. You must get a fine view up there. Ride there as often as you want. I like you talking to me, that is if it's all right with you?'

I gave Edward an apple just to say it was fine and there was no need for him to go on about it. This was my first experience of a quiet and mutual understanding and it was very pleasurable. Never again did I serve the Dallows another drink. My life had changed and I was different. I roamed the vast reaches of the Dallows Estate on Edward's back and everywhere I went, save the mansion itself, where I was known as 'that damned Coco', I was treated with a great and natural respect, which at first was odd and almost uncomfortable, because now that I didn't have to please anyone except myself, I began to wonder who in fact I was. It was a funny time in my life, I can assure you.

It was during this period that Compo, who had been a silent voice in the household for some time now, came forward with a leafy suggestion. Sam, the new drink-server, told me all about it. Apparently, Compo had the theory that everything alive had to make money or else it would die or be stolen in order to survive. He mentioned this in relation to Lord Edward and the herds of wild elephants that now roamed the Dallows Estate.

'What we must do,' he said, 'is turn the Estate into a Safari

Park and charge visitors to view this motley crowd. This will pay for their upkeep and generally satisfy curiosity and speculation as to the whereabouts of the water-drinking Lord.'

Lady Dallows gave the idea her blessing with an ethereal wave of her hand. She had stopped reading romantic novels and was learning to fly from an Indian manual. She hoped one day to surprise her guests by cruising down the table two feet above their heads. Cynthia thought the idea wild and exciting and she gave her husband what he wanted: 'Darling, you're a genius!' Secretly she thought that the visitors would eventually drive Edward and his mud loafers out of the way entirely and back to foreign climes. He was certainly too big to get through the doorway of the mansion now and it was foolish to pretend that such a beast could head such a household. Nor had mixing with the other elephants done anything for his vocabulary and diction. She sighed and filled the emptiness of her life with bitterness against Edward and 'that damned Coco' whom she said was a menace to society! I was amazed!

Visitors came from far and near to view the majesty of the marauding elephants. For the most part they stayed in their cars and trailed us at some distance and we didn't mind that too much. Sometimes a voice would be carried to us over the wind. 'Which one is Edward? Which one is the chief? See that little fellow on his back? That's damned Coco.' And there was laughter, ha ha ha and ho ho ho. We soon got tired of it, of being spied on, and our excursions took us further and further beyond the grounds of the Estate into wilder country where the sun baked the ground into cracked and dried biscuits and marula grew naturally and the vegetation was thick and lush. Edward and I were both happy. We travelled on and on and the ground swayed beneath me and the great curved tusks of Edward reminded me that I was not dreaming but really moving through the world. If I knew where Edward was leading me he didn't seem to know where he was going, if I sort of felt lost he seemed purposeful. It was often like that between us. The cloistered sanctuaries of sherry rooms and champagne slippers were another lifetime away. At night we made camp around dark pools of water and many were the startled eyes that joined us there to drink. And at night the undergrowth seemed to whisper secret messages and I was filled with a sense that we must in fact be going somewhere and that someone knew we were on our way. Often in the dark hours then I would slip off from the herd to stand alone in the night to wonder who I was and what I was doing. Beneath the stars this seemed like a luxury to me.

One night I wandered off from the herd into an empty plain beyond which lay a ridge. I stood there feeling small and mysterious while above me the moon was a golden orb like a golden apple which I could stretch my hand out to pluck if I felt like it. Then I became aware that I was not alone. Edward was standing not twenty yards off, his eye merry and bright in the moonlight. He was a massive shape with warrior tusks of ivory which hung from him like huge traditional ceremonial swords. He swayed over to me like a man in boots wading through a pool and sank down beside me so that we were about eye-level. His trunk moved around in the dusk like some independent alien creature.

'Do you want an apple?' I said, not sure if I had one or not.

He shook his head. 'I don't want anything except never to go back to the Dallows Estate.'

'But you have duties to assume,' I said without thinking about what I was really saying.

He nodded. 'You speak like a Lord, Coco, and you are right. I've known that for some time now. Compo's genius may one day destroy the world and wrap its remains in cellophane paper. His powers must be limited and my sister must be kept occupied so that she does nothing of consequence, for she has only a limited vision, which like a little knowledge is a dangerous thing. I believe Lady Dallows is now fairly safely old.'

'It's you who speaks like a Lord, Edward,' I said and indicated that I wanted to ride on his back. He helped me up and rose to his feet.

'Which way, Lord?' he said.

'That way, Lord,' I replied and pointed at the toothed ridge that lay in front of us like a parapet against intrusion.

We mounted the slope towards the ridge. Even as we went up the slope I knew something was about to happen. I wanted to say something to Edward but I couldn't find the words because I didn't know exactly what it was that I wanted to express. Up we went and the breeze breathed all around us. My mouth was open and in my heart, it seemed. And then with a final little scramble we were on top of the ridge looking down on my dream, the only dream I've ever remembered!

Before me blazed a thousand fires like a thousand stars and in their light I saw a teeming people with their arms outstretched as though to hold up the low bright moon.

We stood silhouetted on the ridge like that and suddenly the people gave a shout, drums began to beat and without more ado we went down to these people to fulfil a prophesy and become a living legend.

For a thousand years, as long as the Dallows Estate had thrived, these people had waited for the arrival of a two-headed

Lord who could see both sides of the world at the same time. They said we were that Lord and when I learned that the name of this place was the name of the place I had originally come from but could hardly ever pronounce, I could hardly contradict their story. Here I was, made a Lord and, like Edward, found I had come home to claim my inheritance, which was different from his, while our knowledge of the world remained shared and the same.

With the knowledge came the awareness that Edward and I would soon be parted. Our duties lay before us. He knew he had to return to the Dallows Estate just as I knew that for now I had to remain in the light of these blazing fires. It was as though we had to walk in different directions around the world in order to meet up in the middle and exchange an apple. I would never have dreamt life was like that.

A few days later I watched my true friend, Edward Dallows the 57th disappear over the toothed ridge. He was a Lord and he was an elephant. I would never forget him. I knew that because he was what he was, he could never forget me either.

CHIMERA

THE SIGN FLASHED 'Chimera' and you both made your way down the steps, and the first thing you saw was a couple, or maybe even three people, having sex against the wall opposite the bar. You were sure of it. You looked away, but she did not. She said something, but the music was so loud, you wouldn't have heard her. The tables were sticky to the touch, and you did touch them, didn't you, to navigate through? And the barman stood polishing a pint glass with a white tea-towel whilst watching football on a giant TV screen. She felt in her handbag for her purse, and leaned awkwardly against the chrome of the bar. The DJ pressed an oversized earphone to one ear, and swayed in the way of a tiger in a cage. His T-shirt said something unreadable from that distance. She had to lean right over to order the drinks and her small breasts pressed down against the bar. The barman rolled his eyes at something she said. You'd stopped noticing the detail of her, as people do a painting that's been hanging on their wall for too long. But you noticed her then. You noticed the way she walked back, balancing the two drinks like it was a magic trick of some kind and you were impressed.

You sat, the two of you, at a round, wooden table that rocked because one leg was shorter than the rest. The drinks jerked as if about to tip over. You picked yours up and held it. When you tasted it, there was a feeling of pepper and dirt and some kind of acid, at the back of your throat.

Beneath you, the floor vibrated, because of the music. You could feel it in your breast bone and wondered if it was good for your heart, never mind your hearing. You were sweating, and you were sure the place was sweating too, from the walls, from the ceiling. You expected that at any moment there would be a deluge, like a sprinkler going off.

She picked up a laminated menu from the table and you watched her study it. It might have been the drink, but you thought, you fantasised about asking her to marry you just then.

'Are you hungry?' she mouthed, or maybe you thought she did. Maybe she just looked like she'd say that kind of thing just then.

'Is there vegan?' you said, trying to impress.

'Are you mad?' she definitely said.

Fair enough, it was Digbeth, after all.

In each dark corner, something like smoke rose, or so it seemed to you, unpeopled, and vaguely medicinal. Spectral. Had there been windows, you'd have expected headlights to have shone through and illuminated disparate images of women, mostly, in various poses and states of undress. A man in a long skirt seemed to just appear, with a small dog on a piece of rope. The way he moved made you think he was begging for cash, or was about to, and you looked away. When you looked again, he was gone.

'Did you see him, that man?' you said.

She nodded, vaguely, said, 'You have to be really thin to pull that look off.'

The barman materialised from a shadow, adjusting his belt, and took your glass, even though you hadn't yet finished your drink.

'You look old in this light,' she said. 'Older.' And her face was close to yours, or you wouldn't have heard her, and her hand was on your thigh, and it felt like you'd expect mercury to feel inside a thermometer. You realised that, opposite, a man sat alone, his stare persistent and challenging. His head so bald, it shone like a halo, his fingers intertwined beneath his chin, the buttons of his shirt opened low, something like a crucifix glistening. When two semi-naked girls passed, he didn't seem to notice until they kissed at the bar and muscles of their tattooed legs, like dolls' legs, strained in their high-heeled shoes.

'What do you want to do?' she said.

You thought for a second, said, 'This. All this.' And your voice ululated.

But she didn't mean that though, did she? And when she laughed, even that couple, or threesome having sex, or whatever, stopped – you're pretty sure – momentarily.

And they all looked at you, just then, didn't they?

You needed the toilet, but she said it was time to go. You'd never been in an Uber before and she kept checking her phone all the way. You asked to see what she was looking at but she said it was none of your beeswax, and to get your own phone, and you said yours was better than hers but it was charging, and she said, 'Of course it is.'

You got home in time, and she sent you to your room. 'Sssh,' she said. 'They'll be back soon.'

You're frightened of the dark, she knows that, but she turned off the light.

The excitement had made you tired, so you never even heard your parents come home, did you?

THE CLEARANCE

THE ESTATE AGENT had been negotiating almost an hour when he smiled a genuine smile, probably because he realised he had clinched the job, the fat commission, decisions had been made at least verbally on the rates, the guide price, the basic terms and conditions and now he was being asked to field a simple, all too familiar enquiry, so he was in a safe zone, he could relax, he could stop playing with the knot of his tie, maybe take it off altogether, relax, all he had to do now was explain with a smile how hopeless it was of neighbours or friends to want to buy the property of the deceased that was going empty, literally empty as the clearance crew were apparently on the way with their van, well, he would say in so many words, these people from across the road, so flimsily related to the recent owner, had next to no chance, and once he had explained that in one or two anecdotes, particularly the one about the gardener who had reckoned he had a special claim which didn't set money at the centre of his takeover of the property, his appropriation was necessary on account of winter pruning and the shape of the birch tree, he would tell the brothers this and then they who like him were sitting inside on the last garden chairs would sign the papers, he would leave behind the brochures with their blue skies and wide-angled views making England look like Barbados, their gleaming bathrooms and their fine floor plans neat as any architect's, all he had to do from now on was pass the time, a month or two, three at the outside, sat not exactly in splendour, as the lighting at work fell well short of splendour, but in his nicely swivelling chair at the back of the office, where he could turn his computer screen away from scrutiny, his walk from the front to the back having been preceded by a delightful nod from Lauren on reception, and then he would go through the motions he was familiar with, walk the line between the obsequious and the professional which was once a tightrope but now was second nature, yes, second not first, his first was on an altogether different, finer plane, and given all this that he knew, this knowledge from experience, he could now drop his guard, what could possibly reverse the obvious, the brothers would sign, the elder blond one he guessed would scrawl illegibly and the younger sign with more careful, looping letters, yes he had clinched it, it wasn't as if he was going to wreck his own efforts, draw a knife from his briefcase and behead one of the brothers, heavens he wouldn't even know which one to go for, the tall blond with the ponderous remarks or the suspicious younger one with the dark eyes and long lashes, just a hint of kohl, no, he wouldn't do any of that or go off the edge some other way, say he was off to the kitchen to bake them a cake, declaring that was his passion and there would be no buts, he had the packet of almonds and the peaches ready to slice in his briefcase, nor would he risk making a rugby-tackle on the cat that had followed the hopeful neighbours inside, and – he debated whether to mention – if anything could ruin their chances of buying the property of their sadly deceased neighbour it was

bringing the cat in, that was almost as bad as taking out a cigarette, those were the days, when there was smoking all round
and ash falling on shoes because it was all so tense, nowadays
the tension breaks with a strident word or tea getting spilt
somewhere, a strident word even between strangers, which
they all were, particularly the neighbours, whose chances were
already next to nil, so he smiled as they at last retrieved the
cat and left, he smiled at the brothers and finally imparted
his thought, his knowledge, You would be amazed, he said,
how many times I've heard someone loosely connected to the
deceased imagine, the moment their neighbour dies, how they
can get a foot in the door and gain an advantage so they might
buy the house for themselves or their relations before anyone
else, at a lower price, and they never do get to do it, and yet
they go through this palaver which any estate agent worth
their salt will listen to thinking these people have lost their
heads, they've been hit by some quiet thunderbolt, it's as if
they've forgotten how lives work, how business works, forgotten there's a sky over our heads and earth at our feet, of course
it's a personal calamity for the family but with the greatest
respect for those who are no longer with us it's plain that
two and two are still four and in human nature nothing has
changed, we're all hurtling through space the same as before,
don't you see that way too, do you think we're hurtling or
just going slowly and steadily about the place, by the way call
me Mr Mazurka if you prefer but otherwise, please, almost
everyone calls me Maz.

In the kitchen glass smashes. Only an old jug, apparently.
That will be Dimitri, who is here to help himself in the house
clearout. This is allowed him in his capacity not as a blood

relation, only via his marriage to the niece of the deceased, who would be Jennie. Would be, because she hasn't been introduced and that somehow made her less substantial, and so, Mr Mazurka had decided, the best way to acknowledge her insubstantiality was to hesitate to think of her by name. Dimitri, who unlike Jennie had been introduced, partly because he was active all over the house in his search for items of use, a search that had brought him in and out of the living room, Dimitri is an anxious young man who apparently has a reputation for dropping things. He arrived with this reputation, deserved or otherwise, much as he arrived with the VW bus with the pregnant Jennie and with the clanking mudguard he insisted on calling a fender. The brothers blithely declared this information, this personal failing, in front of them all, in front of Dimitri, who given these allegations of incompetence could be forgiven for hiring lawyers or lighting candles under the brothers' toes, the elder adding that Dimitri was originally from Estonia, blathering on about him like this in the very first few minutes, when they all stood making small talk before retiring to do business in the conservatory, through which the sky was not blue, more a butcher-paper sky, butcher-paper was not part of the usual estate agent vocabulary but was he the usual, Lauren at work clearly didn't think so, he certainly didn't, the usual agent would see the sky wasn't blue and the sun wasn't out and refuse to accept this, indeed preferring to alter it, by returning to take photos the next day, or whenever, even on a Sunday if the weather played along, but now, he found himself saying to himself, the great spanned canvas of the heavens was the colour of glue that comes on a glue-stick, it might have rain drops stuck to it this very moment, although on the other hand water wouldn't stick with that glue, certainly not with the cheap brand they had back at the office. Equal to the young man's ability to drop things, the elder brother added in a further superfluous remark, adding it the moment Dimitri left to dash up the stairs to inspect the contents of the loft, is his ability to put things back together again, which is how come he has a workshop and how he runs this VW bus others would have long ago put aside. Dimitri simply puts too much in his arms, the younger brother said, I imagine he likes to take all of Jennie in his arms, the elder added, and she was an armful, and indeed she was, as he Maz the successful agent caught a glimpse of for himself at the moment of opening the front door, which his professional self noticed had got stuck at a rogue rail at the bottom, a detail which really needed fixing or best of all got rid of asap, pronto as Lauren would say, if she didn't say subito, I'll have it on your desk subito Mr Mazurka. As for this young man it's not for me to judge the flowers of Estonia, he thought as he unzipped his briefcase, even were he to become crowned county agent of the year, and he might, anything was possible, if crowned he wouldn't use the power to dispense judgements, and now he was not sure he wanted to be served up such a detailed, slightly damning picture of a fellow human being but what could he do, what is said has been said, so all he could think about this Dimitri was how he fills his arms and moves off, unable to see the floor, it's been alleged, the ground in front, anything in front of him except cars, buildings and tree trunks, and Jennie of course. He seems incapable of altering this quirk of his, the elder brother says, with a smile. This time, this smile, unlike his own, is one that puts the estate agent on his guard, he is being told things that appear irrelevant, not to say unkind, and yet in spite of that the fate of the Meissen china Dimitri was purloining, removing from the kitchen, was in the Mazurka book surely party to the whole cosmic conspiracy, to the way everything has to be the way it happens to be, from the timing of his own birth to the dark demeanour of his wife first thing every morning, from nothing to Adam and Eve to now and back again, from the timber posts of the Anglo-Saxons to Taylor Wimpey down the road, from the firing of all porcelain to its precarious path through the ever dangerous world, yes with so much going on at once accidents had to happen and there it is, the turn of the china, as the Meissen hits the floor without for an instant considering bouncing. It's all right Dim, he hears Jennie say in a sharp voice which has no difficulty reaching from the kitchen, swerving around the hallway and through the living room and all its boxes packed ready for the big clearance, past the clump of house plants and right into the little conservatory, it's all right sweetheart, the place is different now, something has to give, it's all right you know.

Did you realise estate agents here are vilified, Dimitri?
Vilified?
Hated. Have nasty things said about them. Careful with that teapot.
No. I didn't know. Why?
It's because they're crap at their job.
So? We're all crap at something.

All crap at something. As he replaces some unwanted papers in his briefcase he, Maz, should he have said call me Maz, hears this little exchange and repeats it. It takes place solely inside his head. He has imagined it; a miracle he can do this; but given its negative sentiments, a reverse miracle. The exchange is crap, the idea crap, a cliché about estate agents. All crap at something? All splendid at something. He makes two fists as he sits in the conservatory, fists of determination, which he manages to make as if they were office ergonometrics that should be practised every so often when in a sitting position. After handing out coloured company pie charts with secrets of the market – you appreciate the paradox, Lauren: we have some facts and we call them our secrets and then we reveal them all, then saying they are facts, whereas we could have simply said in the first place here are some facts, ah-ha Mr Mazurka, then you are a fact agent not a secret agent, your cover is blown, did I do that, I'm always blowing something around here – he repeats the fists exercise so the brothers know it is just that, making fists for-the-sake-of-it and not the determined act of will it really is. I Maz will do a good job now that I have here found another house, do those fists now, another home, another loose ship tossing in the darkness of the universe, so that instead of wandering like a lost beast in the deep it is now fed light from the miraculous Mazurka generator, standing out on the inky dark expanse if not exactly prancing across the waves, a vessel whose ownership I can hand across to whoever steps forward with the right words at the right time, the right guesses, the right impressions, the right music in the background. Yes for him, Maz, director of operations, soon it will turn simple, he will be coasting, on autopilot, on the smooth glide through that post-contract phase. This pleases him no end, as he will be able to continue that inner Mazurka life, which for all he knows may be shared by other agents, that is, while blue-shirted and suited, leaflet-bearing on the outside, driver of a smartly decalled car, inside himself he, or it could be we, are artists, dancers, magicians, we produce the unexpected, not only rabbits out of hats but hats out of rabbits and images from nowhere, straining and striving like pony riders galloping through the night, reaching phenomenal creative waystations no one can describe, indeed why should they bother putting words to them, when our ethos is action, selling and buying to keep everything circulating, in other words alive, oh Mr Mazurka give me an agent with action any day of the week, Lauren would say, one to bring down walls with barely a rise of the shoulder, put our competitors to the sword, whatever you say Lauren he would reply, as long as success remains our byword, as it will, so long as our resources stay well oiled, as I intend they will, and having said that with as natural a gaze at Lauren as he could muster he would after a few more graceful steps down the office floor be swivelling silently at the back desk, thoughtfully, embellishing his thoughts about we agents being artists and magicians, thinking that, what is more, our intuitions rarely fail, it is as if we have our own extraordinary satellites circling up there, relaying information on potential buyers, causing them to take to the phone at the exact moment, leave the right messages, mouth the right figures, this magical technology at the same time beaming down brumming sounds of discouragement to neighbours who would like that foot in the door on behalf of their grown-up child, often newly-wed and wanting, brumming equally into the ears of the cat who fancies getting a paw in, a claw or two, although in the inner life of the agent and the outer life too already he knows, as an onomastician, as an aficionado of name-giving he knows, this house could not possibly or ever belong to any man who like their child had been around for more than twenty-five years and have the name Nathaniel.

The younger brother takes a book from the bookcase, after all
the books will be gone in an hour or two, once the relations
have taken their keepsakes and the clearance crew are here, the
bookcase will be gone, the carpet under it will be gone, even
the ceiling directly above may be gone if it contains asbes-
tos, and it may do, while the memories which involved these
books, the words and pictures, the dust jackets and covers,
the delights and thoughts inside, depicting lives and deaths,
such erudition and scenes of extraordinary sex, the imprints
on minds of all these contents, and even memories of the
removing and replacing of the books in this bookcase, will
after flaring, for however long they flare, likewise start to
flicker and to dim on their ever downward-falling path. The
brother takes the book, breathes in very publicly in what seems
like an expression of admiration, and moving smoothly, the
word is segue, could be segue, segues over to the cheap stone
fireplace which the eventual buyer will surely rip out within
the month – the neighbours across the road will at their family
pow-wow have already jotted a note to the effect – to stand
importantly, leaning an elbow on the mantelpiece, where he
splays the covers open at an early page. Ah, he says: Kraszna.
He glances at the big portrait of a man in uniform over the
fireplace. Is that this Kraszna? He replaces the book. He hasn't
signed the contract, yet. He will. That's how he will tell this
to Lauren back at the office, he was always going to sign, and
after my spiel it was doubly certain, oh Mr Mazurka, Lauren
would say, doubling everything, you're so right, if anything is
worth doing it's worth doing twice. Who's that a portrait of?
he asks the brother, for small talk's sake. Alistair, the brother

says. Ah. Alistair. Not, er, Kraszna then? he says tentatively.
God no, says the brother. As they both move away from the
picture, stepping carefully between the boxes, the elder brother
starts talking about the plants in the pots outside the window,
then about Japanese anemones, which he says grow tall and,
the younger adds, are so hard to spell. Abruptly the elder
stands. We're just going upstairs for a conflab, he says, you'll
be fine left to yourself for a moment Mr Mazurka, won't you.
Of course he will, the younger says.

Of course he will. Some rain falls. The way it so evenly covers
the patio is a wonder, a splendour even, he thinks, to an
estate agent who has seen so many patios, so many wonders.
The voices upstairs drone. Has he said too much, too little?
Suggesting calling him Maz was a suggestion too far, or was
it. It wasn't meant to be real, it was simply to say they were
now all in this together, their interests were aligned, they
would loose one sole arrow that needed joint guidance to fly
to its common target. But the suggestion may have sounded
too intimate, cast a shadow, made a nick in the fine Mazurka
canvas, a scar that was always there, irreparable, on the face of
his endeavours. The revelation about what to call him, what
name he in that unguarded moment said almost everyone calls
him, wasn't even true, Lauren for example had in three years
of working days stuck ironly to calling him Mr Mazurka.
Upstairs the drone breaks into laughs. What else? Has he
been too estate-agently? Or not enough? The sight of the rain
on the patio is joined by the consoling sound of a broom and
dustpan on the kitchen floor. He will, he will, he will what,
he's forgotten. The rain is light but steady. He would like to
make something, some sense, of the little lawn. But does a

lawn have a sense? Look at it. Because they have blades that collect water differently, and have different shades of green, blemishes on its surface stand out, while beyond the sodden square of land the soil of the flowerbed darkens: the sort of details an artist would notice. Again, had he not become an estate agent he would have become, or liked to be an artist, or a musician, after all did not artists, like musicians, often form a loose community of the open-minded, the curious and the encouragers of others, making it possible both to be an individual and to belong, there was bliss in the idea, he feels oddly at home in it, comfortably at home in just such a community, he can imagine it so vividly, there in the conservatory, that the thought produces an actual inner glow of happiness. As he catches the only rose in the garden nodding under its weight of rain, and the leaves of a camellia twitching, and he stops to further analyse his character, much as others stop before their mirrors, he is aware, or perhaps has simply decided that, in compensation for his daily work, he is drawn to outsiders, less reputable types, floaters, foreigners, people who are not so at ease in an office or just waiting for a train, it's they – here he could list many famous names, names he liked to rotate so new ones turned up and old names dropped out – they who have the charisma, who may or may not be frauds or charlatans, who are not quite scientists, not quite doctors, not quite cashiers, estate agents, they ignore the mould they're asked to step in, ignore it or kick it to one side, they create their own lives, even their own professions, that much was true of many of the names he currently had, the ones he'd newly promoted, those which had arrived so to speak at the front of the revolving stage of the famous and not-famous, pushing to the back a couple of really well-knowns he was no longer so sure of. A window bangs upstairs. In annoyance? To stop rain entering? Something, he had no clear idea what, makes him shudder. Could it be a fear of uttering the names of these latest heroes, they were names he hardly dared utter even to himself, and if uttered he had to keep them strictly to himself, well Palladio or Mackintosh might mean something to someone, someone who has actually stood back from a building and looked at it, but the great Jonathan Silver, well, if anyone knew he revered Jonathan – or any of a spate of names he dared not utter, the Van Alens, Sullivan, Antunes, enough, speed them off the front of the revolving stage – he would be in trouble, the kind of trouble where someone walks off in the middle of a conversation and says somewhere else you know old Maz he's retirement material if ever there was any. Crazy thoughts, Lauren would say. That maverick Mazurka. How he stares out of windows. With his mind on the outsides of buildings and their insides, on professions, here come the auctioneers in their van, wait, vans plural he can see from the conservatory, driving up to make the clearance. A brush with crime too – what is to stop them signing papers, loading up and tonight filling a container bound for Kazakhstan? – has its attractions, he realises, its plus points, as the leather-waistcoated crew of two arrive at the door. Dimitri dashes in and out. The brothers reappear, quietly smiling. Seeing their parking is blocking the way of the clearout Dimitri and Jennie decide they may as well leave. Dimitri stands at the door holding a green chair in front of him, there is an obvious attraction in the plush upholstery but he will never get it through the door holding that way, is he waiting for someone to take a photo of him standing there or what is he waiting for. Jennie can be heard telling him to put it down, the VW is piled high to the roof. Yes Kazakhstan is conceivable but why go all that way, moreover why not go where the money is and the authorities are stretched, say to France, that would be quite far enough, now if he had a removal crew, he began thinking, getting no further as words are being exchanged with the newcomers and there is much backing up and shouting and a lurching van, goings-on which he can follow without needing to even slide back the conservatory doors. Dimitri ties more knots to the rope around the mudguard. Up they step and in they swing. The wing mirrors refuse to be reset. They wave and drive off anyway, ejecting a cartoon poop of violet smoke.

So what to do with him? says the younger brother, nodding at
    the portrait.
Was it him? says the main man for the clearout. Barnaby.
No no, he died long ago. It was the. . . the woman of the house
    who just died. My brother and I don't care for him, didn't.
I'll take him, says Barnaby.
Where?
We might get one or two p for him. It's in oils.

He must keep his eye on the ball and not imagine the deal was done, not see himself if necessary retrieving his pen, something he had to check every time, there were more pen-pinch-ers than pens he sometimes reckoned, he must keep focused and not see himself checking he had his V5 Tecpoint, ensuring the copies of the contract were in the right hands, zipping up his case and already leaving the house. But the thought was too tempting, and soon, surely, he really would be in the car, thinking how the possibilities were infinite as he returned (in carefully circumscribed triumph) to the office. Drawing

alongside him at the lights, a famous film director might discover him; in full daylight there would be a meteor turning
the sky to a flash followed by a shower of lightdrops, drops
of light instead of rain; he might spy a badger at the roadside
in distress, lay it carefully on the back seat with a little fruit
and, if it showed interest in the fruit, an earthworm or two.
Of course all kinds of dire possibilities were possibilities too
but it seemed to him that in the clever patterns of the universe
these had been assigned to his wife, or at least her side of the
family, while the wonders had been left to him. He would
avoid the A road, the dismal carriageways had been surely
made for all the pessimists such as them. His roads were never
dreary. His roads had trees, fields, bridges, canals, features, if
features was not too trite a word, they had biplanes droning
overhead, terrifying owls patrolling the hedges and deer in lay-
bys, fawns that for him would stay standing, never scattering.
He would seek these out. By seeking he would find. Life teems
with splendours, Lauren, don't you agree? I do Mr Mazurka,
claro I do. And yet, who but he knew what was really in the
mind of a great estate agent? He could hardly wait to hear the
soft click of his car door shutting, to display the sophistica-
tion of not sitting in the driveway working his mobile but
moving off smoothly towards the main road. Now I have cast
off, he would think, a little like Captain Cook setting off for
the southern continent. Cook, Gagarin, Aldrin. Or what if
he was simply himself? With the steering wheel in his hands
the mere circling of a roundabout might feel like a majestic
gesture, look, those earthlings have the time and the inclination to sweep around curves when they might head straight
on, they are things of beauty, look at that one in that striped
machine, on a three-quarter circle, are not those public dances

of theirs a fine sight. Then there would be the joy of exchange in the glances when he returned triumphant to the office, particularly the looks between himself and Lauren, his flush would become her flush, yes he would say quietly, knowing the power of modesty, they chose us because we're good at it, aren't we Lauren. You ride out at dawn Mr Mazurka, she would say, lasso the wildest studs, bring them back into our corral. I suppose I do Lauren, I rope and throw and brand 'em. Yee-ha, Lauren would reply, tossing one of the flowers from her vase into the air. Part of him was ecstatic at such antics while another part would prefer her to be less raunchy but then she wouldn't be Lauren and look the elder brother, wouldn't you know it, seems to be one of those pen-pinchers, he's put the pen very close to his teacup when by rights it should be more in the centre of the table.

You should be in amateur dramatics, Lauren.
I am.

Mr Mazurka?
Yes?
Tell us where to sign.

THE THINKER

THIS MAN I once knew was the one that made me lose the plot a bit. Well not really him but, well, it wouldn't have happened if I hadn't met him. He was THE stand-up guy in the village; he didn't walk around with a can of beer in his hand and no-one ever once heard him shouting. A real kind sort that you don't see very often. Everyone got on with him, they'd shout and swear at each other but when this man, Peter, walked past they'd stop and say: Alright, Peter, good to see you, mate, take it easy, yeah. And he'd smile and say thank you and walk on. I'm making him sound like a do-gooder but he wasn't. He went to parties and did what other people did. I thought he was a bit simple when I first met him but when you really get talking to him it turns out he's a thinker; one of those *real* thinkers who can *really* work stuff out. I'd been talking to him whenever we were out with the same crowd and eventually I got to going round his house a bit. He lived on the side of the road that's got the field leading on from the back garden. We'd have a cup of tea and really talk. It might not seem odd to other people but round here it's hard to find someone to have a proper conversation with, like about the world and stuff. I was new to thinking and he was seasoned so he questioned me all the time, telling me that this is how

I'll find out what I really believe and saying about Socrates and stuff.

In the middle of the field that his house backed onto he showed me something one day, a small opening that you could just squeeze through, in the middle of the barley, that led down to this cave of hard stone with a texture of sandpaper. It was all wet and smelt a bit like a pub. We went right down and the smell got worse. Almost mushroomy. And that was when we saw it. A little old hunched-up man in a cage. You'll understand why I lost the plot. I mean, I knew there and then that I'd not be the same person again when I came back out. Peter lit a fag and just watched me with a smile. He looked more confident than I'd ever seen him look before. I was straight and asked him, *The fuck's goin off here, mate?* The hunched man seemed to flinch at my voice. He was nearly naked. Peter told me the hunched old man was the last of the *closed-caskets*. I didn't know what he meant when he said that so I asked him and he said he'd been studying them and they lived in the woods and they'd spend a lot of time underground like slugs or moles, digging around and living off of grubs and stuff but also feeding on dead animals and bones and even the dead bodies in the graveyard and that's why they were called closed-caskets. Cos they've got teeth that can bite through nails. People used to hunt them at night and they thought they were all gone, it's lucky that witches like Karen from the Quad were still putting spells on people's houses to protect them, that's what he told me, but that wouldn't last for ever. I ignored the fact that Karen was a witch and I told him he'd lost the plot and, to clear things up, I asked if he was saying this man was like a fairy or a woodland creature or something and he said something like that but he didn't know much more about him at the minute. I was having a hard time believing all of this and I had to raise my voice with him, it was hard but I said, *Peter, what the fuck are you doing, pal?* He told me that he found him in here and he didn't put him in the cage and he didn't know what to do, that's why he brought me down. He said that he thought we were mates and asked me why I was being so aggressive. I felt bad about raising my voice and told him so. I don't think Pete had ever been spoken to like that; no one wants to be mad at Peter.

I sat down on a rock and said, OK, OK, *let's come up with a plan.* I stood up and started pacing.

*We can either   ermmm   well
leave it here and pretend we never found it   or   or
like,   ring the police or summet   or
fuckin kill it.   Like whack it on the head with a rock
or summet.*

Pete was too nice for all of this and shook his head. I'd snapped. I could tell he'd brought me down here to make all of the decisions. Pete was a thinker, not a doer. That's why he'd never had a job. I asked, *Well, does Golem fuckin talk?* He didn't answer me so I asked the creature, *Do you fuckin talk, Golem? Look, here's my ring, you want it?* Peter told me not to wind him up, he was sheepish and very uncomfortable. He told me that I'd make it angry but it was too late, I already had. It went mad in the cage, it rattled and jumped and with one bite it took a chunk from a metal bar. I just ran. I grabbed Pete as I went past and we ran straight back to his house and locked and bolted the door and stared out of the kitchen window that overlooked the field. Quietly. Pete ran the tap and I asked what he was doing and he told me he was just putting the kettle on. I nodded, good idea.

The brew did help to calm the nerves and we started talking like normal again. Well, I did. Pete was still a bit quieter than before. I asked him how long he'd known about it and he said he'd been feeding it for a couple of years now. He got his phone out and showed me pictures of these snares and traps he'd built for catching animals. He said that sometimes he'd sit and eat with it. It'd rip apart a squirrel raw and Pete would sit there with like a chicken kiev or panini and eat with him. He showed me a painting, *Saturn Devouring His Son*, and that was exactly what it looked like. He said it helped him to sit with the closed-casket and see himself as 'animal'.

Pete was found dead a few months later. The police looked into it and it turned out he'd been skipping treatment for a cancerous tumour. Everyone was talking about it. His death affected the community and, as no-one knew his family, I was getting a lot of the commiserations, which felt weird. I know it's mad but I'd carried on Pete's snaring and was chucking food down this hole. One day I even made a panini but couldn't bring myself to go in and see if the creature had come back. There could have been a huge pile of rotting animals down there for all I knew. I thought of how Pete could be hiding in the cave and eating it all and laughing at everyone thinking he was dead just because they'd seen his body. He got you questioning things, Pete did, even after he was gone. He always asked what I'd do if I knew I didn't have long left to live and I'd assumed he was trying to get me to think without 'boundaries' or something but it was really because he knew he was going to die. I don't think I ever gave him any real help on that one. He was the thinker, not me.

That's where the story ended until a sign went up outside

of Pete's old house one day. AUCTION. There were to be no viewings, the house came as it was left due to Pete having no family to clear it all out. The only pictures on the website were of the kitchen. I was curious and all of the commiserations must have gone to my head because I felt a right to see what was in there and take anything valuable. The things that were valuable to Pete would probably end up in a skip if the next person was left to decide.

It was easy to get in. I had a hammer in my pocket but the old wooden back door went through with a quick kick. Being stood there was a strange feeling. The last time I'd been in that kitchen we'd fled for our lives and now it seemed quieter than anything.

In the living room, the floorboards were black and covered with rat droppings that had been trodden down over time. There was nothing else in the room apart from a single-seater settee that had been chewed up and a tall lamp behind that was still left switched on. I could hear the rats underneath the floorboards scratching and scuttling and I could feel the floor moving. A couple of them popped up and ran towards me. I slammed the door on them, then breathed in deep before turning to the stairs and working my way up. It looked like upstairs was his space for studying. There were loose pages and books that lined the floors. There were symbols that even the rats were afraid of. And the walls. They were paintings. The sun and the moon were painted on either end of the landing. On the sun side there was a bathroom and an empty box room, the walls tattooed with stories that were almost hieroglyphs. I studied them, touched them, put my cheek to them. On the moon side was his bedroom. A dark room with flattened cardboard boxes on the floor for a bed, a loose sheet and a pillow. The walls were painted black. It was clearly a tunnel, textured like jagged soil and stone. As you looked left from the door, the tunnel started and continued around the windowless room until, there it was. A study in all its detail. The creature. Its features so crisp that my breath was sucked from me. I could see it breathing and smell its stench. It was impossible to tell if it was a painting or if it was alive. Either way, it was captured on the wall. The hammer was heavy in my pocket. I took it out and began. It was a mess. I washed my hands, peeled the hieroglyph wallpaper from the walls carefully, rolled it up and left. I could hang it up at home and begin my study. I had a lot of work to do.

GEORGINA PARFITT

MIDDLE GROUND

AT SCHOOL, THE primroses were coming out. Brighton was eleven, and every day now there was something new emerging.

The girls at break time had a thing about the primroses. It was a signal – the first primrose under the lime tree, the first milky-yellow flower to flop free from those dark, wrinkled leaves. They lay beside it on their tummies, chins touching the mud-soft grass. From here, the primrose was the whole foreground.

They had learned about foreground already in Art, and often went around the field with their eyes wide, pupils dilated, trying to take in as much of the scene as they could. The background – which they had learned was usually a hill or a mountain – was sprawling and difficult to comprehend here: it consisted of the fields beyond the fence, which were always changing, pathways of uneasy trees between them, and beyond, no mountains, just more of the same. Mud, crops, grass, distance. The foreground, however, was whatever they stood in front of or whatever they held in their hands. It could be anything they wanted it to be.

Brighton was looking at the primrose, but she was not one of the girls in the front row. She lay on her belly in the triangle between two other girls and instead of resting her chin on the ground, she propped herself up on her elbows and watched the flower between those two girls' faces. She was watching the girls' faces as much as she was watching the primrose.

The light – so cold and white it didn't really feel like sun – touched the girls' cheeks and exposed the down on them. White-blonde on one girl, pale brown on the other. Girls were just creatures when you looked at them like this, Brighton thought. Then they got up – Maria and Laura – and became giants as they stepped over the other girls. Lace-trimmed ankle socks.

'It's begun,' Maria said.

Brighton turned over onto her back to keep looking at them as they walked arm-in-arm around the trunk of the lime tree, examining the other tuffets of leaves that might soon produce primroses. The grass had already wetted Brighton's shirt on both sides.

'One flower and eleven girls,' Laura said.

'One of us is going to do well next year,' Maria said.

The girls had a thing about the primroses predicting success. Every year, there was a threshold and some girls passed it while others failed. Last spring, the primroses had signified which of them would be best at singing. They all wanted to be singers, but not every girl had the talent. From the music room, they would look out at the new primroses, thin as tissues, and see the body-tight costumes of singers on *Top of the Pops*. Some of them would have a special future; they could feel it in the air.

This spring, the primroses signified high school, where they were all headed. Not everyone would do well at high school. They had known older girls, sisters and friends and neighbours, who had gone off to high school last year, and now, when they saw these girls around the village, it was clear whether they had done well or done badly. They either strutted or they slumped along the pavement with their book bags falling off their shoulders. Their hair either bounced and flicked or it frizzed. Was it a transformation that had occurred? No, it was more like a revelation. The truth of each girl had been there all along, high school had only revealed it; Brighton knew this in a way that made her stomach ache.

Now Maria and Laura turned to address the other girls, who were still lying in the mud around the first primrose.

'But which one of us is it?' Maria asked. 'Who does this primrose *refer* to?'

Laura weaved around the bodies of the girls. Brighton held herself fast to the ground, as if she were the primrose, the tough roots of it, the papery bulb, the green, hideous leaves, trying to conjure a delicate wisp of a flower – up – from her face for Laura to see.

'I think I know,' Laura said.

'I think I know, too,' Maria said.

The bell rang and they all got up. As they crossed the field, back to the concrete playground, they floated for a moment, buoyed up by their secrets, before they lined up again outside the classroom and their minds turned back to English and sitting still.

After school, Brighton took her shoes off outside, a fat fringe of mud around the soles. She went straight upstairs, taking her plate of bread and butter with her, to sit before her doll's house.

She had had the doll's house since she was very small – they found it at a charity shop and Welly had spent a whole week repapering the walls and painting the tiny window ledges with the same cream paint she'd used in their own living room. Brighton had been obsessed with the house at six, seven, and eight; in fact, if she looked back into her memories of those years, it was the doll's house she saw. Tiny shadows of tiny silverware. A perfect corner of rosebud wallpaper where she could place her fingertip to collect the dust. She called it spring cleaning.

Over the last year or so, Brighton hadn't spent as much time with the house. Fifteen minutes, here and there. She might recentre the dining room table or pick up a tiny vase of paper flowers that had fallen over in the night, but, for some reason, she hadn't wanted to stay too long. As if she might see something in the house that would disappoint her, or might suddenly fail to see something she had seen before – the dining room table, for instance, might start to look like a tiny circle of balsa wood with a fat coat of clear nail varnish on top, and not an Edwardian antique at all.

But since the spring term started, Brighton had been going back to the doll's house and spending hours there. She didn't know what she did there exactly. Mostly she just watched the rooms, while in her mind a track murmured along; the track didn't have words as such – it was more of an undertone, whose rises and falls indicated drama.

Sometimes she would just lie in front of the cut-open rooms of the doll's house and eat her bread – breathing through her nose as she chewed. The feeling of watching the house and filling up with soft, sweet bread was like magic, like managing to slip into another life.

Once the first primrose had emerged, the rest came thick and fast. Overnight, another four had broken through. The girls flew straight to the lime tree at breaktime for an emergency meeting.

'So, girls,' Maria said. 'That's five.'

'About half of us,' Laura said.

They looked very serious, like doctors breaking bad news on TV.

'I feel really nervous,' Robin said. Someone rubbed her arm.

'I think we should stand by the primrose we think is ours,' Maria said. 'Then we'll see, if people are – *deluding* themselves.'

'That's something we'll need to deal with.'

These were words they'd learned this term – deal, delude.

The girls edged around the primroses that had bloomed and stood two per flower.

Nobody took themselves out of the running.

Laura laughed and shook her head. 'I knew that would happen.'

'Let's move things around a bit,' Maria said.

She left her own primrose and went around the tree, taking the wrists of girls who were deluding themselves, and pulling them – gentle but firm – away from the spot they'd chosen. *Sorry* she said to each girl as she repositioned them.

Brighton and Robin were sharing a primrose. They were friends – they had been round to each other's houses for tea – but now Brighton willed Maria to take Robin's wrist and leave her with her own primrose; she willed it so hard she thought Robin might be able to hear. Maria stood in front of Brighton and Robin with a look of concern on her face. For a moment, Brighton thought it was because she was trying so hard to choose between them, but then she realised that it was because neither of them belonged with a primrose.

'Sorry you, and sorry you.' She took Brighton's wrist and then Robin's and dragged them both away from the flower. 'I guess this one's mine then,' she said.

The boys didn't know how primroses worked, but they were going through their own thing that term, so when they looked over and saw the girls on the field, they seemed to understand that it had something to do with high school. They were doing some *adjudicating* of their own. In games, boys were flying over the field, leaning their chests forward, slicing their hands back as if they were running in the Olympics. Any time one of them missed a ball, another would scream – reel his head back and scream at the sky. They were always screaming in frustration with each other. This meant something, Brighton could tell, like their primroses meant something.

Off the field, some of the boys were getting nicer, and some of them were getting meaner. Brighton found she could hardly look at them these days, because she didn't know which way they would turn.

The nicest one was Evan. He sat next to Brighton a lot because his last name also began with a 'C,' and Brighton had always felt better with him than with the other boys, as if having a C-surname made them similar in other ways too. He was softer and more studious than the others – when he was drawing a shape on squared paper, his fingers pressed at the ruler seriously and carefully – but he was still a boy, and his voice had grown an extra dimension that spring like some of the others. It could go one way or another.

As the spring term advanced, the boys began looking

sideways at the girls. Brighton crossed the playground and felt it happening. She looked down at her skirt in case it had blown up and was showing her knickers. Mistakes like knickers showing, wet patches, calling teachers *mum* or *dad*, they all seemed to happen more now. But Brighton's skirt was fine. She crossed to the corner of the playground where the grass of the field met the concrete. Something about the way the boys were looking made it feel like she'd had no choice in walking over there. Then they stopped looking and were back on the field, screaming.

There were two more primroses by the March half-term, but the girls didn't redo their auditions.

There was a sense that everything had been decided already, or even that the primroses didn't matter much now anyway. Most of the girls stopped going down to the lime tree and instead hung around the edges of the concrete playground in groups. It wasn't over yet but Brighton did feel that she had landed on one side of the primrose equation, while Maria and Laura had landed on the other, and that there would be fewer and fewer chances to change her fate, as the year sped towards summer.

Still there were moments when it seemed like it was possible for the whole thing to turn around.

The day they came back from half-term, there was a bake sale. Mrs Winthrop, the supply teacher that everyone liked, gave Brighton and Evan an extra job while the rest of the class was working on dressing tables and decorating cupcakes: it was to go out of the school grounds, across the road, and down to Mrs Lewis' house to get more change for the *float*. Brighton and Evan knew which house was Mrs Lewis' – the big, set-back house with the frightening dead vine still clinging to it in crispy bushes. Often, when they were arriving or leaving school, Mrs Lewis would appear from under the vine and watch them.

'Mrs Lewis will have change,' Mrs Winthrop said. 'Here's ten pounds.'

She got out her purse from the pocket of her coat. This was the first time a teacher had done anything like this in front of them. They saw bank cards and loyalty cards and the thumbed corner of a photograph. Brighton imagined a primrose, in the centre of Mrs Winthrop, lighting her from within like the flame of an oil lamp.

While Brighton stared, Evan took the money. He took it cautiously, and folded it in half to put into his pocket. Brighton saw him as a man-to-be – how one day he would fold money from a job and slide into a car, pat the dashboard.

As they set off, out of the school building, Brighton felt the jealous glares of other girls. She and Evan crossed the empty playground. The sun was now allowed free rein over everything. It was more like summer. They took the path to the school gate, and found it surprisingly easy to open; the latch was a simple iron seesaw in a groove. Once out, they both giggled. The road, with its tufted grass banks and loose clods of old tarmac, may as well have been an avenue in a city.

They criss-crossed from verge to verge, making the most of the freedom. Evan climbed up on the grass and ran his hand along the flint wall that bordered the field opposite the school.

'We should take the long way,' he said.

Brighton laughed. 'Yeah. We should try and take as long as possible.'

There wasn't really a long way to Mrs Lewis' house; she

was the school's only neighbour and already they were at her garden. So they kept walking past the house and started down the long track that eventually led to the village. The track was perfect: the way it disappeared into the distance, the way its narrowness made everything else seem larger – the fields, the sky. There were thickets along the track and tumbling masses of cow parsley and even blousy, bright-red poppies. When the sun went in, Brighton saw even more between the tangles of the thicket: tiny thorns and spider-webs. They followed the track until they couldn't see the school anymore.

'I guess we should be getting back,' Evan said.

But they stayed there for a few minutes, surrounded by farmland. Back at school, the smell of the air was always hot dinners – custard and beans. But out here, the smell was just air and mud. Brighton felt that it was possible she would enjoy life after school a lot, that there would be more and more moments like this for her.

'Well,' Evan said, looking at Brighton straight-on, in a way he never would have looked at her on school grounds. 'This was great.'

Brighton nodded. 'It was great.'

'The letter C. I'm glad to share it with you.' He held up his hand and they high-fived. His palm was very warm, and Brighton was sure that it felt different to how a girl's hand would feel, but she wasn't sure.

They were soon at the start of the track again and Mrs Lewis was waiting for them in her driveway.

'Did you get lost?' she asked. She was smirking; she didn't mind. They hadn't thought that maybe Mrs Lewis had been warned that they were coming and would be looking out for them.

She took them inside her house. People had said it was a mansion, with a swimming pool inside, but it wasn't. It was just a farmhouse, full of old furniture and old carpets, with dog hair drifting through the rooms. Mrs Lewis took them to her kitchen and made them each a Ribena. Evan handed her the ten pound note like they were doing a deal.

Before they left, Mrs Lewis shook both their hands. She said: 'I hope you both go on to do great things. And if you don't, that you don't worry too much about it and just try to be happy.'

Brighton was on a high as they came back to school, and it was breaktime, so everyone was outside watching for them to return. She wanted to go straight to the primrose patch and see if anything had emerged for her, but as she crossed the playground, one of the boys in the year below – the one with the white-blond hair – called out:

'Do you love Evan then?' He was running, following the netball lines that had been painted on the concrete, swerving, as if stuck in an orbit. Then he stopped and looked at her – dead on – and in a flash seemed to see everything – everything she was and everything she ever would be. 'You're just a bit too ugly for him, Brighton-girl,' he said.

She laughed and carried on walking, but she didn't go to the primrose patch; she walked a loop of the field instead and went into the school building through the side door. She wasn't crying yet, but she knew it was coming.

At the doll's house, spring sun fell through the tiny window into the dolls' living room. On the dresser, the plates and cups wobbled every time Brighton moved. She imagined herself to be the wind, a force that moved on all sides of the house. In the bathroom, a pink china toilet had come away from the wall in the latest storm and she bent a pipe-cleaner doll so that it sat on it, embarrassed.

Brighton was staying later and later at the house, lying on her belly past her bedtime, feeling her backbones and hips begin to set in that position. But as she watched the rooms and moved the objects around, the act felt more like playing pretend than it had before. When she moved a doll to the window, it wasn't as if the doll was deep in the business of living, watching the garden, thinking about roses, but like she had been put into a pose and was now expected to stay there. Every night, as the moon lit her own house, Brighton watched the dolls' rooms. She was trying to work something out - something that would help her in the daytime - but she never got far enough and by morning, she was back to square one, walking to school with her hands on her thighs to keep her skirt down.

In Art class, they were drawing their first still lives. It was wonderful, Brighton thought, a big, unexpected joy, to be able to spend a whole hour looking at an object on the table, and trying to draw it. Nothing else was expected of them, and they all - even the loud ones - spent the hour in silence.

When they went outside again after class, Brighton saw that the world was a tumbling assembly of still lives: even trees blowing, even football pitches and farmhouses, and church steeples and roof tiles, and even boys running, they could all be drawn, she thought.

The girls had been keeping away from each other; they had had enough to think about without the group talk of horse riding and high school and song lyrics. They were coming back together though, in these final breaktimes before the summer, pairs of girls would drift across the playground and join another pair and make a four. Maria and Laura began to conduct them again, waving to gather them and saying things to rally them, like *right then, girls* or *we need a talk*.

They were trying to learn different dances, and sometimes they would make a game of it. One girl would try to spin without moving her head. This was something Laura had learned at ballet, and the rest of them had learned from Laura. It was good to be able to spin many times on the spot, but it was better to be able to spin just once and keep your head perfectly still. The girls took it in turns to try, but Laura and Maria always got two tries because they were the closest to getting it, and sometimes Brighton and Robin got skipped over.

As Laura span, and her grey school skirt lifted and settled, Brighton practised her own spins by the wall – not at full intensity, but at a sort of half-speed – using the flints to push off and stabilise herself. She would be able to do it, she knew, if she could just practise for a while. Already the balls of her feet were learning how to turn tightly around one spot.

'Woah, Brighton.' Maria shook her head in disbelief. 'You think your spin is more important or something?'

Brighton laughed.

'I guess it's funny,' Maria said.

'I can practise while I wait for my turn,' Brighton said. 'There's no law against us doing spins at the same time.'

Maria shrugged. 'Okay.'

The routine relaxed. While Laura and Maria kept spinning in turn, the others practised at random intervals, their bad spins landing heavy, splay-footed on the concrete. For a while, it seemed like they were having fun; Brighton even landed a few near-perfect spins and watched her skirt float back down to her legs, panting, like a real ballet dancer at the end of a solo. Then she felt a pair of hands take hers - suddenly she was spinning like a wheel, against her will, from her arm sockets rather than her feet. It was Maria. She was shorter than Brighton, so Brighton had to lean back further to keep them balanced. The toes of Maria's school shoes ground into the concrete; as they picked up speed, Brighton thought she saw them smoke. She tried to laugh but couldn't quite get enough breath. Maria's face was blurred in front of her, but it was so close that she could smell it - Maria had a sweet, ferny smell. And her mouth was moving, saying something just to Brighton: 'Look at yourself,' she was saying. 'Look at yourself.'

Brighton looked down instinctively, but she couldn't see herself really, only Maria's toes, and her own toes, and then, just for a moment, her skirt waved up and she saw her own pink, chubby knees, her thighs and the underneath bit of her knickers.

Maria let go and Brighton fell back against the wall. She and Maria were both laughing, but it was Maria whose legs had become lean and brown like a high jumper, and whose knickers were black like a woman's, not white like a baby's, and whose hair was gleaming and had settled right back where it started. It was Brighton who was blushing, not just on her face but on her calves and knees and arms and neck. That was the truth, and everyone was looking at it.

A few weeks before the end of term, summer had arrived on the playground. It was as hot as it would get before they all went away for the holidays and spent six weeks in their back gardens, in paddling pools, by the coast, or abroad in holiday homes and caravans.

The school fete was held on the field and the teachers dragged hay bales out to make a seating area for parents beside the beer tent. There was a row of barbecues where one of the dads would cook sausages, and a row of trestle tables where mums were lining up bottles of shampoo and wine for the tombola. Arriving on a truck were the swing boats, a giant wooden frame with three boats, carved like gondolas, hanging from the frame by iron rods. The whole structure was painted fresh each year, primary colours, red and yellow and blue. Everyone loved the swing boats. At fifty pence a ride, they were the most expensive thing at the fete, but they were worth it. You got to ride for five minutes, swinging up above the school and down again until it felt like you were flying.

Kids who had left the school last year and the year before came back for the fete. It was like a reunion. They met each other at the gate, now with high school haircuts and makeup on and actual skin-tight flared jeans. Brighton found she couldn't tell which of them had done well at high school. They were all glorious, she thought. They were beautiful. The whole fete was for them, so that they could have two hours of fame in the sunshine.

Brighton and Robin queued up for the swing boats and watched the fete going on around them as they waited. Evan and his friend were next in line and got the swing boat next to theirs when the operator finally called them up.

Brighton leaned back into the wooden shell of the boat. It creaked. It was warm, from the sun and from the previous rider. Again, Brighton had the feeling that there would be many moments like this ahead, moments of leaning back and feeling the sun on her face.

Evan's voice came from the next boat, which was already creak-soaring beside them. 'What are you doing? It's not a bath.' He was teasing, but it was nice somehow.

The point was to pull the rope hanging from the frame and draw your end of the boat up and back; then you could let go and the boat would drop, and swing, wobbly and shallow at first but then higher and higher, and stronger and stronger. Brighton and Robin got theirs going, and soon they were swinging so high that Brighton could see right over the frame, over the conifers at the end of the field, and over the lime tree. She could see several villages – not just Hibwich but Tivenham and Windham and clusters of houses she couldn't name – and other far-off things she'd never seen before: a windmill, a pigsty. If she turned to look down, over the school, she found that the grass whirled as if she were falling onto it and the people were just shapes and voices, that they blurred into one another, someone's face becoming someone else's feet, a belly, a pair of hands, a ponytail.

They were going so high that her bottom and lower back came away from the boat for a second at the top of the swing and then slammed back into the seat on the way down, but even this was not unpleasant. She found that she wasn't scared. She was making it happen. She was pulling on the rope harder each time they swung, and each time she did, she saw things differently. Nothing stayed the same, not even for a moment.

STILL LIFE

IT WAS EARLY in the morning and the ceiling above our bed was washed in blue ambulance light. I heard a door banging in the street. Pushing myself up from the bed, in the dimness I could see through the window a man in his pyjamas, sitting on a wall outside the house opposite. The paramedics asked him what was wrong and he held his chest tightly, explaining in a laboured way that he was a taxi driver. With a limp elbow he gestured towards a door blowing open in the wind. They tried to make him go back inside but he told them he'd prefer if they didn't, because it was a complete mess. He was embarrassed, he kept saying. I went over to the window and while they were listening to his heart, the man looked up at me over their shoulders. Stepping back into her sleep-warmed hand on my back that was asking what had happened, I heard her tell me to come back to bed. I lay down on the clammy sheets and listened as they attended to him and then I fell asleep.

The day after, the drawer containing our passports, which to my knowledge had been undisturbed for a long period of time, was left slightly open. I try to isolate this moment as a specific event, something with a clear beginning and end so it's easier to understand, when really everything organised itself so gradually that I'm still only approaching the reality of how things were all these years later. The cheap drawer, the chest it was part of and the room it sat within are still, despite the time that has passed, well defined when they appear in my head. Sometimes, I suspect that other people can hear the drawer's contents rattling around inside of me while I walk through the quiet reception area at work, or on my way home when I'm walking down a train carriage, trying to keep my balance as it sways. Everyone, I think, carries a room like this around inside of them.

Our passports were kept one on top of the other in the drawer so we wouldn't lose them. Some days I found it slightly open, others sticking out of the cabinet like someone had opened it fully in a rush, and then, more often than not, tightly closed, pushed deep into the drawer's enclosure. Observing this closely for a few days I decided to arrange the pages and the angle at which they touched in a precise and almost elaborate way, so as they would register the smallest tremors from the hands that might touch them. Daily I looked in there to take readings and check for movement, as a scientist might check an air pollution meter or a surveyor assesses a datum on a subsiding building. I thought also of looking for footprints in a remote and humid rainforest.

Cracks creasing the walls were what I expected to see coming from the drawer, aggressive rising damp perhaps. Instead the changes were small: misaligned edges, a crimped corner, the pages left open at a visa for Puerto Rico, 2016. I thought it was still warm on one occasion. She had been looking through the pages of her passport regularly.

At the time I started to track changes in the passport pages, the photographs began turning. I first saw it in the

Instagram photos she posted when I was visiting my parents in Birmingham. I could see that she had turned around any photo that contained me, or us, to face the wall and I wondered if any of the eighteen people that liked the photo had noticed our room contained just the backs of photographs and paintings, with their hanging mechanisms and backing scribbles exposed, rather than holiday memories, doodles and degree certificates. Flipping them to face the room again was useless; whenever I went out, even to smoke a cigarette for a few minutes, when I got back some would already be facing towards the wall again.

In a way we spoke, and we spoke about the future, in bold and definitive plans that did seem like what people should do after living together for a while. Over email, she sent checklists of what we cover, left holiday brochures on the bed and decorated with candles bought for a nicer home we might have one day. There were also the phone calls:

I can't quite hear you.
   You're still so nice to me . . .
   Why wouldn't I be nice to you?
   I'm staying at my friend's house tonight.
   What was that? I'm making dinner, what would you like?

She would say one thing in such a way as to suggest something else she couldn't quite put words to, and it was at this point, I think, that what she thought became lost in the different shapes and densities of silences around us. Or else, she was trying to affect something deeper in me than could be reached by language.

Words are empty rooms when they enter into common

usage. Some arrange comfortable sofas, a bookshelf and warm lighting within themselves. Others, those words and strings of words that are taboo, contain that many furnishings it's impossible to move through them. Linguistically they are the equivalent of what you might find an obsessive compulsive hoarder living in: piles of yellowing newspapers, used ready-meal packets, mountains of tins for the end of the world, food for a dog that died twenty years ago.

It is obvious now that the rented room in that small house contained too much for two people to successfully cohabit. Our predicament was not unique. We were the same as most people who lived in the centre of London at that time. It was something known but perhaps not explicitly said enough, that the meaningfulness of most relationships was based on the fact that people needed to be together, in those tiny rooms, to make life affordable.

It was a small rectangular room with a large window (we were lucky to have that), with glass that was coated with opaque plastic to stop the cold coming through. This defused the light and blurred the view of the large plane trees outside, making them somehow look like they were moving slowly even in high wind. The cars moving past in the distance appeared as though they were moving under water. Birds were always at a glide rather than flying.

You entered the room through a door which sliced the corner off the rectangle of its broader shape, described by our friend who was into Feng Shui as 'a bad omen'. A large Victorian fireplace sat in the centre of the west-facing wall and two large, identical wardrobes flanked both sides, pointed out by the estate agent as 'his and hers storage solutions'. When we started living together there was a discussion about keeping to these opposing sides, apart from when we were sleeping. For the first few weeks this worked well; however, over time, our possessions became mixed up and intertwined, began to bleed into each other. I didn't know what was mine anymore, and she, I thought, felt the same.

It was not uncomfortable. After a period of constant movement our possessions eventually found their place, became content even and were tailored to our restricted, cramped movements in the room – claustrophobia was there, albeit somehow kept at an arm's length through our simple knowledge of the space we both needed, and what went where. If something did need to move, we knew where it could go before being moved back again after a particular movement was performed. Turning a light on, reaching a plug socket, opening a cupboard. It was the books that took up the most room. They were neatly lined up in bookshelves along the north-facing wall and in regimented stacks around the fireplace. One book couldn't be moved without shifting all the others, making them seem completely immovable until the profile of the stacks they were part of began to change. Instinct told me that something had changed, and I knew this was true even before I had chance to look. She had started to take the books that were hers and place them back on her side of the room. The leftovers like barcode.

When I got home in the evenings, I would notice that she had moved other objects around for me. She constantly shifted rugs, moved vases and lamps into different constellations, and as with stars I visualised whole images and stories in these moving arrays. Looking at it all, sitting on the edge of the bed, I felt like some kind of inner city beachcomber uncovering meaning and intentions in discarded items, taking Tarot readings from household objects to register the parts of her that were absent and present.

I stopped cleaning so that I didn't miss or misinterpret anything, and it can't have been long after this that she tendered notice on her half of the contract directly with the landlord. I received documents in the post and I had to pay for the keys she hadn't yet returned. Despite this somewhat final move, she didn't stop living in the flat. She was at least half present, and as we'd shared a bed for so long it was uncanny when she wasn't next to me. I assumed she was there a few nights each week and the odd weekend, getting under the covers when I had fallen to sleep and leaving before I had woken up again, a head-shaped indentation left in the pillow. I only saw her outline in the darkness during this period. Sometimes she would leave in the middle of the night or return at a similar time and stay for a few hours. If I was travelling she wouldn't be home when I returned but I could tell from the subtle traces left behind – crumbs, a teabag left on a spoon, a chair positioned to look out the window – that she had been living there. How did she know when I would get back? Maybe she had been in the room with me and somehow left without being seen. Maybe she was always there. How many times had she been to the door and, listening closely with her fingers on the door handle, realised I was home and turned quietly away? I think she walked around our room and approached the bed while I slept, like some kind of dream.

Following the rearrangements, her possessions started to disappear. I came back from the supermarket and saw there was a collection of small strips of dust along shelves where her books had been. Another time, I ran back to the flat soon after leaving to get a forgotten train ticket, and found L-shaped indentations in the carpet where her small coffee table had once been placed. They perhaps spelled out the words CELL, TOLL or NULL. On another occasion, I stood looking out the back window towards Battersea Power Station and turned around to find a set of strange, hollow rings of dust where her candles and lamp had once been arranged, and faint rectangular shades on the walls where her pictures had hung. I sounded out words with the same multiple 'o' and curved geometry in them without being able to discern exactly what she wanted to say: anteroom, backwood, airproof, coordinates. It was feasible that if these domestic glyphs or scattered, spatialised letters were combined together, and scribbled carpet stains were used to fill in the gaps, they could have read: chronologically, colloquy or apoplexy.

I built up my courage and left messages in reply for her too. I managed to retrieve a woman's bracelet from an old bag in my cupboard – given to me by my first girlfriend, I think – and placed it on the bedside table (in the shape of a 'c' for Catherine), but it didn't elicit any kind of response. This made me check the passports again, and I had to recognise the fact that hers was now gone, leaving mine behind as a pale shadow of its absence.

As the room started to empty out its contents, the picture of how things were between us began to get clearer, rather than diminish. In the end – what I presume was the end – the only thing she left behind was a black bin liner full of rubbish. Spilling the contents on the floor I divined a parallel world in detritus, used the dream life of debris to determine who she was.

In the times, dates and locations on old receipts I mapped

out alternate travel plans to the ones she had told me about – trajectories across the country that didn't quite make sense. I studied ambiguous markings on business cards and on the inside of a matchbox, deciphered frustrated and anxious interactions in the folds of a napkin. Our past reality became fictional as I extracted opposing narratives from the banality of to-do lists, and in birthday cards where the sender had reduced their name to five hangman dashes instead of letters.

There was a box of photographs, half of which I had seen before, the others completely new to me. The first few were of churches in Florence that she had taken on a research trip and had shown to me at the airport when I collected her. I noticed that some of them contained a man, who before I must have thought was part of the same tour group. The pictures she hadn't shown me were taken by someone else, and caught her looking up to ceilings and contemplating paintings, or smiling in a blur and pawing the camera away.

I organised these things into groups: first by how they were scrunched up and compressed, then size, next by colour, and finally something approximating what I thought was the chronological order of what had happened. They were left neatly laid out on the floor for a number of days, until I noticed a gardener was burning leaves in the park over the road. I persuaded him to add them to the piles ready to be burnt, and I watched from our window while I prepared my own things to move out. Everything was packed into small, identical boxes and then wrapped in blue plastic to protect them from water damage. Packages that were left all over the city in the vague hope someone wandering the streets might find them all and reconstruct their contents into a fully functioning room again, maybe, as I imagined it at the time, in some anonymous apartment block on the outskirts of Berlin, Almaty or Madrid.

Dismantling the remaining furniture, I put the pieces into bags and disposed of them by the railway tracks. Then I made sure the room was completely empty, hoovered, wiped down the skirting boards and window sill, closed the window and shut the door before locking it for the final time. Walking down the stairs to the building's entrance, I put on my rucksack and decided to get the train back to my parents' house via Wolverhampton rather than Birmingham. On the way out, I checked again to see if she had collected her mail, and I spotted that she must have come to retrieve it as I was cleaning the room. The landlord had told me to post the keys through the letterbox when I was finished, and that's what I did.

I still think of all the dust collecting in that room, the low ebb of yellow that was fading from the bulb as I closed the door, and how, if a sound, however quiet, is trapped in a perfectly sealed enclosure it will continue to reverberate forever.

Whenever I walk past the building, I sometimes stop and sit on the wall outside the house opposite. Today, there are the silhouettes of a couple in the window of the house where we once lived, moving around awkwardly in silence as if they're playing a part in an old-fashioned movie. One of them opens the blind, another closes it. Later the blind opens half way, the window opens fully and someone looks down towards me. She appears behind him and draws him away, maybe to finish cooking dinner, maybe back to bed. I try to make myself believe I've never been inside the room and can't even imagine what it must be like in there. That I can't remember the slight difference in height between the bathroom and bedroom door, or the floorboard by the bed that made a cracking sound when you stepped on it. The way we thought rain dropping on the skylight sounded like pigeons falling on the glass. Where I'm sitting on the wall, the shadow cast by the plane tree makes the streetlight above me turn on before it's completely dark, and once the others follow suit, I know someone in that room will switch on the light.

LEONE ROSS

WHEN WE WENT GALLIVANTING

RICHIE MET ATHENA Righteous-Fury on the same day the tower block where she lived got up and started walking.

Richie was scooping his hangovered behind out of an acquaintance's yard after a night of group-drinking. The lift was dead. Last night it had seemed hysterically funny getting up to Floor 29, like climbing a concertina. When they finally arrived, gasping, strung out in the corridor like paper bird decorations in the wind, looking at the stars, Richie saw he was too drunk to get down again.

It was a distinct tremor in the concrete that had woken him, but he'd only realise that later, confusing the tremor with a need to urinate. He slipped out the shaking front door, leaving a snoring crowd splayed amongst Rizlas and pint glasses.

Richie didn't notice the fluorescent blue liquid running down the tower block walls, hissing and fizzing. He slunk down the corridor. Didn't tower blocks usually sway in the wind?

A woman three doors down flung open her door and walked out, orange robe flailing. Richie would have skipped on by, but for the transparency of the woman's nightdress, exposing prodigious breasts and a bigger belly. She was the largest person he'd ever seen, like marshmallow foam, beautiful eyes wide and head cocked. There was no way to get past her without full body contact, and he was sure that would be like a hurricane: swept up into trouble.

– You feel that? asked the woman.

– What? said Richie.

Her reply was drowned out by a yawning, squealing metal sound, like all the cutlery in the world scraped against corrugated iron, and a sudden, meaty stench, as if they'd been rammed face-first into a butcher's shop.

The tower block began to move forward.

Gaping, wordlessly screaming, Richie glared over the edge. No, he was not insane, the entire structure was *walking*, as if he'd hitched a ride on a stone monster. Things were falling off the building, bits of furniture and clothing and was that a bicycle coming for his head?

The large woman grabbed him by the scruff of the neck, pulling him inside her apartment and out of the way of the falling bike. It was a perfectly organic motion, like a wise mamma cat with her kitten. Richie crouched in her hallway, heart thundering. He choked a thank-you, noticing the heart-shaped mole on her shoulder.

WINNER OF THE ANGELIC BODY AWARD, said her orange robe.

Outside, metal boomed.

Her name was Athena Righteous-Fury. Richie recognised her type: she was a fixer, always consulted by community. Her day job was swimming instructor, she said, and it was her personal mission to teach everybody in this blasted tower block to swim; she'd been doing it for years. You were supposed to get lessons at school, but around here pools were mostly shut, or shit, and teachers believed their kind had heavy bones anyway. Some parents came from countries where swimming was for rich people; others were too tired to bother.

– Make me a cocktail, said Athena Righteous-Fury. – You look like you'd be good at it.

Richie was a trainee bartender and felt validated by her presumption. He made his best Bamboo from stuff in the kitchen: sherry, dry Vermouth, Angostura bitters and orange.

– Saves on water, said Athena Righteous-Fury, the glass almost disappearing inside her remarkable fist.

She sent a child to collect the respected people in the building and danced around her front room, waiting: for Mr Burt who ran the local cheap-goods store; Aspidistra, a grandma who'd lost her left breast to cancer; the bisexual choir who sang pop songs; the 17-year-old who planted corn and excellent white roses in the communal garden. A whole hour had passed, and word was out: a helicopter buzzed at the window, men inside gesticulating.

The newly minted Tower Block Emergency Group established the facts. Electricity was off. They had a week's water in the tank if careful. Rose Girl and her pals would check door to door and make a list of people short on food. Most people still had the internet, but all computers and phones were to be confiscated immediately to conserve battery life. They had to communicate with the outside world, and there was no point everybody running out of charge. One person per floor would hold a phone, another a laptop. Mr Burt would monitor the news 24-7 and no one should touch the lifts, they were bound to be fucked like always.

Since he was at the meeting too, Richie piped up. Setting rules was all very well, he said, but normal people would certainly disobey.

- Of course, said Athena Righteous-Fury. She was chairing the meeting in her nightie, skin exposed and undulating as the tower crashed forward. No-one seemed phased by her nakedness. - What you do is factor in the disobedience. Don't it, Mr Burt?

Mr Burt nodded.

- Oh, said Athena Righteous-Fury. - And somebody need to talk to the tower block and ask it what it want.

As the group rocked off down the jerking stairs, Richie asked how Athena Righteous-Fury was going to spend *her* day. She looked mildly surprised.

- Swimming lessons start soon, she said. - Make me another cocktail.

The tower block moved at a steady, rhythmic pace: purposeful, as if it were finding its balance. Richie peered through the kitchen window, mixing Athena Righteous-Fury a Bees Knees: gin, lemon and honey. The tower block skirted other buildings where it could, only driving deep furrows through parks when it had to, stepping over furiously beeping cars and people shaking their fists below. Residents lingered on corridors and balconies, looking out at the vast city, taking their washing in, chattering, and pointing. Crying children were slapped or comforted. A married man with conveniently handsome features arrived, knocked, and headed for Athena

Righteous-Fury's bedroom. The subsequent noises suggested he appreciated an angelic body.

Afterwards, Athena Righteous-Fury liked Richie's bright pink Clover Club so much she had two: gin, lemon juice, raspberry syrup and a frothy egg white.

There were more helicopters buzzing now, from news shows. People sent messages up to say they'd seen themselves on television, waving at the cameras, in Toledo and Latvia and Port Antonio and Laos. Blue liquid ran down the sides of the roaring building and into the corridors. Athena Righteous-Fury scooped a handful and sniffed.

– Like cocoa butter, she said.

She stood on the balcony, listening intently, stroking the concrete, watching flocks of surprised clouds, shushing Richie when he tried to talk and taking reports from slickly organised minions.

By afternoon, somebody came running up to say the police were coming.

Athena Righteous-Fury put on a yellow polka-dotted bikini, her navel piercing playing hide-and-seek in the velveteen folds of her belly. She gathered a bag full of swimming goggles, snorkelling equipment, and purple swim-caps for people with large hair. She'd been teaching local people to swim in their bathtubs since someone pooped in the local pool and shut it down. The main thing was to teach breathing and floating, she explained. Respect for water.

– What about the police, said Richie.

– I suppose they're upset we're heading for the rich people, said Athena Righteous-Fury.

She'd only managed to get through two lessons before Mr Burt and the Aspidistra came up with three-score and ten people, all fussing about Babylon heading their way. The news said the tower block occupants were dangerous criminals from somewhere else, set on destroying the country, but everybody knew they were only a few hours away from a fancy part of town and if the block tore through that, very powerful people would have less money.

Mr Burt said they needed to give an interview to explain there were innocent residents here. Athena Righteous-Fury said the Rose Girl was the best choice.

– What about *you*? said Richie.

– Too fat and too drunk for them, said Athena Righteous-Fury, splashing water over a happy man learning the breast-stroke in her bathtub.

– I thought we was saving water, hissed somebody.

For the first time, Richie thought Athena Righteous-Fury looked worried.

Rose Girl was interviewed at 5.17pm. Richie held up a phone so Athena Righteous-Fury could see it all as she coaxed a teenager in a white swimsuit to duck her head up and down in the sink, breathing to the side for the crawl.

Rose Girl was pale and conventionally pretty. Her flat was tatty, ferns and potted lemon trees everywhere. The interviewer asked her why and who and how and was she a bad person, were they *all* bad there, and Rose Girl had to yell NO over the sound of the tower block stepping around a playground.

– Breathe, said Athena Righteous-Fury. – Swoosh-*brrrrr*-one-two-three. She glanced at Richie. – Go number 128 though 147 and tell them I teaching them in a group, today.

– We're just like you, said Rose Girl on TV, her face shaking.

Athena Righteous-Fury said Richie should go make Rose Girl a Mai-Tai for good measure, so he did.

At 5.57pm, just as Richie decided to kiss Rose Girl, the police attached a bomb to the underbelly of the walking tower block. Someone's dog on a bright red string sniffed it out and howled so hard Mr Burt's lookouts jumped up from their beer.

Before anyone could hatch a plan, the tower block belched out a vast quantity of blue viscosity, swamping the bomb, splashing in the faces of the lookouts and soaking the police vans driving alongside.

The drenched police cars hit brakes, *eerrrks*.

– I see, said Athena-Righteous-Fury, when Richie ran up to tell her.

The tower block stalked past the fancy part of town, leaving the TV cameras behind. The bright, late summer sunshine filtered platinum; birds Richie didn't recognise swirled the building's circumference. The land changed, sloping into golden-green expanses of rapeseed; fluffy white sheep; a bigger blue sky than he'd ever seen.

Richie went back down to squeeze Rose Girl's hand, then found Athena Righteous-Fury on the 16th floor. She was flat-out running between apartments, a bag of swimming stuff bouncing against her hip. Richie scowled; he'd have been leading the troops and making speeches if he had half her gravitas. He told her so; something about today had him speaking his mind.

– Move out of my way, boy, snapped Athena Righteous-Fury.

She swept by him in a crocheted, lavender bikini; he knew her nipples better than his own.

He'd seen his drinking companions from last night, all eyes to the heavens. There was a lucid sense of prayer emerging from this place; a woman in number 27 had sung hymns all afternoon and now he couldn't imagine a life without her wheedling, glossy voice.

For the first time, Richie was quite sure he was going to die here.

He'd go foraging for Pina Colada ingredients, that was what he'd do.

The tower block accelerated as darkness folded in. Most slept.

One fat woman did not sleep, going door to door like a dark tremble, clear and firm and soothing.

– Teach you to swim, sis?

It is not a request.

Hot dawn hit the tower block and made it dance: skank one-time, pirouette, a jitterbug, wine-down low, stop for a moment, hammer-time; flairy, 6-7-8. The inhabitants felt the air quicken, the urgency deepen, felt the promise of completion; hushed and afraid, they gathered on grey and crumbling corridors, hundreds, looking, straining, holding hands. Snatches of panicked chatter, like bursts of static. Some newscasters said the tower block had been shot down. They spoke as if the block was a monster, an unholy thing, but around them here it breathed and jigged. They clutched its parts, cheeks to walls, some kneeling and putting their palms to the ground.

Ahead, the endless sky, as if conjured only for them.

Richie stared, trying not to cry. His parents and two older brothers said never come to places like this. He would steal back his phone if he had to, call them and say he was. . . what? Safe? He'd had leftovers for breakfast: Athena Righteous-Fury's cold fry plantain, bully-beef with plenty scallion and scotch-bonnet. Then she'd made morning love with another neighbour, a session that seemed to go on so successfully long that Richie stopped using the sofa cushion to block the sound.

He put his chin on the railing. Athena's hand fluttered around the back of his neck, fiddling, light, ticklish; a jolt; the smell of condensed milk. He turned.

She was holding a megaphone; she was wearing her goggles; she was naked and glorious.

In the distance, the new blue sky glimmered. Richie clutched the railing. The tower block tried the lindy-hop, then a lambada: ohhhh look at that pop-locking, wooo-baby.

– Such a beautiful day, someone said.

– Just wait, whispered Athena Righteous-Fury. Her angelic body simmered. Richie thought he could hear it.

Crunch-crunch, the pebbled shore, crackling underneath the tower.

The sea.

The residents scuttered backwards, hands raised.

Richie turned, looking for Athena, but her face was set on the crowd, all the men, women, the small ones, fierce-fierce, convinced she'd done enough.

She was, after all, a spectacular teacher.

You haven't done enough, he thought.

She lifted the megaphone.

– TAKE A DEEP BREATH LIKE I SHOWED YOU! bellowed Athena Righteous-Fury.

One. Two. Eyes closed.

Breathe.

Trust.

– THREE!

He'd skived on swim school days.

The oiled tower block plunged into the creamy ocean, fizzing and sinking and sighing. Its walls melted, water pouring into every home, pulling objects out: loaded bookshelves, thin yellow cushions, ancient hi-fis, curried cookers, love letters stiff with tears, stinky shoes, pet toys, red polyester underwear, cho-cho and guineps, clothes hangers, cinnamon lotion, 104 kinds of medicines, snapped earrings, give-thanks journals, blood-pressure cuffs, naughty games, lamps that purr, blackberry-flavoured condoms in cupboards.

Richie had the sensation of cold all over his body, then calm. He was happy he'd learned so many cocktails, but he would have liked to kiss the Rose Girl.

No time to wonder if drowning was a pleasant way to die.

Then that strong, swimmer's hand on his scruff and he was up in the air hollering, fitted like a cork between Athena Righteous-Fury's breasts. He tried to fight but she had him fast, spluttering madly, her strong thighs pushing through the ocean. She was smiling and watching for every beloved forehead: pop-pop-pop! up through the water and safe; waving, calling out to neighbours: where Dave-where Miss Sue-I-see-you Putus Mr Burt-oh-yes where-Mrs Trudeau third child-see-her-there Miss Annie, hello now.

Pop-pop-pop: everybody accounted for, swirling, diving, exclaiming, checking, clambering over the stone blocks rising to the surface amongst them.

– Look at what I can do!

- Ooh, you *pretty!*

A baptism. A cooling. Heads down, backsides up.

It took Athena Righteous-Fury fifteen minutes to teach Richie how to swim. First the float, where the trick was to relax; then the breathing; flip you over; done.

- Which stroke you want to learn?

- Butterfly, he said, and she called him a contrary blood-claaht and taught him the butterfly stroke. Forevermore he would think of her, backstroking through buoyant bricks and mortar, her nipples round and wet and pointed up to the sun.

MARK VALENTINE

Qx

'DID YOU NOTICE,' said Michael Brampton, 'that there was a copy of Stansby's *Black Queen Dances* in there?'

They had emerged from a large second-hand bookshop ten minutes before and were now resting from the foraging that had occupied them for the last hour or so, and were sipping at coffees in a corner of a nearby café.

An earnest couple were playing at chess at the next table, in silence. They stared at the pieces and at each other about equally.

'I did happen to notice it, yes,' said his friend John Wickham. 'But I've got a copy. And so have you, I'm sure.'

'Well, yes, I have,' admitted Brampton, 'several in fact. But I don't quite like to leave it there. It's not a bad price. I wonder if I should go back. Or do you think I ought to leave it for somebody else to discover?'

'Yes,' said Wickham. Brampton often valued the terse common sense of his friend, but it soon became evident that this was not quite what he wanted to hear.

'I suppose so,' he responded, doubtfully. 'But it could just sit there for some time yet. I feel as if I am somehow being called to it.' He often had mystical urges that seemed usefully to accord with his own inclinations. The couple playing chess also seemed to him a sign.

'Well go on then,' said Wickham, who did not much care one way or the other. 'I'll wait here.'

'Yes, I think I will. Perhaps there might be something inside it that I am meant to find.'

As he went eagerly out on his errand he noticed that the woman was doing decidedly the better at the chess game, and the man's brown eyes were sorrowful.

The book was still there. He picked it up and looked at it, and almost put it back again. Perhaps after all it was the destiny of the book to thrill or to stir or to guide someone new to it, who needed it far more than he did. It was a novel about a particular set of chess pieces, in which some of the figures seem to come alive and to be encountered or at least glimpsed in unlikely places.

There was no inscription in this copy, only the moderate pencilled price and, as he flicked through some of it, he could see no marginalia and nothing fell from the pages. This was mildly disappointing. Even so, he did not think he could let the book go. He took it to the desk and paid. It was raining lightly when he got outside and he tucked the book inside his jacket.

Back at the café the man had conceded the chess game and the two were talking quietly, with long pauses. The woman held a cup of black coffee close to her face and the fumes rose around her. Her eyes mirrored the coffee.

'All right?' asked Wickham.

'Yes, got it. Nothing obvious, though,' said Brampton. He pulled the book out of his jacket and looked at it again. The lettering on the spine, perhaps once gilt, had faded, and could now only just be discerned. Maybe that was why no-one else had found it. You had to look closely to know what it was. The paper was of good quality, still crisp, opaque and clean. Sometimes Brampton had the fancy that simply turning the pages of a book that had been long unopened might be a ritual act, releasing something. Not dust or stale air, or not just that, but an influence. He wondered what there might be in this copy of Bliss Stansby's *Black Queen Dances* that was now out in the world.

The chess couple were rising to go. The man put the chess board and the box of pieces back on a table that also had a pile of dog-eared glossy magazines. It perched on top of a copy of *Romantic Interiors*. They gathered up their coats and satchels and piled up the crockery neatly. They had a habit, Brampton noticed, of staring at each other, direct into the eyes, quite often. It was as if they were reading each other's thoughts. Yet they did not seem to be partners exactly: there was no easy familiarity between them. They might have not long met. As they approached the door, he thought he heard the word 'Dances' emerge through the hubbub, perhaps spoken by the woman, and he thought she might have looked back. But he could not be sure of the word or the glance, and could have imagined them.

For a few moments he wondered if she had noticed the book in the shop too, and was telling the man with the melancholy eyes that she had intended going back for it. What would have happened if he had not himself taken it? There opened out a different perspective in which it was she, and not he, that had the book: perhaps his own interference had prevented what should have happened.

He briefly entertained the thought of dashing after her and handing her the book, without a word of explanation. But that would be another matter again, not the same as if she had herself obtained it. It would not do.

There were a few crumbs of shortbread biscuit left on the saucer. Brampton licked his fingers and pressed them down on these, then tasted the sweet flecks.

It was getting late, the February dusk drawing in. The café windows were dark screens. When he looked once more at the door, the chess players had gone and he still held *Black Queen Dances*. He began to turn the pages again. Towards the end a slip of paper was caught tightly in the book's gutter. Gently he eased it away from its niche. There was a brief handwritten text: Qx, and then two further blurred characters. He frowned. Where had the Queen moved? What had she taken?

ALINAH AZADEH

THE BEARD

IT'S INSANELY HOT in here. The man shuts the door behind him, and shuffles in his cluster of thick, black, woollen robes towards the far end of the room, away from the window, out of sight of the eyes below, protected from the queues passing through the military gate into the building.

He sheds the robes first, to get some relief, then takes off his silver, square headdress, placing it on a huge, ornately carved walnut desk.

He's always been complimented on the volume and beauty of his beard, the thickest and longest in his close circle, with its enviable twists and curls, its signature indigo-black colour giving it motion, the light catching its shiny ridges. Many men coveted this beard, not just those within the justice department but among all the powerful government cliques. The beards of The Eminent Ones were the most substantial, commensurate with the power they wielded.

The man is panting, exhausted as he lowers himself onto the edge of a creaking sofa in the corner, sweating from the summer heat outside, and the stifling atmosphere of the courtroom. He has just finished pronouncing a series of sentences – thirty ritual cuts each to the forearms and calves, and varying periods of incarceration – for a long line of young women. *Down like dominoes.* He recalls the first defendant: on the video clip he was shown during the briefing last night, the girl's bright red hair rippled around her shoulders, her face increasingly ecstatic as she began to sing, at first quiet and moving to her own melody, then to a rhythm played by a young man with a small drum. Around them, a growing crowd, all smiling and waving at the camera.

Eventually, emboldened by those around her, she'd climbed onto the roof of an old, silver Mercedes, and sang the crudest of slogans across the crackling urban darkness. The girl stood tall, like a ship's mast against the sky, conducting a mass singalong to the music: *Freedom, freedom, freedom will be ours.* The man watched the screen as the girl lifted her arms, saw the delicate fabric of her neon orange shackles, stretched taut between her swollen wrists, glistening with the exquisitely embroidered gold initials of the man who owned her. Raising your arms above shoulder level – without explicit permission – was banned in public for women, was regarded as an act of heresy, yet this girl had offered them up into the night air triumphantly, as if she had just landed on the moon. It was the third night of full-blown demonstrations, triggered by the disappearance of yet another student caught disseminating anti-state propaganda, and this was not the girl's first transgression. Last year she'd had her feet bound together for a week, after being seen dancing in public.

Totally out of control, these little bitches, the man mutters to himself. They were supposed to be the children of the Great Coup, but they were nothing more than a public disgrace. *A serious threat to the moral fabric of this state and our reputation across the world!* he'd intoned before sentencing. Just another whore to silence, who didn't learn from her mistakes.

He enjoyed every single pronouncement of guilt he had made; thousands of them over the many decades since he first began working in this court, right at the beginning of the glory days of The Black Coup, as it had also come to be known. Named after the black robes The Eminent Ones wore, parading through the streets on the day the Palace was brought down. Named also after the viscous, black tar lines daubed across the eyes of the murdered Royal family, their decapitated heads hung by their hair from the ornately gilded balconies where they once made speeches, back in their days of pomp and spectacle.

He runs his palm over his sweating, shiny scalp. Too little left. He sighs.

The sudden hair loss had started yesterday at dinner over stew, then continued – in *public* – during a Judge's Council this morning. He had been listening desultorily when a series of beard hairs began littering the light cream table in front of him, like contorted fleas. He swiftly scanned the room to see if anyone had noticed, but everyone was distracted, so he sat back and stroked his beard casually, as the entire Council did when reflecting on dilemmas together, all very natural, moving his hands down to catch the renegade hairs loosening from his chin, slowly manoeuvring them to his edge of the table as discreetly as possible.

The pockets of his robes are full of hair, now.

He knows he needs a credible cover story for the inexplicable shedding. Perhaps he can say he has developed a rare skin condition, like alopecia, to explain the patchy beard? No, that would be seen as inherent weakness.

The powerful man unbuttons his white under-robe and the stiff corset beneath that. He wore extra layers today, to cover the changing shape of his body. Once a lithe revolutionary, a radical student used to hunger strikes and heroic abstinence, he's had many years as an Eminent One with an obedient wife, an affluent household, a useful and regular concubine, and many rich and tasty meals washed down with good wine. Slowly, he has expanded in all directions, can no longer see his genitals when he stands up, his hairy belly rising like some ancient, grassy, burial mound to meet him when he urinates. But he has grown proud of this belly, a symbol of his moral and actual wealth and status.

No, other things are changing.

He puts on his glasses to check if it's still happening. He scrutinises his nipples, those two previously rubbery, dark brown discs punctuated with thick, black curly hairs, crowning his flabby chest. The skin around these nipples is lightening, becoming completely smooth and hairless. And he swears they are starting to swell, as if injected with water. His belly, once seething with dark hair like spider's nests, is now bald in the middle. *Like a doughnut, a human doughnut!* A tiny, lonely crater of smooth skin which both shocks and fascinates him. How is this happening?

The man moves even closer to a long mirror in the corner to inspect his face. His beard is not thinning out naturally as might be expected with age, but conspicuously dotted with balding areas in the most irregular of places. He has occasionally fantasised, with a flicker of shame, about shaving this beard off completely, wondering what it would be like to run his fingers over smooth skin daily. Like a young girl's skin. An innocent skin. The skin of the women who once ruled this land centuries ago, with their false beards and baby-smooth flesh underneath. Of course, it would be utterly against protocol for someone of his status and role to do this, an outrageous insult to The Teachings. His beard is interlaced with seven threads of high-grade gold, delicately spaced out and woven into his skin at the chin-line, identifying him as an Eminent One and ensuring fraud is impossible.

He will not be afraid. Abruptly, he looks down.

His penis, his most prized feature after his beard, is shrinking back slowly but steadily into his groin. *This can't be. Not that!* What will people say if it gets out, that one of the most notorious judges in the entire state is losing his masculinity before their eyes? *Someone is responsible for this*, he thinks, furiously. Toying with his diminutive penis, he wonders if it's his wife, conscious of his many infidelities, spiking the stew. No, she's too dependent on him to risk that. And so broken, she wouldn't dare. A political enemy, an inside mole perhaps, doctoring the air-con system. *Security's too tight for that, after the attempted poisonings last year.*

For a moment it occurs to him that this is divine judgement for what he keeps in the bottom drawer of his office desk, reappropriated from the previous regime's Unholy Archive of Imperialist Disrepute. He'd removed the single, battered pornographic magazine discreetly, before it was logged and 'filed' away for safekeeping. The artefact has been so well used – inspected and *analysed*, he reassures himself – that its pages are worn thin. And the images of flesh, hair and open red slits amorphously merging into one another through the wafer-thin paper, like a psychedelic landscape, are now too familiar to be quite as thrilling as when he first opened it. It was his job to assess the content. Designed to corrupt, hard to resist, even for a man of his moral standing and resolve!

When he pronounced sentence on women, on girls, they

often collapsed, begging him for mercy, already worn and hollow after time in subterranean prison cells, all bail refused. It thrilled him, their tortured faces and pain. But sometimes, intertwined with this frisson of power, and remembering his own estranged daughter, he feels a flash of guilt. A specific thought arises, panicked, from deep in his stomach: he thinks of smoothness advancing, imagines his whole body changed – soft olive skin, curves, moist orifices. Imagines constant access to this new body's comforts and pleasures. He'd never be inconvenienced by a woman again, with their constant demands, failings and substantial overheads.

This man, who is one of the most notorious and revered of all The Eminent Ones, ponders, with a combination of dread and self-admiration, whether he has become so powerful now, that even his darkest, secret desires can materialise and take physical shape?

Over the next few days, the powerful man begins to realise he is not alone. He notices a number of his colleagues shuffling around the courthouse uncomfortably, changing in ways that seem familiar and connected to his own gradual metamorphosis. Their beards are in different stages of thinning: one has a mere crust of a goatee left, gold threads sprouting almost completely alone in several places. He is tempted to reach out to this man, someone he knows well, during a court break, but quickly stops himself, realising his own beard is disappearing so rapidly that there isn't much between them.

Better not to focus minds on his failings. Not yet.

More than a few of The Eminent Ones have double bulges on their chests that were not there before. They are not all heavy men with big bellies like himself, in fact one of them is remarkably slim for a man of his status, yet today he wears a massively oversized, tent-like robe, attempting to balance himself when he walks, in an increasingly clumsy and comical manner, unused to the extra weight in this most unexpected of places.

An atmosphere of insecurity thickens the air around these men as the week goes on. It is disconcerting for them all. Yet the powerful man starts to feel relief. *So, I am not alone. This is not my fault after all.* By midweek, there is an unspoken acknowledgement between them. Sideways glances bounce around the corridors of the courthouse. *If word gets out, this could be dangerous.* They agree to increase the number of bodyguards outdoors, to create a protective layer of defence. Inside the courthouse they worry less: the long-established fog of fear that hangs heavy in the air amongst the defendants and their families awaiting trial on corridor benches, the stress amongst the staff, preoccupied with stemming the chaos of this overflowing building, all this distracts from the judges' transmutation. Those awaiting trial are choked with anxiety, seeing nothing but an uncertain future, the terror of potential punishment, endless jail terms and the threat of separation from their loved ones. The thickness of a judge's beard or the shape of his chest is the last thing they care about in here.

Once it becomes clear that this metamorphosis is only happening amongst his peers, the man calls a Secret Emergency Council, the first in many months. Sitting together around a huge, boardroom table on the top floor of the building, their eyes flitting over each other's bodies with a mixture of shame, relief and growing solidarity, they discuss a proposed update to The Teachings. One of them suggests dropping the requirement to wear a beard at all. *Let's just keep the gold thread?*

Another suggests false beards, like in days of old by the Fallen Matriarchs – but the reference back to the women who once wielded power is too risky and might remind the people of an alternative in these tumultuous times. And in any case, this alone wouldn't be enough, indeed any kind of change to The Teachings, which they had ruled unquestionable, unalterable, never to be challenged, would be too suspicious. *We cannot let the people know this is happening to us at all*, they conclude.

Despairing, they share conspiracy theories as to why and who is trying to strip them of their gender sovereignty, of all that shores up their power. One man whispers that The Pre-Eminent One seems unchanged. *Perhaps he has had enough of us, and this is a sign of his displeasure? He is the only human alive who could make this happen.* Another points out The Pre-Eminent One hasn't been seen in public for several weeks now, *haven't you noticed? We have no idea where he is. It is said he has gone east on sabbatical, but he left no instructions at all.* They stare at each other, and all take note. *Then we must follow his lead.*

Over the next few weeks, these black-robed men, with their distinctive silver headdresses and mini charcoal-grey-clad armies of mute bodyguards begin to slowly disappear from public view. They refuse all private audiences and media appearances and take refuge in their second apartments inside a high security compound, up on the far edge of the city, at the foot of a blue mountain range. They agree to tell their wives that urgent and serious state business will take them away for the foreseeable future, behind closed doors, working to counteract real and imminent threats to the state. They send out proxies to oversee court proceedings, deliver verdicts and suspend weekly addresses to their subjects, forced to trust those around them in lesser positions of power, communicating only via their most trusted aides.

But a smattering of subversive voices has begun to infiltrate the lower echelons of the justice department, spreading rumours that The Eminent Ones are in jeopardy, though no-one understands why. *They are cooking up something. We do not know what, but we will find out.* The diminishing presence of The Eminent Ones is quietly discussed on street corners, at family gatherings, in the markets. The citizens – or subjects as they are labelled, despite the allusion to the long-buried and hated monarchy – begin to wonder if these bearded ones still actually exist. Connections are made between their absence and the longstanding lack of action on rising costs of living, and life-threatening increases in food poverty and homelessness, a ripple effect of sanctions through conflicts with surrounding states. *And all this, whilst we know the wealth from their precious crystal mines continues to flow into the state reserves. Maybe they've pocketed the money and left the country!* Speculation is growing, though still no more than whispers and confidences.

Just one woman thinks she understands: his ex-lover. On the night before he severed their relationship – after seven years of weekly appointments at the apartment he moved her into – she wakes up to urinate and, seeing the bed empty next to her, follows the sound of his muffled voice. Perplexed, she hears lover's talk, coming from the second bathroom, further down the corridor, reserved for him only: *You pretty, pretty thing, look at this body of yours, isn't this beautiful? Ah yes, just there, just like that.* Catching a glimpse of him through the crack in the door, even in the half-darkness, she is relieved to see he is alone, but realises his body is not quite the body she knows and has loved. Utterly confused, a strong sense of self-preservation pulls her away and she tiptoes back to bed, shaking slightly as she slips beneath the cold sheets. She understands why he wouldn't let her touch him now or at any time over the last fortnight, but what the hell is going on?

She knew the end was coming, had felt a sense of dread as their appointments became less and less frequent, when during the last few encounters he'd refused to let her undress him or touch him anywhere except for his shoulders, through material, a short massage. *I must be coming down with a flu of some kind, no doubt, freezing inside the bones, I am sure you understand, my love.* Again, she noted something odd about his profile as he stood in the doorway before leaving. Yes, the landscape of his body had definitely changed, she wasn't imagining it. She couldn't believe it was possible. She knew of one person in the city who had used a black-market operation in a neighbouring country and then never returned, but for an Eminent One, no, it was heretical, impossible, utterly against The Teachings. He would risk losing everything. And so would she. *So, he got rid of me first, instead of confiding in me. He never trusted me, after all this time and so many moments of tenderness between us!*

Since he split from her and left his wife back in their city house, the man spends most of his time, alone, in this second apartment. At least he has neighbours and Council meetings can happen here quite easily, though none of them seems to know what to do about their bodies anymore. Doctors cannot be trusted, they agree, they have betrayed us before. It is as if they have surrendered to this inevitable change and lost all inclination to disrupt its course.

One cold, dry night the following month, the man, cursing the fact that he can now only move around outside in the dead of darkness, *like a fugitive, ridiculous!* is crossing the street from the private park near his apartment, where he often goes to take in the night air before sleeping. By now he has curvy hips, a hairless, stubble-free face, and a pair of bulging breasts that he cannot keep his hands off. Yet nothing about his new and nubile body can compensate for the absence of other humans and he misses those with whom he has known intimacy, however unequal the power balance. Thinking of his lover and her warm smile and touch, he trips over a pothole. The bulge of accumulated beard hair spills from inside his black robe pocket, his safe place, falling out in one mass onto the ground, and blowing unnoticed, against the kerb, as if settling there for the night.

In the light of the fullest moon anyone has seen all year, the cluster of hair forms a sizeable ball, and this ball gently blows downhill, collecting other hairballs which have also slipped from the pockets of Eminent Ones. They attract each other like pins to a magnet. Or a call from a long-lost lover. The discarded hairs, which they have all agreed are the equivalent of sacred relics and not to be disposed of until a conservation plan is hatched, manage to find pathways not only from robes but out from bedroom drawers, or slipping free from the folded pages of newspapers they have been wrapped in. Others escape from desks, bedside tables or from the shelves of slightly open bathroom cabinets. Buoyed by a gentle night wind, this spiky collective swarms, migrating to a particular spot in the centre of the city's main square.

It is the very spot where, half a century before, the henchmen of The Eminent Ones were commanded to make clear examples of those who refused to support the ideals of their new, shiny state, slicing open the throats of adults and children, allowing the square to fill with blood, flooding into the drainage system in the surrounding streets, a crimson invitation to join in their magnificent project, to create a common utopia, free of all abuses of power and redundant, imperialist ideology. This was also the place where anti-state protests would begin, approximately every decade, though never for more than a few hours or days, due to the brutal and well-organised security forces. Huge prison complexes were built on the edges of the city to contain the increasing numbers of dissenters, their population soon outnumbering that of the university campus downtown, where many of the troubles began.

Early the next morning, as he is setting up his cigarette and newspaper stall, a street vendor notices the enormous ball of debris, a metre in circumference by now – shed from the beards, heads and bodies of hundreds of Eminent Ones. He crouches in front of it, playfully poking it with his pen. People passing by stop and stare. Soon, fascinated disgust attracts a sizeable gathering.

From the top corner of the square, the powerful man's ex- lover approaches, weary from a noisy night at the hostel where she has been forced to relocate after his pitiful payoff ran out and her family refused to take her back. *Too much dishonour you bring on us. And you didn't even get a decent parting gift from such a wealthy man!* Full of grief and shame, she stops and stares hard at the mountain of hair, an impenetrable entanglement of blacks, greys, whites, and browns with the occasional streak of gold. It's a monumental version of the cluster of hair she had come across in her ex-lover's robe, rifling through his pockets before leaving their apartment for the last time, looking for a memento, or something she might use for a bribe if she got too desperate. She wondered why he kept the hair; some narcissistic attachment to anything that came from his own body? *He can let go of me, but he can't let go of his own body hair, what is this?* She had dismissed the hair as worthless and somewhat repulsive, but now she recognises it amongst this mass; its wiry, wavy texture and the shades of blue-grey and indigo-black are unforgettable. She has stroked and massaged it many times, at his request, as a form of foreplay.

During what turned out to be their final farewell, he had spoken as if they would meet again soon. *A few important affairs of state to attend to, we will be together again when it is sorted out, do not worry my love. Just a few weeks or so.* But he only communicated with her one more time, phoning to inform her in the language of a business professional that it was time to separate – *definitively* – that they had originally agreed this was a temporary arrangement. He told her where the severance money would be left. There was an odd fragility, a delicate tone in his voice towards the end of their conversation which she remained curious about for a long time. He had immediately blocked her number. Next came the raging silence, and with that, her regret at the losses incurred: two offers of marriage rejected, attachment to her family severed, a career as a nurse cut short because he had wanted her on call. The sense of abandonment was total.

As the woman stands in the main square amidst the crowd, facing this huge spectacle of a hairball, a wave of white anger takes hold of her, charging up through her body and finding voice. She whispers the truth out loud: the origin of this mass

147

of shed masculinity; she exposes her lover's transformation, the cause of his detachment. Whispers her own despair and pain. She leaves enough words in the space to do their work, and then disappears; it might not be safe to stay.

The words quickly weave their way through the crowd, leaving everyone both stunned and compelled by the quiet foundation of the spectacle before them, in all its expended power.

Two students pick up the ball, raising it high above their heads for all to see, emboldened by no security forces in sight, despite the burgeoning crowd. *Is this all that is left of their so-called Utopian state, those cowards? A ball of grimy hair? Too ashamed to show their bald faces now the people are starving and there is no clean water, no affordable fuel, no nothing! People, is this not a sign, a talisman? Surely it has been sent to us by the great forces they say protect and guide them.*

An elderly woman, who many decades before had run into this square declaring herself a revolutionary, ecstatic at the prospect of a new future, a freer society, now steps forward with a lighter. *Let us burn it! Let us show them what we think of what remains of their precious beards! Let me be the one to start the fire, please! I've lost everything because of these bastards!*

And so, a clearing is purposefully and swiftly created and the hairy mountainous ball, on being ceremoniously ignited, turns to a raging fireball in seconds. The stench of burning hair is too much for many to bear. The women use their delicate, deadly wrist shackles to cover their noses against the smell, but then one of them, a young girl recently released from prison, holds out hers just close enough to the fire to singe and break through its centre, casting it with a shriek onto the sweltering ball of fire. The scent of the perfumed fabric brings some relief, and her bravery prompts others in the crowd to come forward, one by one, to do the same. The core of the contracting, burning hairball is smothered and sustained by layer upon layer of coloured strips of cloth. Neon orange, yellow or green, denoting specific class or district, curling in the flames, dancing with each other. Cheering and clapping ensues, singing and drumming fill the square. By lunchtime, a mass celebration is in process. And there is still no sign of the security forces anywhere.

After several hours, the henchmen finally arrive. They have been focused on hundreds of sudden, suspicious deaths across the city and beyond. They don't bother to coordinate a response to this illegal situation; they are all too shell-shocked from the fresh sight of so many unidentifiable and amorphously cross-gendered bodies, dressed in the black robes of some of the most powerful officials in the land, collapsed lifeless on apartment floors, in stairways, on the streets or inside their smoked-glass, armoured cars. They have had enough trauma for one day and the call to the main square, while Special Forces forensically examine the bodies in the cramped morgues on the outskirts of the city, is a welcome diversion.

Disarmed by the triumphant atmosphere, the men push their way through the joyously raucous crowd, barely noticing the unshackled women and girls waving their arms high, in time to the music, in the twilight. The crowd quietens as they move through and past, increasingly nervously, towards the epicentre of this illegal and momentous gathering.

They come to a still, smoking spot, and here they stop and stare at all that is left of their rulers; a charred pile of intertwined cloth strips and an array of singed, curled gold thread,

glued fast like a series of distorted musical notes to the blackened ground before them.

GARETH E REES

THE SLIME FACTORY

THE PROMOTIONAL VIDEO came out of the blue. A real surprise. Nobody had seen Roman Nesterov in public for almost five years. The eccentric billionaire had shut himself away inside his research complex, leaving his spokespeople to deal with nervous shareholders and enquiring journalists. No interviews. No social media updates. No statements. Total blackout. He could have died, for all we knew. Now here he was on my phone screen, standing in front of the Organistrive logo in a black suit and top hat, looking extraordinarily tubby. His once-chiselled features had become grotesquely bloated, and either he had gone totally bald or he had shaved his head. But it was Nesterov alright.

'I have a vision of a future,' he announced to camera in his sonorous Slavic tones, eyes twinkling inside their fatty pits, 'unshackled from our bondage to fossil fuels. Where organic computers run our lives without electricity and transportation is self-sustaining, self-repairing and even self-navigating.'

The lilting melody of 'The Lark Ascending' struck up as the film cut to a panoramic view of hills dotted with sheep beneath a blue sky. Victorian railway bridges arched across wooded vales. Church spires poked above thatched roofs. Fields of corn and barley were crisscrossed with flowering hedgerows. Ducks and geese paddled on a lake as swallows swooped over the rushes.

This footage was surprising because it didn't seem to be CGI, but a real landscape, presumably Nesterov's private estate in the Cotswolds. If so, it was either a digitally enhanced film or a physically manipulated landscape, for it was a far cry from the Britain I knew: the charred moorlands; the polluted rivers; the barren mountains; the drowned cities and filthy air. It looked like the Gloucestershire of the 1940s, not the 2040s.

'This is the place to which we truly belong,' Nesterov intoned, 'and to where we can return, after the fires and flood, the death and disease, and all else we have suffered. Our future lies in the past of our dreams, but we need dream no more.'

As the camera panned across the bucolic vista, the carriages of an extremely long locomotive could be seen vanishing into a tunnel.

'In a special event on Friday the 11th of July, I shall unveil a radical new technology that will save humanity by transforming it. A special invited press audience shall bear witness to our society's rebirth. I do hope you'll join us for the live stream.'

The film ended with a still of people in summer dresses and suits, crowding a traditional branch line railway platform, waving handkerchiefs and craning their heads for an approaching train. The tagline read: *Organistrive: A Better Time Will Come.*

'Fuck,' I said to nobody in particular, the bedsit being dismally empty, as always. Just me on an unmade bed, with dirty coffee mugs and a bunch of flickering laptop screens. I had been awaiting this moment for so long, it took a few minutes to register what I'd just seen. After years of silence, Nesterov was about to open the gates of his slime factory to the media. This was the big one. I absolutely had to be there for the press conference. Not only to write a story about the flamboyant tycoon, but to help Nia find out what he had done to her missing boyfriend.

Nia and I met at university, where I was a visiting lecturer in digital media, and she was studying for a PhD in bio-science. At a house party we bonded over tequila slammers and a shared interest in environmental activism. I'd written about the attacks on the cryptocurrency systems, the airport sieges and port blockades as battles in a class war against the inequalities of climate change impact. The only way for humanity to survive the emergency was to unite against the gang of super-rich industrialists who caused most of the problems yet were the most insulated against the ecosystem's collapse.

That might be true, agreed Nia, but for her the solution lay way beyond the class struggle. She believed in a Marxist solidarity with non-humans, from rocks and trees to insects and fungi. For too long we had treated humanity and nature as separate entities. In fact, she said, sprinkling salt onto her fist, we should stop seeing things as *other* altogether. She picked up a slice of lemon with her slender fingers. It was the othering of things that was the problem. Human beings were not separate. Not really. The human body was a legion of microbial organisms. The human mind was a series of inter-connected operating systems. The human world was but one among many. The world of chalk. The world of tin cans. The world of dust mites. She pushed a shot glass towards me. The world of tequila. Salt, drink, lemon. All these objects were conscious at some level.

Nia licked the salt, knocked back the shot and bit on the lemon, without a flicker of discomfort. If we were to survive ecological annihilation, she told me, human beings had to give up the illusion of stewardship over the Earth and instead forge a symbiotic union with other species, even other substances.

Bang. That was it. Instant crush. I could not resist her militant ontology, raven hair and tolerance of hard booze. We immediately started going out, although we never moved in together. In hindsight, it was not the most romantically involved affair. Nia disappeared into her work for weeks on end, barely responding to my messages. When she emerged, she wanted to eat, drink and screw like there was no tomorrow – and I was more than happy to oblige. Three or four days would pass in a blur, then she'd be gone, as if recharged by hedonism, and she wouldn't give me another thought until the next time she rang my doorbell, both actually and metaphorically.

The subject of Nia's research was the slime mould *physarum polycephalum*, which I knew only as a gooey yellow entity that lived on forest floors. A weird fusion of fungus, plant and animal, it seeks food by snaking out tendrils in all directions. Those which fail to find nourishment shrink away while others establish a perfect network for delivering nutrients. They were the perfect organisms for helping humans design infrastructure systems. Researchers placed oats on city locations on a map of Japan and watched the hungry slime forge the most efficient railway network. They tried the same with British motorways, revealing flaws in the routes of the M4 and M74. Later, NASA created an algorithm based on slime mould to map the cosmic web of dark matter distributed across the universe.

But slime mould's most exciting quality was the way it retained the knowledge of its previous successes and errors in its protoplasmic veins. When slime moulds merged, they transferred this knowledge and used it to improve their navigational abilities. The bigger they got, the cleverer they became. This capacity for problem solving and memory storage had applications in the creation of organic computer chips, which was what Nesterov's company began to develop in the 2020s.

Organistrive had already developed a means of storing large amounts of data as DNA sequences inside plants. 'The complete works of literature of mankind can be contained within a tree,' boasted Nesterov. 'Soon we shall live in Edenic gardens of knowledge.' Now they wanted to develop fully organic operating systems. To do this, they used genetically modified slime mould to create 'Memresistors', controlled by light and chemicals, rather than by wires and transistors. Organistrive's systems began with basic functions like operating alarms, security gates and prosthetic limbs. Then Nesterov embarked on more ambitious projects involving communication, transportation and artificial intelligence.

In 2037, he announced the world's first living computer. It made a worldwide splash on the news. He was all over tech and culture websites, photographed in his trademark retro English gentleman fashions, with headlines like SLIME KING, BREAKING THE MOULD and GROW YOUR OWN. He was even *Time* magazine's Person of the Year. Then, without warning, the eccentric billionaire shut himself inside his research complex, dubbed *Willy Wonka's Slime Factory* by the press, and vanished from public view. His public relations team would only say that he was working on something big, and he needed to focus all his attention on it, away from the limelight.

There was never any doubt in Nia's mind that she would join Organistrive as soon as she completed her doctorate. Her Kenyan heritage not only barred her from most other career avenues and higher level university posts, it also put her in constant danger of internment or deportation. Nesterov had many faults, but racism wasn't one of them. All he cared about was employing the world's best brains. And while Nia was no capitalist, she agreed in principle with what Nesterov was trying to do. A collaboration between humans and slime mould was one way we could transcend the ecological catastrophe. When the oil ran out and old systems failed, our knowledge could ooze through the protoplasmic tubes of new organic networks. Civilisation could endure in harmony with the biosphere. She believed this was what Nesterov wanted, deep down, despite his showbiz bluster. He declared with typical bombast that his biological technology could help humans survive 'the biggest climate disaster since the Younger Dryas asteroid impact of thirteen thousand years ago', and there was the sliver of a chance that he was right. With our options rapidly running out, it was a straw worth clutching.

When Organistrive hired Nia without even an interview, it was the end for us, romantically speaking. She had a destiny in biological engineering. Mine was in journalism, or whatever that constituted these days. I was pleased for Nia, but I knew I was unlikely to see much of her again once she entered Nesterov's private estate. The sprawling grounds included not only his factory, but villages for employees, family and friends, connected by a local railway network, among acres of countryside, fenced off from the public and guarded by a garrison of security troops. With enough wealth, it was possible to continue a twentieth-century lifestyle amidst the disaster of the twenty-first century. You just needed to establish a territory, pay off the government, and protect your land with walls and weapons. There was no protest from the public because they didn't really know what was going on. The media were in the service of the government, and the government was in the service of oligarchs like Nesterov.

The only silver lining to this dire situation was that it allowed me to eke out a living as an independent journalist. I worked anonymously for underground websites, funded by an uneasy coalition of anti-fascist organisations, environmental activists, former media barons and wealthy donors shocked by the obliteration of a free press. We sought every chance we could to poke a hole in the canopy of oppression and let in some light of truth. The mass executions at migrant concentration camps. The hit squads who stole people from their homes at night. The radiation leaks from the subaquatic concrete tomb that contained Dungeness nuclear power plant. The cover-up of an outbreak of sentient bacteria on the ice-breaker *Salvo* which drove its crew insane. These should have been major media stories but they existed only on dark web news sites in pieces by the likes of me, written anonymously out of fear that one night they would come hammering on my door, too.

Unlike Nia, I had never been convinced by Nesterov and his biological experiments. I didn't trust his obscene wealth. His power. His unaccountability. But there had been no way to write a story about him. Despite numerous offers of life-changing money for a scoop, I couldn't get close enough to anyone who worked for him, past or present. The only outsiders ever permitted into his estate were government cronies and hacks from state newspapers. I knew that Nia was my only way in, but I didn't want to abuse our relationship or jeopardise her career. I set up an encrypted message system for her to get in touch if she ever wanted to tell me anything, or even to say hello, but she never used it. That was, until two years ago, when I was surprised to receive this message from her:

I *need your help.*

In the exchange that followed, Nia told me she was still a relatively low-level researcher in the company, developing bacterial colonies to run genetic programs in computers that used DNA molecules instead of wires. It was important work but she was disappointed that the major slime mould project, for which Nesterov had retreated from the world, was hidden from her. Staff were expected to work on their component parts without ever being informed about the ultimate goal. The rumour was that Nesterov's top scientists were building something extraordinary inside the gigantic hangar near the railway terminal of Rodos village, but there was no way to see inside.

None of this especially worried Nia until she embarked on a relationship with Thomas Riese, the recently divorced head of development at Organistrive. He was a charming, intelligent man, but she quickly realised something was troubling him. He cried out in his sleep. He would begin sentences that trailed off, as if he was desperate to tell her something. Often, he alluded to goings-on in the hangar, which he said were stretching the boundaries of what was acceptable. He complained that he was expected to make the most unreasonable sacrifice. On one occasion, she found him in the bathroom, weeping, a razor blade clutched to his wrist.

When Nia mentioned her worries about Thomas to one of the counsellors, they agreed to look into it. A day later, Riese vanished. She searched for him but her access card could take her only so far. There were rooms, corridors and chambers completely closed off to her.

I need to know if he has left the estate, she messaged me, *can you try and track him down? I am so worried.*

It was easy, at first, to research Thomas Riese. Born in London in 2001, he was a third generation German Jew whose grandfather escaped death in a concentration camp at the age of two and emigrated to Britain. There were plenty of articles about Riese's rise to the top of Organistrive, with pictures of him at conferences with Nesterov and tabloid newspaper photos of his wedding in 2030. The most recent was in a *New Scientist* profile.

However, as I began to dig deeper, I noticed something strange. There was no trace of his social media accounts. Many references to him had been redacted. I would click on links to find websites that were no longer recognised. After a few days, even the images I'd found on my initial search had started to disappear. He was vanishing from cyberspace right in front of my eyes. I'd never seen anything like it. It was hard enough to remove something permanently from the internet, never mind on this scale. And why such a focus on images of his face?

Nia thought it could only be Nesterov's doing. Nobody else would have that kind of power. *Something is going on*, she wrote, *something terrible. They say there are things living in the hangar. Big things. Villagers hear them howl at night. A lot of people feel afraid. Yet nobody knows why. Or at least, nobody that's left.*

The situation was becoming tense. Workers were frog-marched by security from the labs or their homes. Their phones would go dead. Intranet accounts closed. Social media accounts gone. Homes boarded up. That was the price of being suspected of sharing secrets with the outside world. The thing is, I never found a trace of any of these leaks. No rumours on the dark web. We were none the wiser about the inner workings of the biotech giant. And it wasn't only the lower-ranking workers, either. Edward Silverman, Head of Research, completely disappeared. Most shockingly, Gordon Tanaka, the Chief Operating Officer, was sacked out of the blue and nobody had seen him since.

If they know I'm leaking this to you, wrote Nia, *I could be next.*

I looked for information on Silverman and Tanaka but my searches brought up meagre results. Like Thomas Riese, they were being wiped from the internet. Nesterov was disappearing people like some biotech Stalin, not only physically, but digitally. The only way I could help Nia was to get through the gates of Organistrive but there was nothing I could do about that. Nesterov's estate was 'in England' only in a topographical sense. Politically, socially, economically – even morally – it was another country. I had no way of entering without being shot on sight. That was, until Nesterov's surprise announcement that he was flinging open the gates of his slime factory.

It was only moments after I finished watching the film that I received this message from Nia.

I have your Golden Ticket. Please come.

And just like that, I was in.

The train pulled out from Paddington and headed west. As

we passed Wormwood Scrubs, I could make out the slimy tops of tower blocks in the distance, poking above the water in what would have been White City and Hammersmith only ten years ago. Once the flood began it happened quickly. From Stratford to Battersea to Chiswick, whole tracts of London on either side of the Thames slipped beneath the waves. The city was the epicentre of a disaster but many of its denizens still clung to the water's edge, gazing out over their lost pasts – the barnacled flyovers, multistorey car park islands and subaquatic roundabouts – still believing the land would rise again.

Out towards the M25, smoke curled from industrial estates into a yellow sky as gulls circled the sewerage pits of shanty towns on the city's edges. We continued at a crawl through the overcrowded suburbs, where I looked down into back gardens with electricity generators, water butts and dirty kids, who prowled the sidings, throwing stones at us. After Slough the train accelerated through a countryside of waterlogged ditches, ramshackle pig farms and polytunnel networks. It was a depressing journey but things looked the same in whichever direction you left the capital. The English landscape was like a series of collapsed studio sets from a half-remembered twentieth-century film, its backdrops tattered, props in shattered piles, mouldering in pools of dirty water.

We arrived in Gloucester, where I joined a small crowd gathering on a platform for one of Nesterov's private local trains. I recognised a few famous faces from the government-allied news organisations. Nesterov had banned cameras, but these preening ghouls were still accompanied by assistants and makeup artists who could help conceal the shit smeared round their mouths from their constant arse-licking. I kept a low profile in case any of them twigged that I was one of those leftist renegade journos they liked to warn the public about, determined to bring down the state, or what was left of it. But as always, they were only interested in themselves and nobody paid attention as I sat by a window near the rear of the train, avoiding the stare of the trooper who stood guard by the doors, clutching a machine gun.

The final stage of my journey couldn't have been in starker contrast to what had come before. Verdant hedges, fields of wheat and wildflower meadows. Windmills and churches. Sandstone terraced houses with slate roofs. Thatched cottages. Tea shops and public houses. Old stone bridges from which couples in Barbour jackets waved as we passed. The vision of England portrayed in Organistrive's video had been realised through extensive replanting, rewilding, rebuilding and re-sculpturing. It was as if I was travelling through a giant diorama, like one of those landscapes built for a train set in a middle-aged man's attic. It was missing only the frozen plastic figurines and the giant human face of the operator rising above their artificial world like a sentient sun. Of course, Roman Nesterov was the top-hatted man-god who controlled this English fantasy.

We pulled into our final destination, the old-fashioned provincial railway station which had featured in the promotional video. All steep gables, baroque eaves, ornate ironwork and touches of Victorian gothic. As far as I could tell, this was a new station, built within the last decade, but the brickwork had been deliberately weathered. The whole place sepia-stained to look like the inside of a teapot. While some of the passengers gawped at its features in wonder, I refused its sick nostalgia. Nesterov was a vulgar magician who used simple tricks to line his pockets. They didn't work on me.

A man with a whistle ushered us off the train and we queued for almost an hour at the turnstiles as we were patted down by security, our phones placed in plastic bags and non-disclosure forms thrust in our faces. I couldn't see the point of a product launch in which nobody could take photos, report live, or even say what they'd seen. This wasn't really a press conference at all. We had been invited not to report, but to act as props in Nesterov's dramatic performance. I tried to hide my fury, not at Nesterov but these so-called journalists. I had never seen a more compliant herd of fascist enablers and authoritarian apologists. Fortunately, the security guard didn't find the mini smartphone recorder I'd wedged expertly between my buttocks. They should have known better than to mess with a pro.

Once released, we were directed through a subway beneath the station and out to the rear car park, where a large crowd of Organistrive's employees, friends and family were gathered in their Sunday best, drinking gin and tonic out of teacups. We were enclosed on three sides by stalls selling drinks, cakes and party balloons. A troupe of Morris dancers jigged to a minimalist drumbeat, surrounded by white-gowned maidens wearing garlands of flowers. In front of the crowd was an iso-lated railway platform built onto the car park, set up like a stage, with a cinema screen at the back and steps on either side, hung with colourful bunting. Two cherry pickers carried cameramen high above, one pointing his lens down at the assembled mass, the other at the stage where a small band of musicians was setting up. I couldn't recognise all the instruments. Aside from a drum kit and double bass, there was a battered honky-tonk piano and an organ made from steam whistles, the kind you might get in an American travelling fair.

The scene was reminiscent of one of those corporate family afternoon events with face painting for the kids and a tombola, had it not been for what was looming behind the stage: the hangar Nia had told me about, a windowless façade of brick and steel with three giant double doors – all closed. Train tracks ran out from beneath each of the doors, all the way to the stage, where they converged in parallel lines alongside it. I wondered if I could slip away and get a closer look, but despite all the festive gaiety the car park was surrounded by security guards, brandishing weapons.

My heart sank. To get to the hangar, I would have to break through this protective ring, pass around the stage, and then run over two hundred metres of train line to reach the building, where there were more armed men standing by the main doors. The best I could do was find Nia. I moved slowly through the body of people, searching for the Kenyan girl I once knew. Eventually, I saw her standing near a cupcake stall, wearing a long black coat. Her hair was almost entirely grey. Face drawn. Back stooped. It had been, what, ten years since I'd seen her? I don't know why I'd thought she'd look the same. A decade working in a lab for a billionaire despot. All that agony over her missing lover. So much disappointment in her career. She looked older than her thirty-five years. Who knows, maybe I did too? I had dispensed with mirrors long ago and can't remember the last time I saw a photo of myself. It was only my carefully protected anonymity which allowed me to infiltrate events like this weird corporate fete.

Nia pretended not to notice me as I approached. Like me, she was aware of the camera on the cherry picker above, and who knew what eyes and ears Nesterov had on the ground? However, she clenched my hand when I brushed past and I stopped beside her, facing the opposite direction, pretending to study the various flavours of cupcake while I said in a low voice, 'You look good.'

'Liar.'

'Well hello to you too.'

Nia didn't smile. Her eyes remained fixed on the distant hangar, dark against the green hills beyond it.

'I wish we could talk somewhere,' I said. 'What's been going on?'

'Nothing and everything.' Nia grimaced. 'I don't know.'

'Tell me what I can do.'

'Just watch – watch what happens next. Then tell the story. The real one.'

'But I need to find a way to get close to—'

'Shhh – they're starting.'

A harassed-looking Organistrive official trotted up the steps to the stage and began speaking to the band, gesturing to where a white limousine with monster-truck wheels approached. With a 'one – two – three', the band struck up a jaunty instrumental that sounded like circus music and ragtime mixed with music hall. The limo doors opened and out stepped Organistrive's Chief Marketing Officer, followed by Helen Allan, the Secretary of State, and then by Roman Nesterov, in the same black suit he'd worn in the video. He looked even fatter in real life, his face almost a sphere, with ruddy cheeks, his eyes reduced to pinholes. He donned his top hat and puffed up the steps, giving a wave to the crowd, who clapped and whooped, waving embroidered handkerchiefs in the air, just like on the promotional video.

Without warning, Nia pushed through the crowd, working her way to the front, until I couldn't see her at all. I clicked the audio record button on the device concealed in my pocket, waited for a few moments, then made my own way through the throng, partly in hope of getting a better view, partly to stay close to Nia and make sure she wasn't about to do something stupid.

As I closed in on the first few rows, I spotted Nia at the front, about five people across from me. She glared at the stage, where the dignitaries took their seats beneath the screen as Nesterov ambled to the front of the stage and unhooked the microphone like a rock star.

'Thank you for coming.'

Applause.

'Long time no see.'

Laughter.

'As you can see, I've been eating on your behalf.'

More laughter.

'But of course, none of it matters, because we are all going to die and everything you care about will be gone.'

Grim silence.

'Every endeavour in human history. Totally meaningless. Forgotten. That is what will happen after this great extinction, if it continues unabated and we don't change. But who is to blame for our predicament? You, for trying to eat and heat your home? The industrialists, for offering these things to you? No, I'll show you how we got here.'

Nesterov waved a pudgy hand at the screen, where a CGI film showed giant sloths, mammoths and woolly rhinos moving through leafy undergrowth. Humans crouched among them, turning meat over a fire, eating handfuls of berries and mushrooms.

'This world was once our Eden,' said Nesterov. 'But during

the Neolithic era, a great crime was committed against nature and, by default, against humanity itself.'

The film cut to Stonehenge in the sun, priests in cloaks bowing, legions of men and women carrying baskets of bread along ceremonial corridors of white chalk.

'In liberating ourselves from hunting and gathering, we rebelled against not God, but against the idea of ourselves in nature,' Nesterov said. 'We became separated. We didn't know it at the time, but it was an act of war.'

Now the film showed a golden field with medieval farmers threshing corn, windmills turning in the background and folk dancers dressed in white gowns.

'For a time we enjoyed our dominion, but then came industrialisation.'

The scene changed to a landscape of mills and factories, chimneys belching smoke, and earth churned up by diggers. This was quickly overlayed with shots of power stations and pylons, motorways, shopping centres and aeroplanes. Flames licked the bottom of the film, steadily consuming the screen until it was all fire.

'The global warming disaster cannot be undone,' Nesterov said. 'More cities will sink. More lands will burn. We are paying for the original sin of the Neolithic. The enslavement of nature for our ends. The pillaging of resources. The destruction of habitats that were really our habitats too. But I want to end that war. Today, in view of this congregation of friends, family, workers and invited press, I propose a new way forward. A fusion of species that might allow us to go back to the beginning. Back to Eden. But with all our astonishing art, science and knowledge intact. A lasting legacy for the future.'

The screen lit up again with the bucolic English scene from

the promotional video, showing a train crossing a railway viaduct in a wooded vale.

'I have been working on the development of organic machines that can think, navigate and repair themselves, allowing us to travel and communicate even if power supplies fail.'

In the distance, there was a metallic squeak as one of the hangar doors began to grind open. Nesterov turned and pointed at it. 'Behold! The world's first living locomotive!'

The band struck up once more with their insane rockney barrelhouse oompah, as what at first appeared to be an early twentieth-century train engine, with a smokestack and pistons, eased out of the darkness and began to approach the stage, where Nesterov beckoned it towards him like you might entice a shy horse.

Once it was in the sunlight, I could see this was no ordinary train. There was no steam. No sign of electrical input. No mechanical noise that could be heard over the music. The engine itself wasn't shiny and metallic, but wet and fleshy. The skin visibly writhed with muscular movement, and I could make out intricate arterial networks pulsing with yellow slime. Along the locomotive's length, tendrils hung down like millipede legs, gripping bony coupling rods and using them to turn the wheels. There was something even weirder about the circular smokebox door at the front of the engine. But it was only as it got closer that the realisation hit me. It was a face, stretched across the entire disc, made of veiny blue skin, taut and translucent. The big eyes swung from side to side, scanning the crowd.

A wave of nausea came over me. Others could see it too. There were gasps. Cries. A scream. The sound of someone being sick.

'This is not artificial intelligence,' Nesterov declared, over the clatter and parp of the music, 'but actual intelligence. The consciousness of slime moulds, plants and fungi, united with the knowledge of human beings.'

I looked across at Nia, whose countenance in that moment haunts me to this day – an expression of unabated horror, as if she was gazing upon the visage of death itself. I could see her body shake violently as the train groaned to a halt behind the stage, emitting an exhausted sigh, now in full view of the astonished crowd. Tears pooled in its eyes as tiny spores floated upward from fruiting blobs on its roof. There was an overwhelming smell, like honey-marinated meat left in the sun. I could see now that there was no driver. No mechanical parts and no fuel. The creature was a mass of sinew, bone, slime and skin. There was something uncanny about the face, too. Something I couldn't put my finger on until I heard Nia scream, 'Thomas! Thomas!'

As she uttered those words, I swear the rubbery, lipless mouth opened and contorted as if it was trying to reply to her.

'That's Thomas Riese! Thomas Riese!'

Nia flung herself towards the stage, but before she could get even a few metres, two guards tackled her to the ground. An anguished bellow came from deep within the train, like a terrified cow in an abattoir. Instinctively, I tried to move towards Nia, to help her, but the crowd surged to see what was going on, trapping me in the crush. She was dragged to her feet and hauled away to the sound of circus music, screaming 'Thomas!' over and over again. Before I knew it, they'd taken her beyond the stalls and out of sight.

'Apologies, ladies and gentlemen,' Nesterov laughed nervously, his cheeks flushed, 'there's always one, isn't there?

Thomas indeed! Good name for a train, though!' The honky-tonk piano trilled in response, 'Dah-dah-dah-dah dah-dah daaaaaahhhhhhhhhhhh.'

I looked around at the crowd. Implausibly, they had quickly composed themselves after the fracas. Most were beaming up at the abomination on the platform. Some still waved hankies in the air. Clearly, Nesterov was insane, and a terribly insane thing was occurring right in front of us, but at the same time, it also didn't feel that way. Not in the reality of the moment, with all the gin in teacups, balloons and Morris dancers, and folk in nice clothes watching intently, instead of running screaming in all directions. Within minutes the horror had been normalised.

'And there's more, ladies and gentlemen,' Nesterov bellowed, clapping his fat hands together as the remaining hangar doors opened simultaneously and two more monstrosities emerged, blinking in the sunshine. Their train engine forms were similar but with idiosyncratic differences in length, colour and bulk. Different animals grown from similar moulds. It was only as they drew closer to the stage that I recognised their hideous visages, for I had studied both faces intently during my search for information and – unless Nia and I had been gripped by the same pareidolic delusion – I could see obvious resemblances to Edward Silverman and Gordon Tanaka.

The two new arrivals lined up in parallel, mournfully lowing at each other, films of greasy fluid spilling down their sides and dripping from their undercarriages. As the crowd burst into excited chatter, fixated on the spectacle, I took my opportunity to force my way back through the crowd until I could escape through a gap in the stalls. I ran full pelt across the car park towards a row of faux-Georgian houses, where the two guards were grappling with Nia beside an armoured security van parked on a cobbled street.

'Stop! Leave her alone!' I pulled out my secret phone and held it aloft. 'I'm streaming this live,' I lied, 'and you're now on camera. Stay where you are.'

The guards stopped and regarded me for a moment, with smirks on their faces. Nia, slumped between them, cried, 'Look out!'

I didn't know what she meant until a few seconds later when I felt something thud into me. There was a lot of pain very suddenly, then everything went black.

You could say I was lucky. They didn't do much damage, the men who knocked me out. They smashed my phone, of course. Obliterated it. Didn't even give back the shattered pieces. But for whatever reason, I was not considered a threat and they put me on a normal train with some soldiers who escorted me in silence to Gloucester, where I was unceremoniously hurled onto the platform.

Back in London, I got straight on the internet to see how the world had reacted to the bizarre events of the afternoon. All I found was a very slick film of the event, edited and manipulated to remove Nia, and me, and the people who screamed or puked at the sight of Nesterov's diabolical creations. This must have been what they streamed 'live' but with delay enough to tweak and embellish. They had digitally touched up and smoothed out the trains to remove the more visceral details.

There was plenty of outrage on social media, of course – the kind of nugatory chatter which the state gladly permitted – but all the government-sponsored news sites declared the launch a triumph. A damned good show. A tonic for the nation.

The fuckers.

I tried to contact Nia on our encrypted channel but there was no reply. I couldn't think where else to look online. Nia didn't have much of an internet footprint. She'd never bothered with social media and her entire career had played out within the Organistrive world. Now she may as well not have existed.

Opinion pieces came out over the following week with speculation about what self-growing, self-driving, self-navigating transportation might look like if rolled out. They admitted these prototypes were not perfect yet, and might not come into service for perhaps five years. That seemed to quell some fears but Nesterov was concerned enough about the reaction to launch a propaganda campaign. This consisted of a family-friendly series of films about anthropomorphic, driverless trains, set in the landscape of Nesterov's mutated Gloucestershire. These were sanitised toytown versions of the monstrosities I'd seen in the flesh. Thomas, Gordon and Henry looked much more like traditional locomotives, their faces infantilised, with that damned circus ragtime playing over the opening credits.

It was appalling to watch, knowing the grim truth these films represented. But I had to keep checking the latest episodes, looking for clues about what Nesterov might be up to behind the scenes. It was the only thing I could think to do. The doors to his slime factory had closed once more and he'd stepped up the military guard on his estate. After my exposure at the conference, they'd have my face and fingerprints logged on their systems for sure. One glimpse of me on their

security scanners and I was a dead man – a disappeared man
– or something even worse.

I put feelers out to see if any of my comrade journalists
were up for an investigation. They said they'd see what they
could do. I didn't hold my breath. Instead, I stayed at home
and drank gallons of cheap wine, reading old novels written
in those eras before I was born, when people believed there
was a future worth living in.

A year later a new character was introduced to Organistrive's
propaganda film series, in an episode entitled 'Thomas's Silly
Mistake'. She was a tank engine from Kenya, and I was hor-
rified to recognise her face.

AK BLAKEMORE

BONSOIR (AFTER ITHELL COLQUHOUN)

SHE SITS, THIS woman, down at her desk. In a little room. She sits down at her desk that is behind a door, and on the door hangs a long dark red velvet dress. This is the sentence she says to herself, in her head:

on my door hangs a dark red velvet dress

and she says it to herself and she says it to herself again until it becomes like a spell. She works, and she remains aware of the dark red dress hanging on the door, just behind her shoulder (as though a woman is standing there and could at any moment stoop to kiss her neck. Powdered face, perfumed wrists, moon's only mansion, o sweet Andromaque).

It is four o'clock in the afternoon.

The desk stands between a window and the door with the red dress. From the window she sees the whorl of blue-pale buddleia, the microflora velveting the brickwork crevice (o sweet Andromaque, moon's only mansion). Cats come and go, belonging to no-one or perhaps to someone. Semi-feral, faces shred. She likes them from here but she would not like them closer up, because they enjoy to kill things with cruelty, and she herself does not enjoy killing anything. But there, sat at her desk, she watches them come and go, commissioners of miniature enterprise, shouldering their way like bailiffs through the courtyard on sooted pedipalps. When their paths cross, grey and white, tabby and grey, they pause in dignified horror to assess one another. Hiss and spit, flash their nasty yellow eyes. This feline perfidy reaches an apogee at dusk, when men slowly draw the furs from the blue shoulders of beautiful women in restaurants all over the city (and in all the other cities as well, she supposes). The cats, they see no difference between here and wilderness. The cats have no singing-voices, but the foxes do. Are there foxes in Paris? No-one talks about them, if there are.

It will be dark soon (to think of you by moonlight, o sweet Andromaque). She sits with her scissors and her pot of paste. Magazines, periodicals, the style pages. The material is to be reconfigured. A smile hovers under her hand, red and bent like one of Salvador's own horizons (cuttings-out, the re-appraisal and movement of the smallest units, the smoothing of the malthouse units – this is how you make bacon cry! this is how you find the purple fragment in the sand!). Her scissors speak as they stroke a supple cheek – her scissors say bonsoir, bonsoir. Her scissors say moi aussi. Outside the vents spread palladium in a darkening sky Sweet William. She remembers King's Cross station, so busy that the men were pressed into the shining concourse, chest-to-chest. A man in a black hat and an astrakhan lifted a posy high above the crush. Lilies and rain on the glass, the smell of exhaustion. That was in England (o sweet Andromaque, so far away).

In the magazines:

Coty, Tangee, The New Yardley Lipstick, polychete. They emerge, eyelessly. Feed on heat from the middle of the earth. A gamine with short finger-curled hair sits on the beach and contemplates an empty sky. Blue swimsuits, polka-dots. Melting knots, a tempered eye. There will always be parties, they say, until the end, when the bone convulses in a fist, the hag-fish drain the marrow out. This is how a woman, the daughter of the sea, enjoys a life. I will peer, she says, as through a lace, broken down, dissolved to morsels. Baroque. Drenched in Vol de Nuit. If there is a man, he is the hull of a white boat that drives between her softnesses (these are her thoughts while she sits in the bathtub, touching herself (!)).

(Note on men: a tall hat, a thin moustache. They fold their hearts away in tailored black. Or an antique divers' suit. Or a prophylactic. She draws The Tower from the deck, which means he will be either Russian or Italian. A fascist, but of course extremely handsome. She pictures him walking towards her across a vast and empty plain, like the floriated fin of the cinema screen. He is wearing enormous snow boots. His breath is rising in clouds up, up to a washed yellow sky.)

And so, she thinks, about last night: a party. A party is a dark room where people stroke at one another like ferns. She goes, because she was asked, but at thirty-three she already feels too old to enjoy being a fern. The woman there who she felt to be the most beautiful was also the only one with cigarettes left (because sometimes you are just that lucky). They talked. Her wrist crusted like a glacier, broke open (at thirty-three you are a woman of experiences. At thirty-three you are a hand that holds out a smile, stretching it between thumb and forefinger like a gauze, here, for you, and how is your husband? Yes, I think we have met in London – a cat, splendid Bast, turns her liquified soul around. The clash of ice in tumblers, ice filling his big rude laugh ramrod. She doesn't like anyone around her here, but still.

To take off your clothes, snip! The most beautiful faces, isolate. Upstairs, in the room with drapes the colour of moss, the woman lifts her arms over her head and contorts them like statuary to find the hook of her dress and it is perfect – and the other watches from the bed, already arranged in her slip, and she thinks, it is perfect and it will never happen again and only I was here to see it and remember it and even I will not remember it comprehensively, how she was like a Maenad in that moment, bearing flowers to a dark and confusing God, as she reached for the hook of her dress. The white underpinnings. The white polyamide strewings. You are on them and they smell dirty of you and so careful, so cautious (o sweet Andromaque). One red-lacquered mouth closes over another, and the watcher's shadow a device on the draped wall, ouroboros. A heat builds, the straps slither on the skin, more frantically, lain down, falling down like rain on a wide green lawn. Their shoulders shift and narrow and sharpen like ritual knives as they turned one toward each other, and when they open their eyes again they look through splinters embedded in colour, stop, pause in dignified horror to assess, tails lashing, teeth rattling in the pink. I will be in the night and the night will be in me, (half-furred) half-fuzzed in shadow face – she wets her fingers in her mouth and wipes her black pencilled eyebrows and her red lips away. Mimatrice. When my whiskers sprout, all the fine jewels that are placed on my body melt (in cancer, moon's only mansion). A spoon of sugar water, you.

(an image of a bed, still unmade, whose occupant has recently departed)

It is night-time in Paris and at the train stations there are people kissing each other goodbye. And there is this woman, sitting down at her desk in a little room. She knows that she could put down her scissors, and leave her magazines and her desk and her little room. Go down, past the smoking culvert, past the alcove where the waiters suck at their skinny little roll-ups (and sometimes speak to you, salut, bonsoir, ma belle). She knows that if she did they would be moving all around her in the darkness, and she would hear them but she would not see them – there, there would be sounds and singing, maybe, in the darkness—

COMMON GROUND

'I'M GORDON FROM next door,' he said, standing on Erica's doorstep, holding out a hand for her to shake. She had been expecting the postman, and for a moment she just looked at this man, at his neat silver hair and his well-trimmed moustache, his buttoned-up cardigan and his hand, which, when she took it, was cool and dry.

For a few months, that was how she would refer to him: 'Gordon from next door', or just 'Gordon'. Now she calls him 'Mr Granger' or 'that man'.

'I've just moved in,' he said. 'I thought I'd come and introduce myself.'

'I'm Erica,' she said. There was a pause, during which she thought she ought to say something like, 'You'll find us all very friendly round here,' but that was not quite true, or, 'Let me know if you need anything,' but she would rather he did not. The two of them listened to Erica's kettle coming to the boil.

'I haven't found my kettle yet,' said Gordon. 'It'll be in one of the boxes.'

Erica nodded.

'The problem is,' said Gordon, 'the boxes aren't labelled, and there are so many of them.'

'Ah,' said Erica.

'I've no milk anyway,' said Gordon.

She asked him in, and he thanked her and stepped into her hallway. She thought of vampires, who could not come in until they were invited. She closed the door behind him.

Gordon was looking at the piles of paperwork on the kitchen table.

'I'm in the middle of marking some work,' said Erica.

'I can see that,' said Gordon.

Erica got an extra mug out of the cupboard and set about making the coffee.

'I've seen you,' said Gordon, 'in your garden.'

He would be able to see her from his back door, or from his bedroom windows. Handing him his mug of coffee, she said, 'I've made it milky so it ought to be cool enough to drink straight away.'

He set the mug down on the table and took a seat. When he was settled, he said to her, 'Is there a Mr . . . ?'

'No,' said Erica. She sipped her coffee, which was too hot after all and burned her lip.

Gordon looked around, eyeing the framed photographs on the sideboard. There was no picture of her ex, not in her kitchen, not anywhere in the house. Her neighbour could go through this place with a fine-tooth comb and find precious little evidence that she'd ever had a husband. She had not said his name in years; she refused to talk about him, even to their daughter.

Gordon was looking through the window, admiring her tree. 'You have a cotoneaster,' he announced.

'Yes,' said Erica. 'Cotoneaster frigidus.'

'A member of the rose family,' said Gordon knowledgeably.

A rope ladder dangled from the lowest branch, like an invitation to climb. Erica had planted the tree herself, before Sophie was born. Later, Sophie had used the rope ladder to reach what she called her treehouse, though there was no house there, no structure, just the tree itself, within whose cradle of branches Sophie liked to sit. But she liked it too much; she spent hours in that imaginary treehouse, while Erica was alone in the house, washing up or hoovering or marking papers at the kitchen table. Erica would call to her, through the window, 'Are you going to come in now?' and Sophie would call back, 'No, not yet, I like it out here.' What if someone abducted her? One day, Erica would look out and find her gone, the branches empty. She liked to have her daughter safe inside the house, but Sophie was too independent.

Erica had imagined losing her daughter in so many different ways. In the toddler years, she feared her climbing a bookcase or a chest of drawers that had not been fastened to the wall and would crush her. When she was older, but still so little really, the fear was that she would go beyond the end of the garden, which was not allowed, and drown in the river. When Sophie was in her teens, Erica worried about her getting into cars with boys who would try to impress her with terrible speeds on the winding roads.

'You have a child,' said Gordon, 'or children?'

'No,' said Erica, eyeing the rope ladder. 'That needs to come down.'

Gordon moved to the window, watching the fieldfare that had come to eat the cotoneaster's berries. He said, through the double glazing, to the oblivious bird, 'You're a beauty, aren't you?' Gordon would have stayed there all morning, drinking Erica's coffee and admiring the birds, if she had let him.

He popped round for milk and sugar and onions, and sometimes she let him come in. They drank coffee and watched for fieldfares.

He asked her if she would like to swap keys.

'What for?' said Erica.

'You know,' said Gordon. 'If you go on holiday and want me to feed your cat, that sort of thing.'

'I'm not going on holiday,' said Erica. 'And I don't have a cat.'

'But you know what I mean,' said Gordon. 'If you're not here when a package arrives, or if you lock yourself out.'

'I don't intend to lock myself out,' said Erica.

He came round for jump leads, which she did not have, and asked her to go for a drink.

'A drink?' said Erica.

'A drink,' said Gordon. 'A glass of wine, or whatever you want.'

'No,' said Erica. 'Thank you.'

Gordon bowed his head on her doorstep before walking away.

The next time he asked, she told him, 'No, please don't ask me again.'

'It's only a bloody drink,' said Gordon.

Each time he asked, he was angrier. She stopped asking him in for coffee. If he wanted an onion, she gave it to him on the doorstep. He told her that they had a lot in common. She did not think so at the time. He liked military history, which left her cold. He chain-smoked on his back doorstep every morning and every evening, and she could not stand the smell.

Now she sees what they have in common.

The next time he knocked, it was to tell her that her tree

dropped its leaves into his garden, spoiling his lawn. He'd had enough of it, he said, and he was going to cut her tree down.

'The tree is on my property,' said Erica. 'Cutting it down would be trespass.' She knew her rights.

She saw him later, out in the sun without his sunhat, red in the face, up a ladder with a hacksaw, cutting off the branches that hung over his wall.

But her leaves still blew his way and he could not stand it. 'And the roots,' he said, on her doorstep, 'go under my lawn. The roots are on my property, and I don't want them there.' He told her he was looking into chainsaws.

She stopped answering the door to him, but when she marked her students' work at the kitchen table, the cotoneaster with its missing branches was always at the edge of her vision.

Now she sits with her back to the window. She pulls another piece of work from the pile and looks at the opening paragraph. She shakes her head. Her red pen scrapes through the page. The students complain about her. They say she is too harsh, too set in her ways, and getting worse. But *this* and *this* and *this* – she purses her lips and prunes their work with blows of her red pen – is simply unacceptable and she will not allow it in her class. She has to tell them over and over again, and still they keep on making the same mistakes. She sees the looks on their faces when she hands back their brutalised work. She knows how they talk about her. They say things like, 'She's got it in for me.' But she does it because she cares, she really does care, about them and what they could achieve, under her guidance. She wants them to understand what she expects of them, and for them to be better, to deliver, or there will be more red marks; there will be a gradual lowering of grades; there will be penalties.

⁂

'We're moving to New Zealand,' said Sophie. 'We' was Sophie and her boyfriend, one of those boys who had come, after all, in his fast car to take her away. She said it cheerfully, as if it were a wonderful thing to be going so far away from her mother, thousands and thousands of miles away from her mother, who had never lived anywhere but here in this town.

'For how long?' asked Erica.

'Well,' said Sophie, and she did at least have the decency, then, to look ashamed, 'indefinitely.'

'But what about your job?' said Erica. It was a better job than anything Erica had had at that age, but Sophie just shrugged and said there were jobs in New Zealand.

'You'll regret it,' said Erica.

That's what her own mother had said when Erica had a foot of healthy hair cut off: 'How could you cut off your beautiful hair? You'll regret it.' And Erica *had* regretted it, but she did not let her mother see that. She kept her hair short out of stubbornness; she has kept it short to this day.

Erica tried, when talking to her daughter about this ridiculous plan, to stay calm, not to shout, but it had become more and more difficult. When the day of departure finally arrived, Erica refused to drive Sophie and the boyfriend to the airport. While Sophie was at the terminal, Erica was furiously stripping her daughter's bed. While Sophie was up in the air, Erica was emptying her daughter's room. She put the furniture into a skip. If Sophie tried to come back, she would find her bed gone, along with all those little keepsakes and cuddly toys she had left behind. It was heartbreaking to pull down her daughter's posters and hand-drawn pictures, to steam off the childish wallpaper. Erica painted the walls with what she had in the shed – something neutral, muted – and moved in a sofa bed that no one had ever used.

Erica will not pick up Sophie's phonecalls or open her letters, which come less frequently now. Sophie will be busy. She was pregnant when she left, so by now there will be a baby, presumably. The last time Erica went to the pharmacy, she found herself looking at the baby things while she was in the queue, looking at bibs and spoons and nappies. The pharmacist had to raise his voice to get her attention. 'Just my prescription,' she told him, moving forward.

By the time she got back, it was done. The branches of her cotoneaster were lying like a tangle of limbs in her garden, next to the severed trunk, the rope ladder drooping over them. So that was that. She would not speak to him about it; she would not give him the satisfaction.

The stump was still alive; it would need treating or it would rot, become diseased.

She can imagine how he is feeling now: righteous and miserable. There is no going back. When he stands on his doorstep with his cigarettes, what he will see is his ugly stump, the fieldfares gone.

The roots are still there, of course, snaking under his immaculate lawn, reaching in every direction. He will have trouble getting them out.

DAVID BEVAN

THE BULL

AFTER HALF AN hour, I left the wake without saying goodbye to anyone and drove up to the reservoir. I pulled in before the bridleway and walked to the lookout at the top of the stone steps. There was no-one around, just an old man crossing the embankment. He stopped and bent to say something to his dog. It looked like he was asking it a question. Was it the same one I had? How did I become this person and not another? Wasn't that the question you searched your whole life to answer? I watched the wind plait myriad reflections of the bracken-clad hills and the grey September skies. After a few minutes I turned away. It wasn't the reservoir I needed to see again.

I started walking slowly up the lane, where it narrowed between the farms. The air was damp with drizzle and earthy with the pungency of sheep droppings, drifting over from the fields either side of the dry-stone walls. For half a mile the memory tracked me like a shadow, then it stole up on me. My dad and I had once walked this way when I was a child. The lane led to a small, untended field that overlooked the reservoirs further up the valley. There was something in that field, something vital to do with my dad and me. Fragmentary images began to flutter in my mind. I laid them out in sequence as I walked.

A flock of neighbours gathered in our small front room, my mum looking all flushed and glowing, my baby brother being passed around like a rugby ball wrapped in a towel, my face aching from the smile I was forcing. Was it my mum who had felt sorry for me and suggested the walk? Or was it my nana maybe? It wouldn't have been my dad. He wouldn't have been indoors amidst all that fuss and flap.

I had a vision of him as he was then, standing in the alley next to the broken-down skeleton of his motorbike, long boned in his oil-stained jeans, a mop of dirty blond hair and his large angular nose, dark blue eyes under serious brows, his big hand held out towards me.

'C'mon then, Bluebell, if you're coming.'

It was summer. The sun high and bright, the air drifting with clouds of blown dandelion clocks. The neighbours out in force, pruning their hanging baskets and shouting out congratulations to my dad on the birth of his son. I remember old Mrs Riley said something about how nice it was to see him out walking with his pretty daughter, how proud and happy that made me feel. I like to think maybe my dad felt it too. For a while on that walk he *had* seemed happy to me. At one point he'd asked me, what did I think of my new baby brother then? I think I must've made some sort of a face because I remember how he'd laughed, throwing back his head and making a funny honking sound through his nose. I'd never heard it before. Yes, I think for at least a while that morning, my dad thought he might get past things.

He worked at the meat-packing plant in the next town. Even as a little kid, I knew he hated it there. I remember how sometimes, in the middle of his tea, he would flare his nostrils and put down his tray. He'd go into the kitchen then, boil the kettle and start scrubbing at his fingers with soap and a scouring brush. When he came back in, his hands would be all red and swollen like the bloody cuts of meat that he'd bring home sometimes. My mum told me once that he'd worked in the mill before it closed. He was a different man then, she said.

At the time of our walk, he was off work. It wasn't because my brother had just been born; they didn't go in for paternity leave much in those days. It was because of an accident that happened on his shift. Michal, the Polish man my dad was working alongside, had tripped and fallen into one of the giant offal tanks. Dad couldn't save him, but he'd watched him drown in all that gore and filth. They gave him two weeks of sick leave; no one had heard of post-traumatic stress then. 'Taken a bit of a knock.' I remember overhearing my nana saying that to someone in the street. I was just a child. It wasn't until years later that I found out what had happened.

With every step along that damp and pungent lane, my memories gathered closer in. At the start of the walk, he'd taken me to some of the places he'd known as a kid: the mill-pond with the rope swing, tied and rehung so many times that it looked like vines in a Mississippi swamp; his fishing spot by the pony bridge; the pool where he swam under the waterfall; the reservoir, of course. By the time we'd got up to the lanes, I must've been getting tired. I remember the thrill of him hoisting me up onto his shoulders and the joy of riding up there. Tipping back my head and breathing deeply, I remembered the smell of him: coal tar soap and cigarettes; something else raw and metallic underneath that, sometimes faint, sometimes strong, always there.

Up ahead, the lane split in two around the base of a steep hill crowned with gorse and hawthorn. Past the hill one arm bent back on itself, turning into a rough track as it climbed up to join the pack-horse path. The other arm sloped away to the right, narrowing still further and growing a tufted green mohican as it wandered away through a corridor of trees. That was the way I went. Through the trees, stepped back from the lane, there was an abandoned house. As a child I'd been frightened by its empty windows; they'd seemed blind to me. I was surprised to find it unchanged. Maybe it was too far out to have been renovated, but perhaps there was something else. Even though the trees were animated with whispers, it seemed that the clocks had stopped at that end of the lane many years before and that it was a place haunted by more than just my own memories.

I could see the field now, a few yards further on, where the lane petered out. The barred wooden gate was just as it had been, bound in baling twine and swung open into the field, a silent invitation. The field sloped away, through swaying grasses to a collapsing stone wall that overlooked the second reservoir and the high moors beyond. In the far distance, long, dark hems of rain dragged the tops. I walked the few steps towards the open gate, then stopped. My heart thumped in my chest. It was still there. In the bottom corner of the field, listing over, like a slowly sinking ship, sunk in the nettles and ragwort. Still there.

Suddenly, I was there too. Chasing after my dad as he strode through the long grass towards the strange, dark container, the grasshoppers ticking off one by one, creating a corridor of silence as we passed through them.

'Some kind of an old animal box,' he muttered as he stalked around it. It was built with heavy timbers and had a slatted iron ribcage. At one end there was a huge door with great hinges and a massive, bolted lock. At the far end, there was an open grille with metal bars. Hung from a giant stud nail, on a twist of barbed wire, there was a rough square of wood. It had some hand-painted writing on it. My dad reached up, turned the sign, then read it aloud: 'Beware of the bull.' He looked at me, raising his dark eyebrows. 'Shall we have a look at him?' In one movement, he scooped me up and lifted me towards the metal grille.

'No, no, I don't want to.' I screamed and kicked.

'It's OK, sweetheart, he's not in there any more, I promise,' he said.

He was wrong. I could sense the black eyes glittering in the darkness. I knew that if I as much as glimpsed the bull somehow I would end up in there with him. 'Let me down, let me down,' I cried.

When he did, I ran back across the field towards the gate. Halfway there, I turned and looked back. My dad had both his hands on the grille and was looking into the container. It seemed like he was standing there for a long time. When he walked back, he had his head down and there were two deep lines etched between his eyebrows. When I reached for his hand, he offered it distractedly but didn't speak.

The vividness of the memory stunned me. Why hadn't I remembered it until now? Perhaps I'd thought it was a bad dream and had forgotten about it? There was a lot about my childhood I wanted to forget. Or perhaps it had always been inside us, my dad and me.

He never did go back to work. After a month on the sick, he was offered voluntary redundancy. When I came home from school, often he would be sitting in the kitchen with a can of lager in his hand and a cigarette burning down to his nicotine-rusted fingertips. When I said, 'Hello,' sometimes he would smile, though it looked like it hurt him to do it. Other times he would just say, 'Hello,' his deep voice dropping the word like a stone in a lake. Over the coming weeks and months, he spoke less and less, became almost mute in fact, but physically he was anything but silent.

'Take your brother up and play, love. Me and your dad are having a talk,' my mum would say. Upstairs I would pull the duvet around our heads and try to read over the muffled shouting downstairs. At the start, it was mostly mum's voice I heard - her, screaming at him. There would be a crescendo and then the banging would start: doors thundering in their frames, plates and glasses smashing. I'd hear my dad's voice then, deep, monosyllabic, primitive somehow. Often he would just bellow a single word: 'What? What? What?'

He never hit us, but the violence in him was terrifying. From my bedroom window, I remember watching him drag a kitchen chair out into the alley, swing it over his head and smash it into tiny sticks. He did the same with the coffee table and, a couple of weeks after that, he put his foot through the TV. The rows would always end the same way, the back door booming in its frame, my dad's motorbike thundering into life, then screaming up the valley road like a banshee. At some point he'd painted the motorbike matt black, even the chrome bits, everything except the headlight. Sometimes he'd be gone for days, other times just hours. When I heard his bike growling like a brute thing under my window, I knew he was back.

I was twelve or thirteen when he left for good. I hated him by then: the chaos and sometimes deafening noise of him; the silence too; the haunted calm in between times, fragile as eggshells. I hated him, yet still I felt a deep connection to him. Physically, I looked more like him than either my mother or my brother. The dark blue eyes and the dirty blond hair, the long limbs that made me feel like a gangly, uncoordinated horse throughout my childhood and adolescence. There were other things too, feelings that I couldn't express but knew on some level I shared with him.

He felt it too. He never missed my birthday. At some point, he would always turn up with a gift for me: a porcelain animal or bird, a horse, a fox, a rabbit, small delicate things, the opposite of him and me. As I got older, he'd bring other things too: a pot of nail varnish, a hairbrush, a bangle. He'd catch me on the way home from school, or be sitting there on his bike at the end of the alley, or he'd leave it on the back step. 'Happy Birthday, Bluebell' was all he'd usually say. Mostly, I didn't say anything at all.

'Chuck them in the bin, where *he* belongs,' Mum said, but I never did. I kept those things in the chest of drawers in my room. Sometimes I got them out and carefully lined them up on the window sill. I thought if I arranged them in the right way, they might help me understand something: why he was like he was, and who I might be. The older I got, the more strained things became between my mum and me. I couldn't blame her really; the physical resemblance between dad and me must have picked at all the scars he'd left behind. No doubt she saw other similarities too. I remember more than once her turning to me and shouting, 'For Christ's sake, Chloe. Can't you speak, girl? I swear you get more like him every damn day.'

Things were no better with my brother in the end, but again I couldn't really blame him. His father had ignored him since the day he was born and over the years I bore the backlash of that. 'Daddy's girl' is what he called me, most recently at the wake that morning. He hadn't come to the service, Mum neither, but somehow I knew he'd make a point of being in the pub. 'Eh up, here's daddy's girl,' I heard him say from the corner, laughing too loud and then masking his face in his pint. I didn't know any of the biker blokes that came. I must've said half a dozen words the whole time I was there: 'Hello' to my nana and 'Whisky and Coke' to the barman.

The last time I saw my dad, he'd come into the barbers in the town. I switched to cutting men's hair as soon as I was trained. Though some still expected conversation, I never offered it, beyond asking what they wanted. Over the years I gained a few regulars, for whom that worked just fine. He'd never come in for a cut before. Seeing him walk in out of nowhere, I felt my heart beat hard in my chest. He was the man he'd always been, a stranger and my father. Lean still, but older, heavily lined around his eyes and mouth, his hair thinner, dirtier, greyer. In his septum he wore the silver ring that he'd worn ever since I could remember. He was wearing a ragged old Motörhead T-shirt. Though he looked burnt out, when I showed him to my station, I felt heat radiating from him, smelled the raw, metallic scent that had always been there.

'What d'you want, Dad?' I said.

He caught and held my gaze in the mirror.

'I was thinking of a mohawk.' His chest rattled with a laugh, then he added, 'Whatever you think, lass. I'm in your hands.'

While I worked, his eyes moved slowly over the dark ink and fine white scars on my arms, the piercings in my lip and eyebrows. I remembered his monosyllabic rows with my mother. 'What? What? What?' The same question rumbled in my head like thunder claps, but my tongue wouldn't unlock any sentences, so I just kept cutting. I found it exhausting, my hands shook a little and I felt cramp building in my fingers. After ten minutes I stopped.

'I'm done,' I said.

He smiled then, thin and quick.

'Aye,' he said. 'I reckon I'm not far off that myself.'

He took my hand then. Holding my gaze in the mirror again, he said, 'Y'know you'll always be part of me, Bluebell.'

Was I destined to become just like him, then? The question had haunted me most of my life. Standing at the entrance to that field again, I felt closer to the answer than I'd ever been, but at the same time I felt unnerved to find myself there. It was as if I'd had no choice in the end. The wind shifted then, lifting the peppery scent of nettle heads to my nostrils. It acted like smelling salts, and a moment later I was walking.

The winters had taken their toll. The whole structure lurched swaybacked like a shot elephant about to fall, the bitumen roof rolled forward in a glowering monobrow, the steel ribcage had slipped its planks, the heavy door stood slant like a drunken man. 'Just a rotten old shed,' I said to myself. Except the closer I got, the less I believed it. 'Beware,' the sign had said. By the time I turned the corner at the far end, I'd become a child again, my pulse skittering like a trapped bird in my throat, my scalp prickling. Two twisted entrails of wire still hung from the stud nail, but the sign was gone. 'It's nothing,' I said aloud. 'There is nothing.'

Clenching my fists around the rusted bars, I pulled my face to the grille to look inside. A sharp, fungal reek of rotted wood greeted my nostrils. With my head and shoulders now blocking most of the light, it took a moment for my vision to adjust to the darkness inside.

The container was empty, and yet it was not. Dusty fingers of light probed its many fissures and cracks revealing ghostly spider webs hung with long-dead brittle insects. Though I could still feel the slight push and rock of the wind against the container outside, inside the silence had the solemn quality of a long-held oath. It drew me in.

Beyond the reach of the frail fingers of light, the heart of the container was purely, thickly dark, like a long fall into a deep well. Though I could not see to the bottom, I kept staring into it. After a while, I became conscious again of the pulse in my throat. I had a vision of myself then, as if from across the field, standing there, looking into the container, just as my father had done all those years before. Seeing myself like that made me think that I must do something, but I didn't know what. The darkness held me. For some reason I couldn't seem to think outside of it.

The realisation came with a sudden sensation of falling.

'No,' I gasped, understanding then that I was no longer outside but in, in there. Tears pricked my eyes, as the hot stink of a huge animal swelled around me. Then, with the roar of great bellows, the darkness began to breathe.

GABRIEL FLYNN

TINHEAD

ONE NIGHT IN March of this year, Tinhead left the house he shared with his mother and brother, walked the three miles of disused railway line linking Hayfield and New Mills, and jumped off the Queen's Bridge, dropping 80 or so feet into the shallow River Goyt. This I learned tonight when, after long contemplation, I decided to leave my flat in Manchester, drive to the Decathlon in Stockport, and buy some new boots so that I could head out early the next morning for a day of walking in the Lake District.

Not having left the flat all weekend, at first I couldn't decide whether to go at all, and then, when I found the courage, whether to drive to Stockport, which was easier to reach and had a larger Decathlon, or to the Trafford Centre, which was further and had a smaller Decathlon that closed earlier. If I went to the Trafford Centre, I thought, I might get caught in traffic and miss the chance altogether. But if I went to Stockport, I was breaking a promise to myself. Once I was in Stockport, I thought, I would be halfway to New Mills and then I would be only a few miles away from Hayfield, the village that had once been my home and to which I had sworn never to return. In Stockport, I would be within the orbit of Hayfield. After all, I had often taken the bus from

Hayfield to Stockport on Saturdays to eat at McDonald's, watch a film at the Savoy or go skateboarding at Bones. In Stockport, I thought, there was every chance that I would encounter someone from Hayfield or New Mills, an acquaintance I hadn't seen in years. Every time I saw one of these former acquaintances they reminded me of the misery and violence that I had been witness to throughout my teenage years, and of the confusion and fear that had governed my emotions at that time. I was not, I thought, standing by the window that overlooked the small gardens behind my new flat, in a fit state to go messing around with my emotions. And yet I deliberated for so long that I altogether missed the chance to go to the Trafford Centre, and had no choice but to go to Stockport.

The town centre was even more miserable than I remembered. It had already been run down in the 2000s and now it seemed to have run down even further. Many of the red brick shops and pubs stood empty, their windows boarded up or broken, and on the streets I saw only a few homeless people and drunks. The warm and sterile atmosphere of Decathlon was a welcome contrast and I spent a good while browsing the aisles and trying on boots. Then, as I walked towards the checkout with my selection, I heard a deep voice behind me saying, 'Rafi? Is that Rafi Orchin?' I knew immediately from the rural accent that this was an acquaintance from the village, though it wasn't until I turned around that I recognised Darren Hallam, cradling two large tubs of protein powder in his arms.

'Ayup, mate,' he said, moving closer to me than I'd have liked. 'I've not seen you in a long time. What are you doing around here?'

'I just moved back,' I said.

'To Hayfield?' Darren said.

'God, no,' I said. 'To Manchester.'

'Nice one, mate,' he said. 'You gonna come out for a visit?'

'No,' I said. 'I don't intend to.'

'Funny fucker, you. You've not changed.'

'I have,' I said, though he paid this comment no regard.

'Do you still see much of anyone? Joey Pound or anyone like that?'

'Not for a long time,' I said, and then I tried to let a silence kill the conversation. I ought to have held out, and almost did, but finally I weakened and said, 'What about you? What's new in the village?'

There began a litany of marriages, deaths, beatings and imprisonments. One mutual acquaintance had had a heart attack at the age of 32 due to his use of steroids, Darren said. Others, former schoolmates of ours at New Mills Secondary, had been convicted of violent crimes or had died of drug overdoses or road traffic accidents.

The long and gruesome list seemed to be drawing to a close when he added, 'Rick Tinsley – Tinhead – do you remember him?' My heart began to pound in my chest and I could only grimace and shake my head because, although I hadn't heard the news, I knew what was coming: Tinhead had finally had enough of this world and like many before him, had jumped off the Queen's Bridge. Before I could say a word, Darren spoke again. 'He killed himself,' he said. 'Leapt from the Queen's Bridge.' I was grateful that my turn in the queue came at this moment because I could hardly contain my distaste for Darren Hallam's use of the word 'leapt', a word he wouldn't have used in any other circumstances, whose purpose was obviously to attribute a fabular quality to Tinhead's death and thereby make it palatable. The people of Hayfield were too narrow-minded to understand suicide, I thought as I turned away and paid for my boots, and it was exactly this narrow-mindedness that had led to the suicide of Tinhead.

The only surprise, I thought when I got in the car, glad to see the back of Darren Hallam, though the smell of his aftershave remained in my nostrils, was that he hadn't done it sooner. A person like Tinhead, in essence an intellectual, who lives in a place like Hayfield is bound to kill himself or die of a drug overdose if he doesn't escape, and it was always clear that Tinhead didn't have the means to escape and would live in Hayfield until it killed him. Tinhead lived in a culture that was hostile to his every need and desire, I thought, as I watched Darren Hallam get in his BMW and exit the car park via the mini-roundabout. He lived in that culture knowing that he could never get away from it. That is always enough to kill a thinking person.

Tinhead wasn't an intellectual in the strict sense, I thought, as I turned the key in the ignition and started the car. He certainly didn't read books, for example, though he was sympathetic to all people that read books and especially to English teachers. Although he didn't read them, Tinhead understood books. In that sense, he was unlike the majority of the villagers, who felt no shame in having not a single book in their garish cottages, decorated for a rustic way of life that none of them in fact had anything to do with. He also knew nothing about politics or philosophy and didn't even read the newspapers. He was an intellectual in the more fundamental sense, in that he was a restless questioner of everything; he took nothing as immutable and recognised the contingency of all modes of life. Most of all, he was an intellectual in the nature of his relation to village life, I thought, as I joined the mini-roundabout. Tinhead was dissatisfied with village life—he found it petty and dull—but at the same time, he relied on the people of the village. He coaxed their narrow-mindedness toward open-mindedness; that was the function the little motor in his brain had been engineered to perform.

He would pace around the village on his own, I remembered, as I drove through Stockport's miserable town centre with its famous viaduct, muttering to himself and drinking cider, always holding the rim of the can with the tips of his fingers, and one would think: there goes a person who cannot tolerate the small-mindedness of this village. But then one might also see him in The Bull, drinking pints with the red-faced men in polo shirts who convened there on Friday and Saturday nights. Tinhead moved constantly back and forth from the periphery of village life to its heart, and he couldn't tolerate either. He revered Carl Atherton, who lived in a shack with a corrugated steel roof that he built with his bare hands on a plot of land near the campsite, but Tinhead would never have built his own shack and lived in it. He was not practical enough to build a shack and, even if he had been, he would have been too lonely there. He needed village life and it needed him, I thought, as I turned on the radio and almost instantly turned it off again because I wanted to think clearly about Tinhead and not be distracted by the voices on the 6 o'clock news. Without a person like Tinhead in its midst, I thought, without a person who demonstrates the dangers of asking too many questions, the village would lose the impetus for repression that sustains its order; while Tinhead, without the village holding him back and restraining his desire to be free, would have quickly gone astray and veered too far from the moorings of social life. It was his critical position in relation to village life that made Tinhead a true intellectual, even though he didn't read books. While conversely, some of the most respected and acclaimed academics, even in the fields of philosophy, history, and literary studies, are not intellectuals at all, but merchants.

One thinks of Tinhead as perennially unemployed, I thought, turning right and not left on to the A6, turning, in other words, in the direction of New Mills and Hayfield rather than back towards Manchester. In fact, he had a job at a factory in Strines that made circuit boards for electronic goods. One of their largest customers was a manufacturer of budgie warmers, I remembered him telling my friends and me while we had been sitting on the bench opposite Ken Rangeley's Newsagents. We had all had a laugh about that, Tinhead included. He knew better than any of us, who were still in school at the time, that the absurdity of spending eight hours a day soldering circuit boards for budgie warmers was just one instance of the absurdity of work in general. We always liked listening to Tinhead, my friends and I, because he saw through the pretensions of the village and he paid no heed to its authoritarian culture, which punished curiosity and joy and rewarded repression and misery. We liked Tinhead because he would always go into Roy's and buy us cigarettes when we were too young to buy them ourselves; he approved of young people smoking, which he understood as a complement to thinking. It was in Tinhead's nature to value thinking, walking and smoking, and to be highly suspicious of work, whereas the villagers on the whole held work in the highest esteem, especially pointless physical work. Tinhead was more suited to walking around the village with a can of cider and asking the big questions. He asked the big, pressing questions that nobody else in the village would ask, the ones that even many highly remunerated professional intellectuals are too embarrassed to ask, like 'Why am I alive?' and 'Why must I suffer like this?' I remembered that when Tinhead asked the big questions, he would raise his eyebrows as far as they would go and then laugh as though responding to a feeling of vertigo. This laugh was an early indicator that he would one day kill himself, I thought. Tinhead's path had always led more or less directly to the Queen's Bridge.

Tinhead favoured hallucinogenic drugs over cocaine, though he took a lot of cocaine too, I remembered. We had taken cocaine together once in Eric Cuthbert's caravan, when I still took cocaine and before I left the village. I was well past Stockport Town Hall now, approaching Hazel Grove, and the memory of taking cocaine with Tinhead in Eric Cuthbert's caravan caused me to reflect that I hadn't seen Tinhead for 10 or 15 years, since the days of dial-up internet. Since then, I thought, he would have spent a lot of time exploring the darkest corners of the internet and would likely have become interested in conspiracy theories. Yes, I thought, as I entered Hazel Grove, Tinhead was exactly the sort of person who would fall for the most outlandish conspiracy theories because he was not complacent and always wanted more answers than anyone in the village was willing to supply, but he hadn't a clue where to look for them. Though Tinhead might conceivably have loved reading books, though he might even have been saved by books, there was no hope for him growing up in a house with no books; with friends who didn't read books; in a village without a bookshop; where he attended a school where books were treated as official documents and were therefore anathema to a person like Tinhead, who mistrusted all authority. It was more than likely that in the years since I had last seen him, I thought, as I came to stop at the traffic lights by the big Sainsbury's, Tinhead had absorbed the wildest conspiracy theories, though he wouldn't have succumbed to overtly right-wing conspiracy theories because he hated militant tendencies and all forms of authority. What would have spoken to Tinhead would have been something like lizards controlling the world. It wasn't hard to imagine Tinhead loping home along the Sett Valley Trail, walking in a way that one recognises instantly as the physical extension of thinking – in Tinhead's case, an ebullient, unstable kind of thinking – with a can of cider in his hand and a few more in his rucksack, coming to the understanding that lizards run the world. One could imagine him standing opposite Ken Rangeley's Newsagents, by the phone box, the bench, and the old set of wooden stocks, which most of the villagers, though not Tinhead, would happily bring back into service, explaining to a group of teenage boys how lizards run the world.

Tinhead's was a gentle, inquisitive and anti-authoritarian nature, I remembered. His eyes were pale blue and conveyed his vulnerability and over-saturation with life. I could picture Tinhead's eyes clearly as I drove along the A6 in the gauzy evening light, beyond the junction at Hazel Grove and into Middlewood. From there, the road climbs towards the Peak District and the gardens between the semi-detached houses are larger, the cars in their driveways bigger and shinier. Tinhead's brother, Ryan, had a more sinister look in his eyes. Were he not so complacent and resigned to his subservient, repressed existence, Ryan would absolutely have been amenable to right-wing militarism, I thought. Tinhead did not consciously refrain from crushing insects, but his instincts guided him to brush insects away rather than crush them. His brother, however, whom nobody ever called Tinhead, though they were both named Tinsley, was the sort who, when he saw a mosquito or spider, destroyed it forcefully and without a moment's remorse, I thought, as I passed the High Lane War Memorial and the Red Lion. Ryan would have displayed the same pleasure in killing birds or even larger animals, I thought, as I drove towards New Mills, the Queen's Bridge and Hayfield. That assumption was not unfounded because I remembered that I had seen him in the Royal one Christmas Eve, probably on the eve of the last Christmas that I spent in Hayfield, and he had told me in Thailand, where he had been on holiday, you could pay $15 to fire a machine gun at some chickens and $100 to fire a rocket launcher at a cow, and that the only reason he hadn't done it was because he found the price too high. Tinhead never would have fired a rocket launcher at a cow, I thought, as I passed the entrance to Lyme Park.

Driving along the stretch of road beside Lyme Park, dark because of the high wall and row of oak trees on one side, I asked myself for the first time what I was going to do in just a few minutes when I arrived at the Queen's Bridge. I was going to pay my respects to Tinhead, I thought, because I owed a debt of gratitude to him. It would not be untrue, I thought, as I drove along the A6, to say that Tinhead saved me from Hayfield. Although it's clear to me now, now that I have long since wriggled free of the village's morbid grip and achieved a certain amount of perspective, that I was never *of* the village in the way that most of its inhabitants were, this was not at all clear during the years that I lived there. Then, it seemed to me that living in the village and going to school there qualified me to be *from* the village just as much as anybody else, a misconception that Tinhead helped me to recognise. I had met him walking through the park and we had stopped at a bench to smoke a joint together. Tinhead was always smoking a joint or about to light one.

'You'll be alright, mate,' he said. 'You'll get away from here.'

'What do you mean?' I said.

'You've got brains,' Tinhead said, I remembered as I drove along the A6. 'You'll get out of here and do something.'

'You've got brains,' I replied.

'Different kind of brains,' Tinhead said, 'very different kind.' Then he said, 'You're not from around here.' Those words had deflated all hope of belonging that had occupied so much of my thinking at that time. Recognising this, Tinhead said, 'That's a good thing. You don't want to be from around here. Have you seen what happens to people who live here?' I shook my head because at that stage, I thought, I still hadn't. 'Look more closely,' he said. 'It's not good. Everyone's fucking mental.' It would not be an exaggeration, I thought, as I lowered the window slightly to ventilate the car, to say that with these words Tinhead had effectively saved my life where he had not been able to save his own.

Even then he had known the fate that awaited him. Even then he understood that suicide was not a force that came out of nowhere and lopped off a life's remaining years, but an idea that resided in the very middle of a life and sought to force its way outward, like the magma in the Earth's core. Yes, I thought, like the magma in the Earth's core. I had effectively given up writing altogether since quitting my studies to save myself from going mad, but I could still turn out an effective simile when I needed one to proceed in my day-to-day thinking and that pleased me because it meant that I still possessed some of the agility of mind that had saved me from the village and, so far, from the fate of Tinhead. A certain agility of mind and the ability to think metaphorically may have been the only difference between us.

The differences between myself and Tinhead, I thought, as I drove around the bend into Disley, could all be put down to the simple fact that I had grown up in a house with books on the shelves and maps on the walls while Tinhead hadn't. When I felt suffocated by the village and its stifling, repressive, petit-bourgeois culture, I had been able to stand at the map mounted on my bedroom wall and run a finger along the Danube, or to read the fine red print listing the names of islands around the Antarctic, whereas Tinhead, I was sure, had no such map. I pictured him in the pebble-dashed house on Pendle Brook Close where he lived with his brother and their mother, in his bedroom, which looked out onto the small play area and the boggy fields beyond. It wasn't hard to imagine him looking out at the fields on a rainy day, wishing that his mind would meet with some object that would stop it in its tracks and finding none, wishing that the secrets of the world would reveal themselves to him in the boggy fields. It wasn't hard, I thought, as I passed The Cock in Disley, to imagine how a boy who looked out of his window at some sodden fields in the shadow of Lantern Pike and felt, already at 16, that there was nothing in the village for him, and therefore nothing in the whole world, would one day walk along the Sett Valley Trail to New Mills and jump off the Queen's Bridge into the River Goyt.

They had a PlayStation, I seemed to recall, and while Ryan's favourite games were *Call of Duty* and FIFA, Tinhead, who had a technical mind, liked racing games like *Colin McRae Rally* and strategic warfare games like *Tom Clancy's Ghost Recon*. But a PlayStation isn't enough to stop an intellectual from going mad in a village like Hayfield. He needed to know about the Bering Strait, I thought, about the Russian Steppe and the Black Sea. He needed to contemplate Moldova, Albania, the Suez Canal and the Strait of Hormuz. He needed the North Atlantic and the South Atlantic, Montevideo and Santiago, the North Pacific, the South Pacific, the Solomon Islands, Alaska; but he didn't have them. He needed books. Even the mere presence of books on the shelves might have saved him. He didn't need Swift, Austen, Dickens, Joyce or Woolf, and he didn't need Aristotle, Kant, Hegel, Schopenhauer or Wittgenstein; he simply needed *Emil and the Detectives* or *The Secret Diary of Adrian Mole*. If only Tinhead had received at exactly the right moment a copy of *Emil and the Detectives* and a free afternoon on which to read it, he might have survived. If only one rainy afternoon he had chanced upon a map of Europe in 1910, had leant in to squint at Austria-Hungary and then looked out the window, looked at the sky, with the words 'Little Carpathians' inscribed on his retina, he might have lived. Instead, he remained trapped and alone, not only in the village but also inside his own head.

I remembered, as I passed the petrol station in Disley, that I had once bumped into Tinhead on a fine summer's evening. He was drinking a few cans of cider on the picnic table by the bus stop and he looked relaxed, at peace with himself. When I told him he looked well, he said, 'I've been studying the universe, mate!' He said this with the zeal and the relief of a person who believes they have finally found the answer they've been looking for all of their life. Even by his own high standards he was drunk, but I took him seriously nevertheless and asked where he had been studying. In reply, he jabbed his finger at his temple and said, 'In my head, mate!' Then he laughed in an unsettling way, pointed at his head again and said, 'In this fucking thing.' I should have understood then, I thought, as I rounded the bend between Disley and Newtown and the green hills of the Peak District came into view in the distance, the chimneys of the old mills in the foreground, that Tinhead would remain locked inside himself until he could no longer tolerate his existence. Naively and wrongly, I took it as a sign that perhaps he could, after all, be saved from the village and that it was even my job to save him.

Not long afterwards, I recalled, as I passed the vintage car dealership in Newtown, I was walking from New Mills to Hayfield along the Sett Valley Trail and I saw him ahead of me, loping along on the stretch of the trail that ran alongside Birch Vale Fishing Lodge. I walked as fast as I could, eventually caught up and fell in step beside him so that we could walk together. He seemed sad and lost, I remembered, as I approached New Mills, and he kept beginning sentences that he wouldn't finish: 'I don't know—' and 'It's fucking—'. I should have left him, or simply walked beside him, but instead I took the opportunity to tell him about the book I was reading at the time, Jean-Paul Sartre's *Nausea*. This was a terrible mistake and an insult to Tinhead, which made me wince with shame as I remembered it, driving along the A6. I began, 'I read this book recently,' as though it were natural for me to say that that, which it wasn't and never could be in the village or even on the Sett Valley Trail, and I had told him about the book, calling it a 'philosophical novel'. Being essentially polite and good-natured, he listened and occasionally said 'right' as I rambled on interminably, describing the whole plot of the novel, which today I cannot stand, and all of the so-called philosophical themes that it tackled. Driving along the A6, I could even picture the dark look that had come over Tinhead as I spoke, the way he retreated to a troublesome corner of his mind.

When I had finished talking and suggested I lend him the book, he offered some polite words in reply, affirmative but vague. We had walked the last stretch together in silence, a silence in which Tinhead was clearly troubled, I saw now, while I had been oblivious. I had tried to persuade him to read a philosophical novel that would have never interested him and didn't even interest me except in what it symbolised, which was the possibility of a world beyond the village, a possibility that was open to me but not to Tinhead. I had not then recognised the differences between us, I thought, as I approached the turn-off for New Mills. I was from a house with books and maps whereas he wasn't, and although I lived in the village I was not *of* the village in the same way as Tinhead.

My parents had moved to Hayfield from Manchester because they thought that they would be happier living in a village, surrounded by fields and at the foot of Kinder Scout. Tinhead's parents, on the other hand, had always lived in Hayfield, just as their parents had presumably done before them. Tinhead's great grandparents had probably worked in the mills in the days when they were still in operation, I thought, as I turned off the A6 into New Mills and passed the Swizzels Matlow sweet factory, which was, I reflected, one of the only employers left in the area besides Ferodo Brakes in

Chapel-en-le-Frith and the manufacturer of circuit boards in Strines where Tinhead had worked.

The last time I had seen Tinhead, I recalled, he was playing darts in the Kinder Lodge with a man I didn't recognise. I had gone there to meet a friend for a drink before I left the village forever and went to university. This friend, who I have not spoken to in years, was the last one I had in Hayfield. My other friends and I had already grown apart as we advanced through our teenage years and the differences between us became more apparent. They wanted to become joiners, plumbers and electricians, while I, having grown up in a house full of maps and books, wanted to become an intellectual. My friend was late to arrive so I had spoken to Tinhead. 'Same old, same old,' he had said when I asked him how life was going. I told him I would soon be leaving the village to go to university. I had expected him to be happy for me, even proud, or conversely, to feel hurt that I was leaving, but he hardly turned, making two dummy motions of the hand toward the dartboard before he finally released the dart. It hit the triple one ring, I remembered, causing Tinhead to shake his head. He was clearly in a bad way that day, I thought, because he was drinking in the Kinder Lodge and a person like Tinhead can never be happy in the Kinder Lodge. New Mills really is a dismal place, I thought, as I was slowing down for the traffic lights at the bottom of the Newtown Road. If you had set out to kill yourself here, you would not be incentivised to change your mind by the surroundings. I turned on the indicator and pulled into a side road opposite the Queen's pub to park.

I got out and the air was colder than it had been in Stockport by one or two degrees, probably because the sun was now setting and I had been gradually ascending during the drive from Stockport towards the Peak District. I crossed the road and stood on the footpath portion of the bridge. It was a long way down to the river, which foamed over the dark rocks protruding from its bed. I wondered if people usually aimed for the footpaths on either side or for the water itself. The former would surely lead to a quicker death because the impact would not be softened by the water, and yet, standing there, in Tinhead's shoes as it were, I was sure that he had chosen to aim for the river. It wasn't difficult to picture it: a fast movement like a crow taking flight, with just the sound of a shoe squeaking on the railing as he pivoted his weight over. It would have been night, without a doubt. A person like Tinhead loves life too much to kill himself during the daytime. It would have taken him several seconds to descend, perhaps as many as four, and it wasn't hard to picture the look of concentration on his face as he dropped; he had a great capacity for concentration, greater than the soldering of circuit boards for budgie warmers required. Nor was it hard to imagine that he found the experience exhilarating; he loved life and found in every aspect of it something to redeem. As the village intellectual, Tinhead made it his duty never to stop seeing the potential for things to be better than they were, even as his fellow villagers gradually relinquished their hopes and sought out more and more ways to deaden their senses. It was exactly this desire for improvement, I thought, and his absolute conviction that life was not simply identical with the worst thing you could say about it, that caused him ultimately to jump off the Queen's Bridge to his death in the River Goyt.

After looking over the railings for a while, but not for very long because there wasn't much to see and the scene was more or less exactly as I remembered it, I got back in the car and drove along the Hayfield Road. First, I fooled myself with the thought that I was going to have a pint alone in one of the pubs in Hayfield, in the same way that one can have a pint alone in London or in parts of Manchester, as a person partaking in a public culture. Then I thought, no, it's not possible to have a pint in the same way in Hayfield. You can go to the pub alone but you are partaking in village life and that is something different. In Hayfield, only the locals can go for a pint on their own, and that's because they are never truly alone. If nobody in the pub remembered me, I thought, as I passed the Low Leighton housing estate, and it was safe to assume the pub would be busy because it was a clear Sunday evening with a chill in the air, I would be taken for an outsider and therefore distrusted.

On the other hand, if they did remember me they would also distrust me. I had always been distrusted in the village because I was not *of* the village, even though I lived there, and I would be distrusted even more now for returning after a long absence. But I had been thinking about Tinhead and I wanted at the very least to contemplate him in the only place where he could be truly contemplated, I thought, perhaps even bump into somebody who could tell me something about the circumstances of his death, though in a village like Hayfield, nobody understands suicide apart from the village intellectual, the role recently vacated by Tinhead. They would be bemused by his suicide and would regard it as cowardly or dishonourable, concepts that meant nothing to a person like Tinhead but mean everything to the people of Hayfield, who wish they were still living through the Second World War. There used to be a pub there, I thought as I drove along the Hayfield Road in my Toyota Yaris, not listening to any music or to the radio but only thinking about Tinhead and Hayfield. There are far fewer pubs now than there used to be.

I reached the point where the Hayfield Road draws level with the Sett Valley Trail, where they are separated only by one sloping field, and I thought about the many times that I had seen Tinhead walking up and down that trail. During the spring and summer months, he used to walk home from work: five miles, starting on the Strines Road, dropping into the Torrs Valley, passing beneath the Queen's Bridge and then following the Sett Valley Trail all the way from New Mills to its terminus at Hayfield. To walk such a long way was regarded as a sure sign of madness in Hayfield, where despite being surrounded by mountains, hills and trails, the villagers wouldn't go to Roy's for a pint of milk without getting in their Land Rovers. This I thought as I rounded the bend by the quarry at Birch Vale and the village came into view. And yet Tinhead walked home every day, drinking his cider, sometimes listening to trance music on his Discman, topless if the weather was good. He walked home, marvelling at the way the evening sunlight fell on Lantern Pike, the way it lit up the gorse and heather, and thinking about the way that there were patterns in all things, one of his favourite topics. That there were patterns in all things was the inevitable final topic in any long conversation with Tinhead. Now he was dead, I thought, as I closed the driver's side window, and Hayfield has been plunged into darkness.

I entered the village as the church bells were ringing 7 o'clock. I drove down Church Street, past Roy's, the village chippy and The Bull, but The Bull had also closed down and been converted into a house. I passed the church and crossed the picturesque bridge that runs low over the gentle river – too low, I thought, to even contemplate as a place of suicide. Finally, I decided to park in the car park of The Royal Hotel.

The air was cold. Just one person was sitting on the picnic tables in front of the pub: a man in shorts and a fleece with a bit of ale in his glass, smoking a cigarette and looking at his phone. He paid no attention as I passed through the seating area and opened the large wooden door with its shiny, mock-brass handle. Inside, the pub was busy with customers at most of the tables in both the snug and the bar area, partaking, as it no doubt pleased them to think, in village life. Meanwhile, a few locals were sitting on stools at the bar itself, neither entirely alone nor with one another. I felt completely out of place as I crossed the soft red carpeting in my long coat, the sort of coat that nobody wears in Hayfield, and I was at once relieved that I had severed myself so definitively from the village and full of regret that I had decided impulsively to drive back there alone tonight on hearing the news about Tinhead at Decathlon in Stockport. I never should have gone to Stockport, I thought, as I crossed the carpet towards the bar, because someone like Darren Hallam was always bound to be there, stocking up on protein powder, waiting to give me news of the village, news that would tempt me back despite myself.

I ordered a pint of ale and the young man behind the bar regarded me suspiciously as he placed the glass beneath the pump. 'And a packet of salt and vinegar crisps,' I said, which caused the man behind the bar, as well as the men at their stools, to look me up and down with renewed suspicion, just as they always had done, because there was something about the way I had ordered the crisps, the way that my request had admitted a real desire for crisps and not just compliance with the custom of ordering crisps with beer, that made it obvious to them that I was not *of* the village in the way that they were. But I'm an adult now, I thought as I took my pint and packet of crisps to a small table in the corner of the pub, and I don't need them to accept me. I've come here to commemorate Tinhead, I told myself, who was my friend, and who was driven to a tragic death by men like the ones sitting at the bar in silence, men who, because they repress everything they think and feel, insist that everyone they encounter does the same. One of these men, a bald and fat-headed local, with great crevices in the skin of his neck, looked over at me with the dead eyes embedded in his hideous face, which was the same garish red as the carpet, and I realised that I was literally writhing with rage on my oak chair in the corner.

I opened my packet of crisps. No, I thought, placing a large one in my mouth and biting down to break its curvature, this is absurd; I hate this pub and so did Tinhead. The truth is that I only came here hoping for news of him, and though some of the faces I could see from my table in the corner were familiar, everyone in the village basically had the same red, unhappy face, and none were familiar enough that I could approach them and ask for news. I could sit here all night, I thought, hoping to see somebody I knew and who knew Tinhead well enough to tell me what had caused him to finally his end his life, even though I already knew and had always known the answer to that question. But the chances were that it wouldn't happen, that I would leave the pub alone and frustrated and drive back to Manchester none the wiser. So I got up, having taken just a single sip of my pint of ale and having eaten only one crisp, and walked out of the pub under the suspicious gaze of the locals.

I let the mock-oak door with its mock-brass handle close behind me and I left the car in the car park to set off on foot, past the cenotaph, past Ken Rangeley's Newsagents, the post office, the old butchers, past The Pack Horse, which hadn't been closed down, and up the hill towards Tinhead's house. This was also towards the house where I had once lived, on Fairy Bank Road at the top of the valley, whereas Tinhead had lived on Pendle Brook Close at the bottom. I was contemplating this difference between us and whether it also accounted for the fact that I had been able to go on living while Tinhead had needed to die, when I saw a figure in the corner of my eye coming down the hill towards me in the semi-darkness.

Immediately, I retreated into a ginnel between two houses and then asked myself why, why was I now crouching in a clandestine manner beside a wheelie bin in a ginnel, as though I were 12 again and playing a game of hide-and-seek with my former friends from the village? Firstly, I thought as I placed a hand on the ground, which was mossy and cold to touch, because I had effectively exiled myself from the village and was afraid of being discovered there, by myself as much as anyone else, and secondly, I thought, because without quite admitting it to myself and without examining my motives, I had been planning to walk to Tinhead's house in the hope of seeing Tinhead's brother, Ryan, and the figure I had seen rounding the corner was him. This was confirmed to me as he passed the end of the ginnel, clearly oblivious to my presence. He was wearing a hoody, tracksuit bottoms and work boots, and he was smoking a joint as he walked.

I crept out of my hiding place and rose to my feet. Now

I had a good view of the portion of the high street leading down to the bend at Ken Rangeley's Newsagents, and I could watch Ryan Tinsley as he walked, emitting plumes of thick smoke every ten or so paces. You could tell just from his walk, I thought, as he passed the old butchers and the post office, that his was a totally different nature to Tinhead's, that walking for Ryan Tinsley was an activity more aligned with fighting and sex than with contemplation. I began to follow him carefully and from a distance through the heart of the village, which was deserted except for me and Ryan Tinsley. As he approached the bend in the high street by Ken Rangeley's Newsagents, I saw that Ryan was not going to continue along the high street but that he was going towards the Royal. I watched from a distance as he entered the pub and then a moment later, I followed him inside.

One of the locals at the bar turned and watched me with his dead eyes as I approached. Ryan was at the part of the bar perpendicular to the part where I was standing. He was making small-talk with another local while the young man behind the bar poured his pint of lager. There was no way for me to apprehend him in these circumstances and I didn't want him to see me now, when there was no chance of us beginning a conversation, so I turned to look at the local sitting directly beside me and our eyes met. We were at an uncomfortable proximity to one another, far closer than was customary in the village, and his eyes were beady and wary like a sheep's.

'Ayup', the local said then.

I nodded and said, 'Evening.'

'Cold, int it?' the local said.

'Bitterly,' I responded, shutting down the conversation entirely.

Now the young man at the bar was standing in front of me, while I sensed Ryan passing behind me with his pint.

'Another pint of the ale, please,' I said, as though I had drunk the last one and was simply getting a second, even though I could see that the first one had been removed from the table where I had sat, and knew that the barman had noticed me leave and come back. He poured the ale and I waved my debit card for him to bring the card reader over.

'Thanks,' he said, in a lazy, absent-minded way that was typical of young people in the village.

I turned and walked across the soft red carpet to find Ryan sitting by the fire in the snug, one hand around his pint of lager, the other holding his phone, whose white light made his face look ghastly, haunted. He looked up at me and said, 'Alright, pal.'

There was a resemblance with Tinhead, I thought, but a distant one. They were the sorts of brothers that cause one to think, strange that they are brothers, rather than, they are clearly brothers. It wasn't only that Ryan's hair was brown whereas Tinhead's had been blonde, but that Ryan appeared altogether more robust. Ryan, I thought as I examined him, had the sort of farmer's physique that was common in the village, whereas Tinhead had been more delicate.

'Do you mind if I join you?' I said.

'It's a free country,' Ryan said, and I pulled a stool from under the table and sat down opposite him. 'How you been, pal? I've not seen you in a long time. You were at uni, weren't you?'

'At Oxford,' I said, meeting his eyes without flinching, because I wished to underline that where in the past I had always fought against my outsider status within the village, that was no longer the case. 'I was doing a PhD,' I said, 'but I had to quit.'

'Right,' he said. 'Fucking hell.'

'It was too much pressure,' I said. 'I couldn't handle it. I had an episode.' Ryan's face looked gentler in the firelight than it had in the white light of his phone, and I now remembered that it was not an altogether mean and violent face but somewhat friendly, though its friendliness appeared painted on, as it were, learned, rather than a result of an essentially friendly, open nature, as was the case with Tinhead's face.

'What's brought you back to Hayfield then?' Ryan said.

Without blinking, because I had prepared for this question, as I stalked him along the high street, I replied, 'I'm visiting my parents.' This was a lie – they had long since moved away to Dorset, where they had recently died, and left me with no connections to Hayfield except for the memory of the unhappy years I spent living there.

'Right,' he said, 'I've not seen them about in a while.'

'They're very old now,' I said. 'How are you doing?'

'Not too bad, pal,' he said, 'not too bad considering.' He took a sip of his lager and then asked me, 'Did you hear what happened?'

'No,' I said, because I didn't want to prejudice Ryan's account.

'You remember my brother, don't you?' I nodded. 'He passed away,' Ryan said.

'I'm sorry,' I said. I was displeased that he had chosen such a euphemistic phrase, a phrase suggesting a peaceful death in a comfortable bed, surrounded by loved ones and completely inappropriate to describe a manic jump from an eighty-foot bridge into a shallow river. 'I'm so sorry to hear that, Ryan,'

I said. This was a minor transgression in the village, where nobody addressed anybody by their name.

'That's life for you, pal,' he said.

'Do you mind if I ask how it happened?'

'I don't like to talk about it.'

'No,' I said, 'I can imagine,' and I kept my eyes fixed on him as he looked into his pint glass.

'He took his own life,' he said.

'I'm sorry, Ryan. How terribly sad,' I said while thinking, I bet nobody in the village has used the word *sad* to describe the death of Tinhead, only the word *tragic*. I watched Ryan's face closely to see whether the word would move him, though when he cast his eyes downwards, pouted slightly, and shifted his stubbly jaw I could not say what was going through his mind. People like Ryan had always been alien to me, just as people like Tinhead were alien to them. 'He was very clever,' I said. 'I always had the sense that he didn't know what to do with all that energy. Do you think that's right?'

'Probably, pal,' Ryan said. 'You probably understand it better than me.'

'Why do you say that?'

'I don't know,' he said. 'You were a bit like him, weren't you?'

'Perhaps,' I said. Then I looked up and examined the various brass objects attached to the exposed brick wall above Ryan's head while he took a long sip of his lager. 'What pushed him over the edge?'

'He always had it in him,' Ryan said.

'Yes,' I said.

'But it got worse when he lost his job at Blue Lighting. The factory closed and he was on the dole for a bit. Then he got a job at Swizzels, boxing up sweets. He was there for about three years - three and a half years.'

'Swizzels,' I said.

'It's what everyone dreads, isn't it? Ending up at Swizzels.'

'I shudder at the thought,' I said, and Ryan intimated a chuckle. You could always get a laugh out of the villagers with a bit of elevated language, I remembered. 'What were those last years like?'

'Grim, pal,' Ryan said. 'You've seen what's happening around here, haven't you?'

'I haven't,' I said. 'What's happening?'

'It's all changing. Going downhill.'

'It looks the same as it always did,' I said, 'except The Bull has closed down.'

'Everything is closing down,' Ryan said.

'I always found it grim,' I said.

'That's because you're a weirdo,' Ryan said, 'you always were.'

'Perhaps,' I said.

'It used to be alright around here.'

I left a pause to communicate that although I disagreed, I did not want to argue with him because I was afraid of his superior strength and propensity for violent behaviour. I looked at the menu standing on the table, bound in red mock-leather, embossed with the words *The Royal Hotel*. These menus haven't changed in ten years, I thought. Once they conveyed grandeur and tradition, but now they appeared outdated, even seedy. 'So it was Swizzels that pushed him over the edge?' I asked Ryan.

'He hated it there. He was smashing the coke every weekend. He wasn't even going out. He used to sit up in his room doing coke and playing *Train Simulator*. All he talked about was train routes: Northeast Corridor from DC to Baltimore, Marsdonshire Lines, the fucking Chengkun Railway from Hanyuan to Puxiong.'

'Really?' I said.

'Really, mate,' he said. 'The Gotthardbahn Alpine Classic and the Fife Circle Line. I remember all of them. If I had to piss in the night, I would hear the sound of the trains when I passed his room, hear his mouse clicking.'

'I had imagined he would have been into conspiracy theories. Lizards and so on. The Illuminati.'

'Not at all, pal,' Ryan said. 'Rick didn't give two shits about that sort of stuff. It was all *Train Simulator* by the end. I knew he wasn't happy,' he said. 'But I wasn't expecting him to go and do that. He was saving up money. He wanted to go to Australia.'

'Tinhead was too clever for Hayfield,' I said.

'Don't call him that,' Ryan said.

'Sorry,' I said.

'Rick was a Hayfield lad,' Ryan said.

'That's true,' I said, looking once more at the brass ornaments and instruments mounted on the walls. 'When did he do it?' I said. I chose these words carefully to indicate that I understood the decision to be Tinhead's own, to emanate from the heart of his being.

'March,' Ryan said.

'Yes,' I said.

'What do you mean, yes?'

'It's a miserable month, March.'

'People survive it,' Ryan said.

'Some,' I said. 'Why do you think he did it?'

'I don't know, do I?'

'But don't you have an idea?'

'No.'

'You must have thought about it,' I said.

'I don't know,' Ryan said. 'Because he was an idiot.'

'Tinhead wasn't an idiot,' I said.

'Don't call him Tinhead,' Ryan said, and I remembered that I had always known him to be capable of turning quickly to violence.

'I'm sorry,' I said. 'That was how I knew him.'

'Don't call him that around me,' he said.

'I'm sorry,' I said. In the village, I remembered, I had always felt under threat from the violent tendencies of the villagers.

'Don't call him fucking Tinhead. His name is Rick.'

'I'm sorry,' I said. 'That's just how I always knew him.'

'Don't call him that again,' Ryan said. He seemed to have retreated to some private place full of grief and anger and I understood that the moment had come for me to leave. We had attracted the attention of the villagers at the next table: a man, woman and dog. I turned around and saw that the locals remained at the bar, drinking their beer amid a terrible silence.

Buttoning up my coat I said, 'Do you mind if I ask how he did it?'

'He jumped off the Queen's Bridge,' Ryan said. This he said without looking at me, without leaving his private place, and so flatly that I knew he had not even begun to think about what the words meant. I nodded in response as though I were reacting calmly to information I had just acquired, rather than to the confirmation of something I already knew and, in a sense, had always known. Then I stood up, bowed respectfully, and left Ryan alone in the snug.

Outside, the air was cold and dry and the church bells were ringing the new hour. I got in my car and started the engine. I pulled out of The Royal's car park and drove through the village, where I saw no other villagers. I crossed the Hayfield bypass and drove fast along the Hayfield Road towards New Mills, relieved to be leaving the Peak District behind.

Never again will I return to Hayfield, I thought. Never to New Mills, never even to Stockport. If I need any more sporting equipment, I'll go to the Decathlon in the Trafford Centre or I'll plan ahead and order it online. I reached New Mills and drove quickly across the Queen's Bridge, where Tinhead had killed himself six months previously, and then I climbed up the hill past the Swizzels factory where he had spent the last three years of his life boxing Love Hearts, Parma Violets, Drumsticks and Refreshers. I drove along the deserted A6 through Disley and past Lyme Park, through High Lane, Middlewood, Hazel Grove and Stockport, glad that I was leaving Hayfield behind forever and glad, I thought as I drove, that Tinhead had found a way to leave Hayfield behind too.

When I got back to Manchester, to Didsbury where I had recently bought the flat with the money I inherited from my parents, I felt relief. I got out of the car and thought, yes, a person like me can live in a place like this without going mad. It's hardly Paris or New York but at least it isn't Hayfield or New Mills. People live in flats and are less suspicious of one another. The air is warmer and more polluted with fumes, noise and light. I looked up at the sky and I was pleased that I could not see the stars as one always could in Hayfield. Instead, I saw sheets of purplish gloom suspended in the darkness. I opened the door to my building and the heat from the hall radiators wrapped itself around my back and shoulders. I was glad to be home. But when I opened the door to my flat and found the silence untouched, exactly as I had left it when I had set out for Decathlon, I remembered that I had still not found a way to cope with being alone.

I put my hiking boots on the countertop and lay down on the sofa in the darkness. My parents had moved to Hayfield as a married couple and had therefore been able to live somewhat autonomously, enjoying those aspects of village life that they enjoyed and ignoring those that they didn't. When they moved to Budleigh Salterton, it was not because they couldn't stand Hayfield but simply because they wanted to retire by the seaside. I, on the other hand, had been deranged by village life, exposed to it from a young age but clearly never *of* it, and had learned to live in a state of alienation from myself and others. But I forgive my parents, I thought. They had only wanted us to have a simple life in the countryside.

CONTRIBUTOR BIOGRAPHIES

ALINAH AZADEH is a British-Iranian writer, visual artist, performer and cultural activist. She has had short stories, poetry and articles published and broadcast. She is the inaugural writer-in-residence at Seven Sisters Country Park and Sussex Heritage Coast, UK, for South Downs National Park, leading 'We See You Now', a decolonial literature and landscape project supported by Arts Council England, which includes the podcast, *The Colour of Chalk*.

DAVID BEVAN is a 2021 graduate of the Manchester Writing School's Creative Writing MA programme. 'The Bull' is one of two stories first published by Nightjar Press.

AK BLAKEMORE is a novelist and poet from London. Her novels include *The Manningtree Witches* – winner of the Desmond Elliott Prize for a debut novel – and *The Glutton*. She has published two full-length collections of poetry: *Humbert Summer* and *Fondue*. Her work has been widely published and anthologised, appearing in the *London Review of Books*, *Granta* and *The White Review*, among others.

GABRIEL FLYNN is a writer based in Berlin. He was shortlisted for the White Review Short Story Prize in 2020 and is currently working on his first novel.

JIM GIBSON lives in Newstead Village, Nottinghamshire, and is the author of a short story collection, *The Bygones* (Tangerine Press).

LYDIA GILL is a writer, teacher and member of the Esk Valley Camphill Community in the North York Moors. She is a Writers' Block North East alumna, and a Northern Short Story Festival Academy writer. 'The Lowing' is her first published story.

MILES GREENWOOD is the Lead Curator at the International Slavery Museum in Liverpool and a writer from Stockport. 'Islands' was first published in *Extra Teeth* while he was living in Glasgow. It was his first short story to be published.

KERRY HADLEY-PRYCE has written three novels published by Salt Publishing and was shortlisted for the Encore Second Novel Award 2019. Her third novel, *God's Country*, was published in February 2023. She has a PhD in Creative Writing, teaches creative writing at the University of Wolverhampton, and has had short stories published in *Fictive Dream* and *The Incubator* and broadcast on Brum Radio.

PHILIP JENNINGS has an MA in Creative Writing from City College, New York and a PhD in English and Creative Writing from Lancaster University. He is a Bridport prize winner and his fiction has appeared in publications as diverse as *Evening Standard*, Unicorn Productions, *Encounter, Penthouse, The Pan Book of Horror Stories, Astounding Little Alien Stories* (Barnes and Noble), *Panurge, Punch, Iron,* and most recently *Personal Bests Journal* (2021 and 2022). He tutored for many years at City Lit Institute and other adult institutes including Roehampton University.

SHARON KIVLAND is an artist and writer. She is currently working on the natural form, fables, and the furies. She is also an editor and publisher, the latter under the imprint MA BIBLIOTHÈQUE. Her novel *Abécédaire* was published by Moist Books in July 2022. A chapter from her new book, *Almanach*, is included in the forthcoming anthology *Prototype 5*.

ALISON MOORE's first novel, *The Lighthouse*, was shortlisted for the Man Booker Prize and the National Book Awards (New Writer of the Year), winning the McKitterick Prize. She recently published her fifth novel, *The Retreat*, and a trilogy for children, beginning with *Sunny and the Ghosts*. Her short fiction has been included in previous volumes of *Best British Short Stories* and in *Best British Horror* anthologies, broadcast on BBC Radio and collected in *The Pre-War House and Other Stories* and *Eastmouth and Other Stories*. Born in Manchester in 1971, she lives near Nottingham with her husband Dan and son Arthur.

GEORGINA PARFITT lives in Liverpool. Her stories can be found in the *Dublin Review, The Common, Ambit* and elsewhere. She is currently working on a collection of Brighton stories.

GARETH E REES is an author of fiction and non-fiction. His books include *Marshland*, *The Stone Tide*, *Car Park Life* and *Unofficial Britain*. His debut short story collection, *Terminal Zones*, was published by Influx Press in 2022.

LEONE ROSS is a novelist, short story writer and editor. Her fiction has been nominated for the Women's Prize, Goldsmiths Prize, RSL Ondjaate Prize and Edge Hill Prize, among others, and 'When We Went Gallivanting' won the Manchester Fiction Prize in 2022. She has taught creative writing for more than 20 years, and worked as a journalist throughout the 1990s. She is editor of *Glimpse*, the first Black British anthology of speculative fiction (Peepal Tree Press, 2022). Her third novel, *This One Sky Day* aka *Popisho*, is published in paperback by Faber & Faber and Picador USA. In 2023, she was named as a Fellow of the Royal Society of Literature.

JOHN SAUL grew up in Liverpool. Widely published, his short fiction has been brought together in three collections with a fourth, *The Book of Joys*, due out next year from Confingo Publishing. Work of his appeared in *Best British Short Stories 2016* and as the contribution from England to Dalkey Archive's *Best European Fiction 2018*. Now living in London, he is a member of the European Literature Network. Website: www.johnsaul.co.uk

DJ TAYLOR novels *Trespass* (1998) and *Derby Day* (2011) were both long-listed for the Booker Prize. His *Orwell: The*

Life won the 2003 Whitbread Biography Prize. Among his recent publications are the short story collection *Stewkey Blues* (2022), *Orwell: The New Life*, and a novel, *Flame Music* (both 2023). He lives in Norwich with his wife, the novelist Rachel Hore.

BRIONY THOMPSON is an East Lothian-based writer specialising in prose fiction. After completing an MLitt at St Andrews University, she pursued a career in policy research. Writing has always been part of that. However, keen to explore her artistic side, she is currently studying for an MA Creative Writing with the Open University. She also works freelance as a copywriter. She grew up in the Scottish Borders and much of her writing is informed by the lives and landscapes of that place.

MATTHEW TURNER is a senior lecturer at Chelsea College of Arts. His essays, reviews and short stories have been published in *Financial Times, Architectural Review, Art Review, Frieze, Gorse* and elsewhere. In 2021 his first book, *Loom*, a story about threads and hidden wealth, was published by Gordian Projects.

MARK VALENTINE is from Northampton but now lives in Yorkshire. He is the author of studies of Arthur Machen (1995) and the diplomat and fantasist Sarban (2010). His short stories are published by the independent imprints Tartarus Press (UK), The Swan River Press (Ireland), Sarob Press (France) and Zagava (Germany). He also writes essays on book-collecting and forgotten authors.

DAVID WHELDON was born in Moira, Leicestershire, then an active mining village, in 1950. His father was a schoolmaster, his mother a nursing sister. He attended Sidcot, a Quaker school. He was the author of five novels: *The Viaduct, The Course of Instruction, A Vocation, At the Quay* and *Days and Orders*, and a short story collection, *The Guiltless Bystander.* He died in 2021.

ACKNOWLEDGMENTS

'The Beard', copyright © Alinah Azadeh 2022, was first published in *Glimpse: An Anthology of Black British Speculative Fiction* (Peepal Tree Press) edited by Leone Ross, and is reprinted by permission of the author.

'The Bull', copyright © David Bevan 2022, was first published in *The Bull* (Nightjar Press), and is reprinted by permission of the author.

'Bonsoir (After Ithell Colquhoun)', copyright © AK Blakemore 2022, was first published in *Tate etc* issue 54, and is reprinted by permission of the author.

'Tinhead', copyright © Gabriel Flynn 2022, was first published online in *Five Dials*, spring 2022, and is reprinted by permission of the author.

'The Thinker', copyright © Jim Gibson 2022, was first published in *The Bygones* (Tangerine Press), and is reprinted by permission of the author.

'The Lowing', copyright © Lydia Gill 2022, was first published in *The Lowing* (Seventy2One/Massive Overheads), and is reprinted by permission of the author.

'Islands', copyright © Miles Greenwood 2022, was first published in *Extra Teeth* issue 6, November 2022, and is reprinted by permission of the author.

'Chimera', copyright © Kerry Hadley-Pryce 2022, was first published online in *Fictive Dream*, 27 February 2022, and is reprinted by permission of the author.

'Elephant', copyright © Philip Jennings 2022, was first published in *Personal Bests Journal*, issue 4, summer 2022, and is reprinted by permission of the author.

'The Incorruptible', copyright © Sharon Kivland 2022, was first published in *The Incorruptible* (Piece of Paper Press), and is reprinted by permission of the author.

'Common Ground', copyright © Alison Moore 2022, was first published in *Eastmouth and Other Stories* (Salt Publishing), and is reprinted by permission of the author.

'Middle Ground', copyright © Georgina Parfitt 2022, was first published online in *Granta*, and is reprinted by permission of the author.

'The Slime Factory', copyright © Gareth E Rees 2022, was first published in *Terminal Zones* (Influx Press), and is reprinted by permission of the author.

'When We Went Gallivanting', copyright © Leone Ross 2022, was first published online at *Manchester Fiction Prize*, and is reprinted by permission of the author.

'The Clearance', copyright © John Saul 2022, was first published in *Lunate* vol 1, 2022, and is reprinted by permission of the author.

'Somewhere Out There West of Thetford', copyright © DJ Taylor 2022, was first published in *Stewkey Blues* (Salt Publishing), and is reprinted by permission of the author.

'The Nights', copyright © Briony Thompson 2022, was first published in *Extra Teeth* issue 6, November 2022, and is reprinted by permission of the author.

'Still Life', copyright © Matthew Turner 2022, was first published in *The London Magazine*, December 2022/January 2023, and is reprinted by permission of the author.

'Qx', copyright © Mark Valentine 2022, was first published online in *Soanyway*, Volume 2, Issue Eleven, edited by Derek Horton and Gertrude Gibbons and is reprinted by permission of the author.

'The Statistics Rebellion', copyright © David Wheldon 2022, was first published in *The Guiltless Bystander* (Confingo Publishing), and is reprinted by permission of the author.

This book has been typeset by
SALT PUBLISHING LIMITED
using Neacademia, a font designed by Sergei Egorov
for the Rosetta Type Foundry in the Czech Republic.
It is manufactured using Creamy 70gsm, a Forest
Stewardship Council™ certified paper from Stora Enso's
Anjala Mill in Finland. It was printed and bound by
Clays Limited in Bungay, Suffolk, Great Britain.

SHEFFIELD
GREAT BRITAIN
MMXXIII